Walter Wager is the author of over a dozen novels, including TELEFON and TIME OF RECKONING. He has been public relations director of ASCAP, diplomatic advisor to Israel's Director of Civil Aviation, a senior editor at the United Nations Secretariat, and a screenwriter for the U.S. Information Agency. A graduate of Columbia College and the Harvard Law School, he also holds an L.L.M. degree in air law from Northwestern University and is an irrepressible world traveller. He lives with his Irish wife in New York City where he is public affairs advisor to the National Music Publishers' Association.

Also by Walter Wager

BLUE LEADER
TIME OF RECKONING
TELEFON
SLEDGEHAMMER

Walter Wager

Blue Moon

Macdonald Futura Publishers

A Futura Book

First published in Great Britain in 1981
by Macdonald Futura Publishers Ltd

ISBN 0 7088 2015 8
Printed by
William Collins Sons & Co. Ltd
Glasgow

Macdonald Futura Publishers Ltd
Paulton House, 8 Shepherdess Walk
London N1 7LW

For Winifred,
lovely Liffey Bird and wondrous wife
W. W.

ACKNOWLEDGMENTS

THIS BOOK is a work of fiction about imaginary people doing good and evil in situations and incidents that have never happened—not even in that extraordinary desert fantasy called Las Vegas.

The author thanks those gracious individuals in Beverly Hills and Las Vegas whose insights, wisdom and generous hospitality contributed to the research for this novel. A lot of people—policemen, hotel executives, gamblers, stars, show business lawyers, publicists and those good chefs at Caesars—helped.

There are two other gentlemen/scholars who answered many questions and provided much information. They are Don Typond, editor of *Model Airplane News*, and Bill Winter, editor of *Model Aviation* and co-author of "Basics of Radio Control Modeling." Their patience and guidance were invaluable.

Last but far from least, there are thanks due to the New York City Police Department's Bomb Squad, to Lt. Preston E. Hubbs of the Crime Prevention Bureau of the Las Vegas Metropolitan Police Department, the F.B.I. Bureau in Phoenix, Arizona, and U.S. Drug Enforcement Administration Special Agent J. David Quilter, an able and dedicated public servant whose expertise includes the training and use of dogs to detect explosives and narcotics. It would be a sin not to acknowledge the assistance of composer-critic-author Arnold Shaw, who enlivens the musical life of Las Vegas, and of Nevada's Gaming Control Board.

BLUE MOON

CHAPTER I

THE TANNED man in the blue suit trailed Alison Gordon east on Wilshire Boulevard, admiring her fine legs and calculating. She'd probably walk north in a minute onto Rodeo Drive, maybe stop to check her appearance in the window of some fancy boutique or jewelry store. Enjoying her rippling walk, he held his breath as she reached The Brown Derby at the corner. She passed the famed restaurant and turned onto Rodeo—and he smiled.

She paid no attention to the window displays at Giorgio's, surely one of Beverly Hills' super-chic clothing shops. She crossed to the other side of Rodeo without breaking stride, ignoring envious glances of middle-aged women in shiny new Mercedes as she made her way north to Van Cleef & Arpels. Stars, tycoons, sheiks, rich widows with excellent face-lifts and gifted dentists who had even more talented tax lawyers all bought their "drop dead" jewelry here. He figured that she *had* to pause to scan the diamonds, star sapphires and blood red rubies that blazed behind the shatterproof panes.

But she walked right by, heading east again on Dayton Way toward Beverly Drive. She didn't look back or show any sign of wariness. Must just be out on some errand, the watcher decided as she passed the Dalton bookstore to enter

Parklane Hosiery next door. He thought about her splendid legs again and grinned in the pleasant midday sun. His orders had been quite specific. He was to do it when she was alone.

She was being followed and she did not like it. What annoyed her even more was not knowing who or why. The stocky man in the blue silk suit might be twenty-eight or thirty, but he definitely wasn't federal. Neither F.B.I. nor D.E.A. agents wore such expensive clothes and even C.I.A. trainees were more discreet in "mobile surveillance."

She bought two pairs of "French Nude—Luxury Sheer" pantyhose, walked out into the glare and made her way up Beverly Drive to The Cheesecake Factory. She considered her passion for chocolate and for this establishment's huge fudge sundaes, then computed the calories to resist the surge of temptation.

Couldn't be a local cop either. The rawest detectives of the L.A. Police Department or the Beverly Hills force did a classier job of tailing. Who the hell was he?

When she reached Nate 'n' Al's delicatessen, she thought about their excellent mushroom and barley soup and the Academy Award-winning screenwriter who had wooed her here—a handsome bearded man who was always going to complete a great tragic play as soon as he caught up on his alimony payments. He'd been a good lover but a bad prophet. His last two scripts had exalted Burt Reynolds and a dozen cars. She paused for a moment as she remembered —a *very* good lover . . .

The watcher shifted the .38 in his belly holster and took cover behind a maroon Rolls parked four shops away.

Perhaps it wasn't surveillance. Maybe he was a hit man. She realized that she was probably being paranoid, and that made her still angrier.

She walked on toward Santa Monica Boulevard, and he saw her turn right suddenly into a parking lot. Several cars entered and left in swift succession, blocking his view. By the time he reached the lot, she was out of sight. Where? How? Puzzled, he wandered uncertainly into the rows of cars, searching.

"Yes?"

He turned, faced her standing beside a brown Bentley. No one else could see them here. This was the time.

"Got something for you," he said and reached inside his jacket.

Suddenly there was a goddamn big .357 magnum in her right hand pointing straight at his navel. It was like some crazy card trick.

"Next of kin?" she asked.

"Hey, take it easy! It's just an envelope!"

It wasn't supposed to happen this way. They hadn't told him that she was so fast, so jumpy.

"Lady . . . please . . . listen to me."

"You listen to *me.* This thing could core you like an apple, so pay attention. Are you carrying a piece?"

The expression in her face said it clearly. She'd kill him.

"Yes, but—"

She waggled the gun, and he stopped talking.

"Pretend you're ninety-three years old," she ordered, "with arthritis. Very carefully and slowly, reach inside with two fingers and take out the piece. Just *ease* it out. Would you do that now, please?"

He swallowed and nodded. She was probably insane. He felt the ninety-dollar Italian silk shirt plastered to his back with perspiration as he extricated his automatic, exactly as she had commanded.

"Now put it down gently—like an egg—on that green Jag beside you, and back off eight or nine steps."

He obeyed. She walked forward, put his .38 in her purse and shook her head in disapproval.

"Your gun is a piece of junk, mister. Now what about my envelope?"

She handled the magnum like a professional. Why hadn't

someone warned him? The noon sun seemed extremely hot; his palms were wet. Moving warily, he took out the cream-colored envelope—still using just two fingers—and held it out to her. .

"You open it. I've got this thing about letter bombs."

She was crazy, but it *could* be a letter bomb. He'd been told to give her the envelope, but no one had said what was in it. Hell, she *deserved* a bomb. He looked at her heavy revolver, braced himself and slowly tore open the envelope.

He pulled out a folded sheet of vellum stationery and thrust it at her.

"Who sent it?"

"Read it yourself," he replied and she guessed that he didn't know. This gunman in the four-hundred-dollar suit was merely a messenger. She told him to slip the piece of paper under the windshield wiper of an adjacent Ferrari and back off, and when he had complied with her order to turn his back she advanced cautiously to scan the note. Three lines of typing. No signature, but the reference to piano playing told her all she needed.

Stiff with humiliation and frustration, he suffered in the expensive Beverly Hills sun. He'd have to come up with a story. He certainly couldn't tell the others how easily this psycho had trapped and disarmed him. Damn it, how long did it take her to read a letter?

"Help you, sir?"

He looked over his shoulder and saw a slim Chicano parking attendant five feet away.

"Got your ticket, sir? What kind of car is it?"

The man in the blue silk suit glanced left, then right before he sighed.

The woman with the .357 was gone.

Thank God.

CHAPTER 2

"AIRCRAFT APPROACHING . . . bearing two-zero-two . . range sixteen miles . . . altitude 4,300 . . . airspeed one-five-five. Stand by, Guns and Perimeter," the radar operator ordered.

Two men in green coveralls on the roof put on Marine Corps armored vests and combat helmets, adjusted anti-glare goggles to cope with the afternoon sun and took seats at a pair of swivel-mounted heavy machine guns. On the landscaped grounds four floors below, and half a mile from the massive stone mansion, other guards at camouflaged security posts checked their automatic weapons and light missile launchers. Using walkie-talkies, each team reported that it was battle-ready.

"Aircraft closing," the radar operator warned. "Altitude 3,800 . . . range eleven miles . . . airspeed one-five-zero. Prepare to engage." He switched to another frequency and asked the pilot of the inbound plane to identify himself and his mission.

As the flier complied, the elegantly dressed woman beside him in the jet helicopter looked ahead at Mr. Spinoza's private mountain. There was no road to the summit from the valley, and trespassers who defied the signs and hiked up would have to cut through three fences—one of them electrified—before they got within a mile of the big house. There were attack dogs, too. Determined to enjoy his golden years and a fortune that the Federal Bureau of Investigation wistfully estimated at "more than $90,000,000," Spinoza was a peace-loving man prepared—thoroughly—to kill anyone who bothered him.

The .50-caliber machine guns on the roof tracked the rotorcraft until the moment Alison Gordon stepped out onto the concrete landing pad, and as she started for the house she saw one of the heavy weapons actually swiveling with her—step for step. A white-jacketed servant let her in, guiding her down the long hall past the paintings and suits of armor to the library. Music. Just before the houseman rapped on the door, she heard the recently tuned Steinway grand. Only her anger kept her from smiling as she recognized the melody.

"Thanks for coming on such short notice," Spinoza said warmly as she entered the room. He rose from the piano stool and walked across forty feet of Carrara marble floor to greet her. The library-living room was big and impressive, with beamed ceilings, oak-paneled walls, elaborate carved bookcases and stained-glass windows from European castles and manors. Her host, wearing gold wire glasses, was gray-haired, no more than five-feet-nine, wiry.

"Your invitation was difficult to decline. How've you been?"

"Busy with my piano and gardening—old man's work."

"Not that old. Sixty-eight next week," she recalled.

"Gershwin's tough at any age. I was practicing when you arrived. Please, won't you sit down?"

She ignored the invitation.

" 'How Long Has This Been Going On?' " she said instead.

"Right. Would you like a beer? You drink Carlsberg, I think."

She shook her head, taking out and lighting a gold-tipped Sobranie.

"You know 'Let's Call the Whole Thing Off'?" she asked in tones edged with hostility.

"What's the matter, Miss Gordon?"

"You tell me, Mr. Spinoza. I'm sorry, I'm forgetting my manners. Brought you two birthday presents."

He opened the flat, square package first, and nodded in approval. The RCA-Victrola recording of the *Rhapsody in Blue* with George Gershwin himself at the piano.

"Thank you. But what's the—"

"Try the other one," she interrupted.

This was unsettling. Her manners had always been perfect. He tore off the paper, lifted the lid of the box and stared.

"What's *this?*"

"That's what I want to know. I thought you were a gentleman, and I'd like an explanation."

He put the box on a Louis XV end table and sat down in a red leather armchair.

"I don't know anything about . . . I can't imagine why you'd bring this *thing,*" he said quietly.

"That *thing* is a .38-caliber automatic, and not a very good one. You might want to return it to your messenger. I took it from him in a parking lot. He's worse than his weapon, you know."

She couldn't stand still. She paced to a stained-glass window that had once graced a princely chapel in Tuscany, turning just as Spinoza spoke.

"Please tell me exactly what happened."

"I don't like being followed by some goon with a piece under his arm, and I won't stand for it. That's not what I expected from you. A hood in a flashy silk suit? That's B-movie."

"Some moron sent a *button-man* to deliver my note?"

"What kind of people have you got working for you?"

"Trash! I apologize, Miss Gordon. I had just asked that . . . well, since this is a very private matter I suggested that the note be handed directly to you, preferably when you were alone. A former business associate was visiting here, and he said he'd take care of it. The imbecile who followed you doesn't work for me. Even before I retired, I never employed garbage."

"That's one of the things that made me so angry. You've never treated me like that before."

Spinoza walked to the sideboard, filled a Florentine silver goblet with mineral water and extracted a tube of yellow pills from his pocket. He swallowed a capsule, washed it down and sighed.

"These men have shamed me and insulted you—both intolerable," he said. "I give you my word this will be made clear to them. I don't know why you came at all after such treatment. I suppose it was to tell me off, and I can't blame you."

He'd probably used this humble routine on women before, she thought. Still, she found it difficult to resist.

"Telling you off was one reason," she admitted and puffed on her cigarette. It tasted harsh. She ground it out, lit another and wondered about the yellow pill. Was he ill? God, she was reacting as if she were his mother.

"Was there another?" he asked.

"Your note said you needed my help, that it was urgent. You're not the sort of person who uses that word casually, and I haven't forgotten what you did for me in that Pete Anthony matter. I *know* it was you, so tell me about this new mess."

Spinoza sidestepped her reference to the narcotics smuggler who'd put out a $20,000 contract on her life. He again invited her to sit down, then poured a glass of the dark Danish beer she enjoyed.

" 'Mess' may be exactly the right word, Miss Gordon. Though I'm basically retired, now and then old friends ask for my advice . . . in unusual situations. Something very unusual has come up, something that happens once in a blue moon. This is all confidential, of course. I'm trusting you not to discuss it with anyone."

Right, the F.B.I., Drug Enforcement Administration, Internal Revenue Service or those other official anyones. She nodded. "Sure. Tell me about the blue moon."

Spinoza hesitated, and she could see that he was choosing his words carefully. Whatever it was, it was something big if the people who now dominated the U.S. underworld had to turn to this cunning old man for guidance.

"I guess you'd have to call it extortion, Miss Gordon. It's the old protection racket, like in those cheap movies you mentioned. This isn't cheap, but that's not the issue. I told my friends not to pay."

"Someone's shaking *you* down?"

"Not me, my friends. I've got a few dollars invested with them but it's really a question of principle."

Nobody shakes down the Syndicate. It's the Syndicate that shakes, and only deranged or desperate individuals would dream of extorting money from the ganglords. She finished her beer and waited for Spinoza to explain.

"They're asking for five million dollars—five million by the first Tuesday of next month."

Election day. November 6th.

"And if it isn't paid?"

Spinoza shrugged.

"They say they'll blow up every casino in Las Vegas. There are maybe twenty-five on The Strip, half of them in big hotels that run at ninety-percent capacity. Thousands of rooms full of tourists and people in for conventions—doctors and plumbing supply dealers, teachers and wholesale grocers . . . *and* their wives. All sorts."

"And there are more casinos downtown," she thought aloud.

"Dozens—for the nickel and dime crowd, the little old ladies in tennis shoes trying to bust the slot machines. Like you said, it's a mess."

"If they could do it, they might wipe out ten or fifteen thousand people—and of course your friends' hotels."

"My friends only own five or six now. It's mostly major corporations in Vegas these days, outfits listed on the Stock Exchange. Hughes, Hilton, MGM—that kind of money. Whole town's changed in the past fifteen years. You've been there. You know."

"Five or six? I won't ask which."

"It doesn't matter which, if they're all blown up. Does it?"

"It doesn't," Alison Gordon agreed diplomatically and realized that her mind had begun working on the problem automatically—as if Las Vegas was worth saving. It wasn't that she actively disliked the city, she had just never taken it seriously enough to judge the place at all. Spinoza poured another Carlsberg for her and half-filled his own squat glass with ice cubes and twelve-year-old Scotch. Neither of them spoke for almost half a minute.

"What makes you think this threat is serious?" she finally asked.

"They sent a free sample of their merchandise. A bomb—a *very good* bomb. Big. Latest in delayed-action fuses. An expert checked it out. He rated it A-Plus, the real thing. You can see it—and the letter—when you get there."

"If I get there."

"Of course. Nobody's taking you for granted, Miss Gordon. You're so good at what you do that you take on the jobs you want, but of course I'm trying to help you want this one. You don't need our mess, but we need you. I hope you don't mind my directness. I've always admired yours."

She sipped the beer and worked.

"A single letter and a bomb. Not to every casino owner, but just one of your friends. Why?"

"Maybe because they know my friends can put their hands on plenty of cash quickly. It could also be they have an idea my friends are the least likely to call in the cops."

She couldn't help it.

"Who needs government meddling? It was Free Enterprise that made this country great, right?"

Her performance was perfect. He searched her face for some sign of irony but found none.

"Greatest in the world," he ventured uncertainly. "That's what I said to them. We're practical businessmen, and we can handle this ourselves."

Without the F.B.I. or tax snoopers crawling all over their casinos and their multiple sets of books. Somebody very shrewd had planned this shakedown.

"Any idea who might be behind this, Mr. Spinoza?"

He sipped more of the Ambassador and reviewed the question for at least the sixtieth time. The international underworld had long honored him as a canny thinker who solved more problems with brains than with bullets. Law-enforcement authorities in a dozen countries still spoke of his sophistication and cunning.

"Professionals," he judged. "This bomb wasn't put together by college kids, although one of my friends suggests it could be radicals."

"Or it could be one of your friends."

Something flickered in his eyes.

"You'll find out. Ought to be interesting for you—a nice change from the usual cases, huh?"

She did not answer.

"My friends will give you plenty of help—full cooperation—"

"I don't know. This might be one for the police."

"My friends can't afford the police—not even the local cops. We just can't have it. That's why we're going to pay you a thousand dollars a day instead of your usual four hundred."

She stood up and slung her purse over her shoulder.

"You're that sure I'm going to take the case?"

"Not for the money, for the safety of those people. You're a tough lady, but your toughness is about *that* thick." He held up his index finger and thumb and squinted between them. "Now that I've told you, I don't believe there is any way you'll risk letting someone wipe out ten thousand innocent people."

"What's so innocent about the people who come to Vegas?"

He drained the whiskey, shook his head.

"I'm surprised at you, Miss Gordon. They're the most innocent people in America. They expect to win."

Ten thousand people? It was probably a bluff.

She started toward the door but paused.

"I don't like anything about this deal," she said.

"Well, neither do I, but I'm afraid we're both stuck with it. Try to see this from my viewpoint. Who else could I ask to do it? You were in the C.I.A. for years; you've dealt with secret outfits and saboteurs before. You're the logical person to handle this. In fact you're the *only*—"

"I don't want it."

"All you have to do is find out the basic facts," he persisted. "I'm not asking you to kill anybody. Look, you get more money than any other private-detective outfit on the Coast—maybe in the country—because you're smarter than anyone else. We need that mind, that experience. It has to be you."

"No, it doesn't. Thank you for your compliments, but no thanks."

Now Spinoza was on his feet.

"I wasn't just flattering you, and you know it. Think about all those people. The ordinary detective firm wouldn't have a clue, but your team . . . undercover veterans like you . . ."

Fine, but who cared about that vulgar plastic city and the gauche conventioneers and tourists anyway? If one bunch of thugs wanted to blackmail another, that was no serious concern of A. B. Gordon Investigations. . . .

It *couldn't* be ten thousand people.

Just another effort by a calculating man to manipulate her. No, not *man.* Client. In a moment he'd offer more money.

"I hope you won't be offended, Miss Gordon," he was saying, "but we're not limited to one thousand dollars a day. I was about to add, this is short notice, and I understand there could be some inconvenience to . . . your staff . . . and to your other clients. We're not limited at all. Perhaps two thousand dollars a day would be an appropriate adjustment . . ."

She said nothing, but he saw an answer in her eyes.

"Sorry I wasted your time," he said. "I appreciate the record."

"*An American in Paris* is on the other side," she told him . . . and wondered why. As they walked out to the landing pad they talked about the brilliant Gershwin brothers, and Spinoza told her that it would take at least a year before he'd try the repertory of another major songwriter—perhaps Harold Arlen. She barely heard him talking. Why was he babbling on so? Didn't he understand that she wanted to pay her debt all right, but this Vegas "mess" was something for a large law-enforcement agency with a huge staff? Why did men think they could con her into anything—everything? She was fed up with lies and bribes, tricks—the insulting tactics bad fathers used on gullible children.

"Thanks again for coming," Spinoza said at the helicopter —and then it happened.

"I'd need thirty thousand dollars up front," she heard herself say.

"Of course," he agreed instantly.

What the hell was she doing?

"Aren't you going to ask what for?"

"No, I trust you."

This man was notorious as one of the most devious princes of organized crime, and she was going to help him protect investments in that fantasy city in the desert? It was preposterous.

"You know why I'm taking this on?"

"Compassion," he replied in tones worthy of an Easter sermon. Spinoza didn't give a damn about why she'd changed her mind, she told herself. He was no better than the talent agents and producers who did sixty pushups and three rip-offs before breakfast. The question was how much worse.

"Make that forty thousand."

"Whatever you say."

They spoke briefly about arranging for her to examine the bomb and the note, and he gave her a name and a telephone number. Area code 702, for dialing the whole state of Nevada. She climbed into the rotorcraft, turned her eyes away from him and saw the heavy machine guns pointing at her again. The helicopter rose thunderously, gained altitude and leveled off at 4,200 feet for the ninety-seven-mile journey south to Los Angeles. She looked down at the green countryside, wondered how much of what he'd told her was true and how much he'd withheld. She needed a cigarette.

When she reached into her purse for the Sobranies, she was annoyed to find that she'd left them—almost half a black cardboard boxful—back in Spinoza's castle. She glanced up into the mustachioed pilot's appraising stare. Maybe the other women in his life succumbed to his mustachioed macho, but Alison Gordon found his sexual pre-flight inspection and pretty-boy "cool" repellent.

She took out her lighter and mimed her desire for a cigarette. He shook his head and pointed to the fuel gauge to signal that smoking in the chopper would be dangerous, then gave her that masterful smile he'd used so successfully in the singles' bars. She gestured ambiguously, avoided eye contact with him until they were walking away from the helicopter at Los Angeles Airport. He reached out and took her arm.

"Give you a lift, hon?"

"It would be a depression, *hon,*" she replied as she

brushed away his grasp. By the time she guided her Porsche out of the parking lot, she wasn't thinking of that pilot at all. She was remembering another, a wonderful man named Harry Logan who had flown B–17 bombers—until less than a year ago. Logan was dead. He had probably been the last of the old-time heroes, a throwback, and she had no reason to expect that she'd ever meet another. Even now, she sometimes cried when the longing for Logan twisted inside her. Well, there would be no love to worry about in Las Vegas. Oddly comforted by this thought, she decided to concentrate on the freeway traffic in order to put Logan from her mind on the way home. She was a strong, intelligent woman, a practical executive who had run her own profitable business for years. . . .

She drove expertly through the late afternoon crush of vehicles, reached her home in only thirty-six minutes and parked the sports car in the driveway. The past was gone, and she had too much to do to indulge in any sentimentality She unlocked the front door of the house, stepped inside, and began to cry.

CHAPTER 3

IT HAPPENED very quickly and made no sense to anyone who saw it.

The tall Miamian in the back seat of the red and black Simca 1000 taxi had a slight hangover. When he heard the horrid screech overhead, Owen Albion looked up at the Royal Air Maroc 707 disappearing behind the white terminal building of Casablanca's busy Nouasser Airport less than two hundred yards away. Glancing off to the right, he recognized the markings on a large jet as those of Aeroflot, the airline of the Soviet Union. He did it automatically. He had been trained to recognize the civil and military aircraft of many nations.

A dozen other taxis, identical to the one in which he rode, inched slowly toward the terminal in a tangle of cars and trucks and minibusses. The traffic jam, the noise and the crowds—of Arabs and Berbers, Europeans, Americans, black Africans of varied hue and even a knot of Asian businessmen—bothered him no more than the tired eyes and headache memorializing the last night of his "holiday" with the pretty English photographer. Blinking in the bright sun, he thought again about her wonderful skin and sophisticated sense of humor. As intelligent as she was sensual, she'd introduced him to the excellent local red wines, translated deftly during shopping expeditions in the splendidly colorful *souks*—and hadn't asked questions. He had a ready stock of facile answers, of course, but it had been such a joy not to have to use them for once.

When his taxi reached the terminal, the noise of the throng grew even louder as tourists, porters, drivers, families and uniformed police cheerfully shouted up a multinational barrage of sound. It was all wonderful, he decided, and he'd have to come back to this friendly and exotic land sometime. The weather and food were good, people were affable to Americans and during his entire five days in Morocco nobody had tried to kill him. It had been one of the best vacations he'd had in years.

As soon as the cab stopped, the Floridian and the driver stepped out almost simultaneously into the buzz and bustle. Albion took a sheaf of limp twenty-*dirham* notes from his pocket while the driver put down the brown canvas suitcase at his feet. He gave the smiling Moroccan two of the bills, aware that the man considered him another tourist who overtipped in ignorance. In fact, Albion knew, the export of Moroccan money was forbidden, and the London banks wouldn't convert this currency into pounds anyway. With his flight to Britain leaving in only seventy minutes, he could get by on the eighty *dirham* he still had left for a glass of that sweet mint tea and a souvenir—perhaps another camel-leather belt. . . .

Albion turned to signal for a porter and found himself staring into the intense eyes of a young Arab in Western clothes seven or eight yards away. The features of the stranger in his mid-twenties seemed remotely familiar, but Albion couldn't dredge up any name to go with that sharp-featured face. He shrugged and began to raise his hand to flag down a porter. To his astonishment, the Arab suddenly drew a large pistol and pointed it at him.

M.A.B.—P.15.

French and modern with an unusual fifteen-round magazine. Nine-millimeter shells, like the Browning High-Power.

Albion identified the handgun automatically as he dove to the pavement, but he still had no idea as to who wanted to kill him. The first bullet flew past, and a Moroccan policeman who had been standing almost directly behind Albion squeezed off two rounds at the gunman barely a second later, knocking the shooter with the P.15 back over a baby carriage and into a cluster of pre-school children. People were screaming in Arabic, French, Berber, Swahili, English, German and several tribal tongues.

Albion yelled too, but too late. The blond European in a white suit who had abruptly produced another P.15 had already shot the policeman in the head. The officer's gun clattered beside Albion, who grabbed it and rolled over expertly into firing position.

Albion was functioning efficiently now. Two-handed shooting grip, three rounds at point-blank range. Three hits. The white suit was splashed with red, and the man in it was a corpse before his face hit the sidewalk. People were scattering, shrieking, fainting, or just staring numbly in paralyzed terror—all the right things to do when caught in an exchange between homicidal adversaries.

Somebody shot the Floridian in the chest. It might have been the Arab whom the policeman had apparently only wounded. It was hard to tell in the excitement and confusion. Then there was more gunfire, the battering sound of some rapid-fire weapon such as an assault rifle or submachine gun. Albion heard at least two ripping bursts, and just before everything went black it occurred to him that he might be dying. He felt baffled and angry for a few seconds. After that he felt nothing, not even the pain of the wound just below his heart.

CHAPTER 4

ALISON GORDON looked down at Wilshire Boulevard nine floors below, swiveled in the large chair and scanned the pink message slips on her desk.

A vice president of CBS had called at 9:50 A.M.

An *executive* vice president at Universal had phoned at 10:00, and at 10:05 the manager of two of the most successful rock music groups in the world had left word that it was *very urgent* she get in touch with him *as soon as possible.* Paul Kaplan of Kaplan, Glass and Sherman wanted to have lunch with her at Le Bistro at one o'clock. She didn't like Paul Kaplan. His tennis game was better than his ethics, and even if he was the richest Harvard Law graduate of the class of '58 she couldn't stand men who called her "babes."

It was 10:20 A.M., and the head of A. B. Gordon Investigations didn't want to speak to any of them this morning. Her mind was filled with Las Vegas. There was no time for delay. She had to discuss the case with her senior assistants, organize their plan and schedule for the trip to the pleasure city in the Nevada desert. She was reaching for the intercom but the box spoke first.

"Mr. Feldman on two."

"Which Mr. Feldman, Ella?"

"Jennings Feldman at Warner's."

Mr. Feldman was extremely happy—and grateful. He had bought one of Alison Gordon's sculptures for his wife's wedding-anniversary present, and she "loved" it. Feldman was a man of taste as well as money, and he wanted to commission another work if it could be ready by December twenty-third—his girlfriend's birthday. Something in the same price range—three or four thousand—would be fine. She lied about other commitments, thanked him civilly and hung up as Hovde entered her office.

"There are two guys outside with a shoebox," he announced in the voice scratchy from a bullet in the throat outside of Saigon nine years before.

"Uh-huh."

"You *expecting* two guys with a shoebox?"

"Everybody's expecting two guys with a shoebox, Don. Is one of them wearing a blue silk suit—sort of *electric* blue?"

"Something darker, I think. Why?"

She opened the desk drawer and took out the .357 magnum.

"Maybe he's got two suits," she speculated as she checked the clip.

"Why the gun?"

"I didn't expect a shoebox," she said. "I suppose I should have, but I didn't."

"*Who's* got two suits? What the hell is going on?"

She smiled benignly, making Hovde more uneasy.

"Sorry, Don. I'm not entirely sure, but my theory is that a client has sent a shoebox full of cash. It's also possible that someone else has shipped us a booby-trap, or maybe seventy-two of those chocolate-covered Goo-Goo bars from Nashville. I'm betting it's the cash."

"Well, I don't bet," Hovde replied curtly. He walked out to the receptionist's desk, signed for the package and took it to the alcove where they kept the fluoroscope machine. He put the box on Alison Gordon's desk two and a half minutes later.

"It isn't a bomb, and it isn't your candy bars either. You really think it's money?"

She nodded, and the quick-release knife up his sleeve dropped into his right hand. Hovde had been extremely effective with that weapon, she remembered. She also recalled having told him that it was probably illegal to carry one in California. Before she could mention this, he slashed the string and wrapping paper. It really was a shoebox.

"Gucci," he read off the lid.

"What else would you expect in Beverly Hills, Don?"

He flipped off the top with the needle-point of his knife and studied the neat stacks of used twenty-dollar bills. Stacks and stacks, each bound with rubber bands—no rings of paper with the name of a bank.

"These didn't come from a bank," she said in reply to his unspoken question, "and there's no sequence in the serial numbers. Our client believes in anonymity and invisibility, and he's got the cash to buy it. If I'm right, there's forty thousand in this box."

She was wrong. She summoned Agajanian from the next office where he was going over the firm's books in preparation for a tax audit. The slim accountant donned a pair of horn-rimmed glasses and totaled the money with the dexterity and precision of a bank teller.

"Exactly forty, Andy?" she questioned.

"Not exactly. Try fifty."

She shook her head and put the .357 back in the desk drawer.

"It was supposed to be forty," she told Agajanian and then turned to Hovde. "Would you put that damn knife away? You're in a Beverly Hills high-rise, not some jungle camp setting up an ambush. About the money, the extra ten might be for expenses—in case we need additional people," she said defensively. Hovde took off his jacket to replace the throwing knife in the arm-holster, listening carefully as she told them about Spinoza and the extortion threat. Agajanian was equally focused; she could almost hear his mind tabulating the details.

"What do you think?" she finally asked.

"Even at two thousand dollars a day, I don't appreciate this deal," Hovde answered. "The client's creepy, the job calls for nine hundred men and three teams of dogs and the whole proposition, in my opinion—"

"Sucks," the accountant put in. "If anybody's counting, I agree with Don this time. You shouldn't have bought this, Alison, and you know it."

"Go on with the rest of it," she sighed, sitting back in her chair.

"That's all I have to say," Agajanian replied. "You're not going to break your word. You were conned into this with that save-the-simple-schmucks routine, so the only thing we can do now is minimize the risks."

"What makes you sure it's really risky?" she said.

"It always is when the client overpays up front. It's *never* worth the . . . hell, I'm sorry, Alison."

The last case on which she had been sent more than the fee requested had started out as a "simple" investigation of the drug-overdose death of a California adolescent; it ended with the slaughter of hundreds in northeastern Burma and the loss of that pilot named Logan—less than a year ago. She looked Agajanian directly in the eye.

"There are a number of risks to be minimized," she said in a voice that did little to hide her hurt from these two men who'd known her more than a decade. "There's the danger of being caught in the middle of a confrontation between two criminal organizations—one unknown and therefore unpredictable—and there are the hazards of colliding head-on with any of our law-enforcement agencies."

"Vegas local police . . . Nevada state cops . . . agents of the Gaming Control Board and the F.B.I." Agajanian couldn't help himself.

"Thank you, Andrew," she said as she pushed a gold-tipped cigarette into the onyx holder. He winced, knowing she only called him "Andrew" when she was furious. His mother had done the same damn thing until the day he went overseas for the C.I.A. all those years ago.

"Al, I said I was sorry."

She lit the Sobranie, ignoring his offering for the moment.

"Other risks?" she asked with a nod toward Hovde.

"Bombs . . ." he replied.

"Yes, we'll need an explosives specialist. I suppose that Thomas Arroyo could handle it. You were friendly with him, Andrew. Why don't you give him a call?"

She was choosing the Navaho to show them that she was in control of her emotions. Arroyo had been with them in the secret air assault Logan had commanded. Agajanian wondered why people couldn't speak directly to each other instead of making these signals. "Right away," he promised.

"We'll need a lot of research, quickly," she continued. "Basic information on the city. Maps of the streets, sewers, power lines. Data on all airports—big and small—within two hundred miles. I think we can exclude Nellis, of course."

The men nodded. It was unlikely that extortionists would strike from the huge military airbase less than a dozen miles from the city that calls itself The Entertainment Capital of the World. Nellis AFB itself had gotten into the spirit of show biz as the headquarters for the U.S. Air Force's impressive and theatrical squadron of high-flying Thunderbird jets whose aerobatic exhibitions dazzled taxpayers and legislators alike.

"I want a rundown on that bomb as soon as possible," she went on. "That—and our command post—are number-one priority. We'll have a lot of casinos to go over, a big piece of territory to patrol."

"No chance at all for perimeter security," Hovde rasped.

"Absolutely none. Whoever these people are, some or all of them are in Vegas—or not far away—already. Fourteen or fifteen airlines pouring passengers in every day, and at least a couple of thousand visitors flowing in and out by car every twenty-four hours—"

"And Vegas is a twenty-four-hour town," Agajanian said.

"The city that never sleeps. Everything and everybody's going around the clock—fast. All kinds of visitors coming through—average stay of about two and a half days, somebody told me last year—and all sorts of permanent or semi-permanent residents. Ministers, hookers, tailors, obstetricians, waiters, chemistry professors—the U. of Nevada has a branch there."

"Impossible to do it without our own communications. We'll need radio-equipped cars, and our own transmitters," Agajanian said.

"That's why Don's going to rent a big mobile home and rig it as a communications van. We'll need three radio operators for round-the-clock coverage; no, make it four. Transmitter with a one-hundred-mile range, and a back-up set. Two-way sets for five cars, the best. You think Fanelli's available, Don?"

"If the money is right."

"Fanelli's crazy," Agajanian protested.

"And the best damn signals man the Agency ever fired. Get him. Tell him the mission's weird and dangerous. That ought to do it."

She leaned forward over the desk and began writing notes and lists on a lined yellow legal pad—a habit she'd picked up during a seven-month liaison with California's ablest but also most driven and ambitious congressman. She covered two pages with scribbles in the handwriting that still embarrassed her, then thrust one at the accountant and the other at Hovde.

"Before we discuss these assignments, let's double check on what we've got going or on the front burner. Don, am I right that you cleared up the stolen painting thing for the insurance company?"

"I did what you said. Turned in the report yesterday."

"How did they take it?"

"Not too well. Seemed unhappy to find out their top appraiser was fingering the jobs. Told me they'd just given him a gold watch for twenty-five years' service eight months ago."

She wrote something else on the pad and looked up again.

"Anything else?" she asked.

"Check's in the mail."

"The check's always in the mail," the accountant said.

"They want us to find some kind of thoroughbred hound worth twenty thousand dollars. Dognapping ring grabbing all the best mutts in Bel Air, holding them for ransom."

She shook her head. "Divorces, windows or dogs—we won't touch them. Any questions about the assignments?"

Whatever uncertainties she might have had about the Las Vegas case were no longer evident. She sounded strong, confident, committed.

"Not on the assignment," Agajanian said, "but I don't understand why you're suddenly so exuberant about this grubby deal."

"It's not as grubby as the high-priced garbage cases we handle all the time," she answered. "You know that old joke about the man who justified shoveling elephant crap in the circus because he didn't want to leave show business? Well, it's time—for a while anyway—for us to get out of show business."

She sounded angry, and it took Agajanian several minutes back in his office to figure out why. She was fed up with hedonistic Hollywood . . . again . . . of course, but that wasn't all. She was irritated with herself as well. It obviously annoyed her that she couldn't resist this appeal to save the lives of these nothing people—porky beer salesmen and foolish old women hoping to win something . . . anything . . . for the first time in a life of losing. Why should *they* mean anything to her? She was embarrassed to face the fact that she could not ignore them. It was disturbing for her to acknowledge that, despite everyone and everything she'd lost, she was still vulnerable.

It was preposterous, the accountant thought, to expect the small, unofficial force that Alison Gordon could mobilize to find a covert criminal group in a city of strangers, a community of more than three hundred and eighty-five thousand permanent residents seething with thousands of transients. She knew that, too, but Alison Gordon clearly didn't care. It was happening all over again. She had made up her mind, and the impossible war had begun.

CHAPTER 5

LATITUDE, 36°-11′ north. Longitude, 115°-08′ west.

Battleground. Antonio Armijo had called this place The Meadows, but that was a long time ago, before all the people came with their cinder blocks, plywood and concrete. Now most of the grass lives in small neat patches called lawns—miniature memorials to what once was. The Paiutes who hunted here are long gone. This place—283 miles northwest of Phoenix and 289 miles northeast of Los Angeles—is cupped in a 2,000-foot-high desert valley ringed by mountains, and dry. It celebrates three hundred and ten days of sunshine a year, gets by on an average rainfall of less than four inches. Temperatures reach 99 degrees Fahrenheit in June, climb over 105 in July and August and hover near 100 during much of September. It is no Death Valley, but it is hot.

Even this late October afternoon, it was 83 degrees and every room in the Lady Luck Motel on East Fremont Street hummed with the sound of air conditioners. The same relentless monotone of conscientious compressors blanketed rooms at the Black Jack Motel, the Lucky Cuss Motel, the Par-a-Dice Inn, the Roulette Motel and more than a hundred and twenty competing establishments—including the Tivoli which offers "XXX RATED FILMS . . . FULL COLOR &

SOUND . . . In the Privacy of Your Own Room . . . QUEEN & KING BEDS—WATER BEDS . . . CONNECTING UNITS—MIRRORS."

The thin balding man in Room 6 at the Lady Luck was not watching pornographic movies. For one thing, this motel, like most of those here in Clark County, offered free coffee and inexpensive baby sitters instead of sexually explicit movies, to attract the family trade. For another, he had seen more than two hundred such films and lost interest—at least temporarily—in nymphomaniacal stewardesses, interracial orgies and baby-faced Oriental women dressed in red leather boots with matching whips. Mainly, though, he was concentrating on the firing mechanism of an M-72 launcher for anti-tank missiles.

His name—his *real* name, not the one under which he was registered—was Arthur Messinger. Precision and dignity were important to this son of a Pittsfield, Massachusetts, electrician. Even in this temperature he always wore a shirt and tie outdoors and he insisted on being called Arthur. He made it clear to his colleagues—he had few friends—that he found such as "Art" or "Artie" intolerable. He didn't want intimacy or affection, just respect. Since violence was his profession, everyone humored him in this idiosyncracy.

"Does it have to be this cold in here?" the other man complained as he returned from the lavatory.

"Yes."

Messinger didn't look up from the table on which the M-72 rested. He had chosen this motel because each room had a dinette section, with a table large enough for him to work on the weapons.

"I'm freezing my ass off," the younger man in the gaudy Hawaiian shirt grumbled.

Arthur Messinger found Stanley Kuziw's shirt—and the rest of his wardrobe—appalling, but he was willing to put up with the vulgar clothes because Kuziw was an excellent driver and the job required a skilled wheelman. Interruptions or distractions while Messinger was checking out a piece of key equipment were, however, not acceptable.

"This temperature is healthier for us and the gear, Stanley. It would not do for me to work with sweaty hands," he said in the tones of a kindergarten teacher.

"You're sure this damn thing will work?"

"It always has, Stanley. I spent twenty years in the Army. Three combat tours in Vietnam. I was an instructor in antitank weapons and tactics when I retired." He reached for the box of 66-mm missiles.

"Just because you were a sergeant—"

"Master sergeant," Messinger corrected and recited his serial number. "Stanley, I know a *lot* about weapons, explosives, mines—the whole number. This is a good plan. We'll all be rich."

For years, Arthur Messinger had lived by another plan—a decent pension with extra income from a gun shop he'd open. Inflation had wrecked that plan. It was the damn politicians who had screwed up the whole country. They sat on their butts and let the world's economy get all messed up, living off their fat-cat friends and ignoring the working people. If it were not for those politicians and the inflation, the former master sergeant would not be here with a person in a loud Hawaiian shirt preparing for a multi-million-dollar crime. Messinger heard the click of Kuziw's lighter and sighed without turning from his work.

"Put that out, Stanley. The room is full of explosives, and I don't like the smell of cigarette smoke. It gets in your clothes in a sealed room like this."

"I'll just grab a couple of puffs."

"I'll break your face, Stanley," the older man promised softly as he slid a rocket halfway into the launcher.

Kuziw stole another drag before he tossed the Winston into the toilet bowl. Arthur Messinger closed his eyes for a moment in disgust. Kuziw was a thief; Messinger considered himself a soldier, and war was his craft. The name of this battlefield was Las Vegas, not Danang, and this time the foe was Caucasian rather than Oriental—and they would be counting dollars, not bodies, after this operation. Messinger told himself that this was a different kind of war, and that he wouldn't have to put up with undisciplined criminals such as twenty-eight-year-old Stanley Kuziw much longer.

"If I can't smoke in here—"

"You can't, Stanley."

"Does that mean the stuff could blow us up?"

Messinger extracted the armor-piercing missile.

"Not without the fuses. I told you that," he said.

Kuziw abruptly put on his gaudy "cool" sunglasses, signaling that he was going out to prowl the downtown casinos and strip shows again. There was a defiance in his gestures. He knew that Messinger didn't trust him out there alone. But this time the older man didn't argue because he recognized the tension in his immature confederate—the restless, stupid thing that had to be released if another kind of explosion was to be averted. Master Sergeant Messinger had learned how to handle men as well as weapons in those twenty years of military service. Whether it was boredom or fear that now drove his driver didn't matter. The reality was that Kuziw was one of those who needed action and motion, flashing lights and bobbing breasts—all available only out there. He had the intelligence and inner resources of an empty vending machine.

"Be back around seven," Kuziw announced.

"Sure. Air yourself out. Blow a couple of dollars on the slots, and grab some sun. Take it easy on the vodka though. Be careful, Stanley."

The younger man jerked a cigarette from an almost empty pack, glared.

"I'm no boozer," he protested.

"Never said you were, Stanley," Messinger replied, "but this town is full of temptations. We've all got to be careful, Stanley."

Kuziw was at the door when he took out the green plastic lighter again and paused to check his reflection in the large mirror. He caught himself about to flick his lighter again and felt a rush of indignation.

"Can't you call me Stan instead of Stanley?" he grumbled.

"I don't think so," Messinger replied truthfully.

The driver slammed the door as he left, and Arthur Messinger focussed on the anti-tank weapon again. The others would arrive with the fuses and detonators for the bombs tomorrow, and that left more than a week to put them in the places he had scouted and selected. It was an excellent plan, although not entirely without its dangers. However, you had to expect risks when you were planning to take this much money from men who had weapons too, and no hesitation about killing. It would be a very interesting little war, Messinger thought cheerfully and walked into the bathroom to wash his hands for the fifth time since breakfast.

CHAPTER 6

PAUL NEWMAN was wearing a blue outfit, and Muhammad Ali was sporting white boxing trunks. Done up in a "Hunchback of Notre Dame" outfit, Lon Chaney appeared both tacky and scary while Sonny and Cher looked even more plastic than usual.

"Weird," Alison Gordon said.

"The King Is Here in Living Wax—Elvis Presley!" Hovde read from the large card in the window.

"ADULTS $3. JUNIOS"—someone had left out the R—"$2." The slovenly spelling on the sign at Tussaud's Museum seemed appropriate for this tired and tawdry street. Once the symbol of glamor and success to millions around the world, Hollywood Boulevard had become a magnet for the most unsophisticated tourists, drugged-out adolescent prostitutes of all sexes and perversions and adults out cruising for fresh "chickens" whose bodies were for rent. A bright-eyed Asian couple—they might be on their honeymoon—paused before the wax museum to take photos.

"Why did he want to meet here, Don?" Alison asked.

" 'Cause he's weird. You just said it yourself," Hovde replied. "You know, I understand this street used to be really something, full of young actors hoping to be discovered . . . twenty or thirty years ago."

She looked at her watch and nodded toward the sidewalk. "That's what the papers and magazines said, but how do we know?" she answered.

"You think it was a hype? Another media number?"

"I think it's time we start walking to the theater," she said. Fanelli had specified the wax museum at three or Mann's Chinese Theater—the Hollywood landmark formerly known as Graumann's Chinese—twenty minutes later. The street was half empty as they walked past the wig shops, cheap jewelry and souvenir stores, and windows offering books, photos and posters about the Golden Age of Hollywood. They didn't speak as they passed the parking lot behind the Holiday Inn, or even when they looked across at the older architecture of the Paramount Theater or the Hollywood Masonic Temple. The sight of the wildly colorful movie house with its pagoda roof and Oriental towers had to be acknowledged, however.

"Now *that's* something. Admit it, Al."

"That's preposterous," she replied, "and pretentious. It's the movie business at its peak, a crass eye-grabber. Hollywood's answer to the Sphinx, bad taste at its worst."

"So you hate it?"

"I love it," she confessed. "It appeals to the child in me. Look at those signatures and handprints in the cement. Who could resist those names?"

Lana Turner, 5–24–50. Bette Davis, 11–6–50. The Marx Brothers, Feb. 17 '33. "For Mr. Graumann, all happiness—Judy Garland . . . 10–10–39." Fred Astaire, Shirley Temple, Henry Fonda, Cary Grant, Jimmy Durante, and scores of others. By "Aug. 21 '46," Humphrey Bogart had left hand and shoe imprints with the printed wish, "Sid, may you never die till I kill you"—a jocular tribute to his violent roles. They watched as a dozen tourists bent over to read the signatures of the legends, the evocative markings that future film students would examine with the kind of scholarly passion now accorded Mayan stelae in ruined cities of

Guatemala and Yucatan. She found herself smiling.

"When I was a kid, Don—"

"You were *never* a kid."

She turned to face the laughing radio technician they had come to meet. "You're still a kid, Gerry," she told Fanelli.

"You were born an adult—a smart and sexy broad." He blew her a kiss across a cupped palm, then winked at Hovde.

"How's it goin', man?" he asked.

"Weird and dangerous. You in?"

"Tell me all about it," Fanelli said affably. As he guided them back onto the sidewalk to cross Hollywood Boulevard to the Hamburger Hamlet, his sly expression told Alison that Fanelli hadn't changed at all. He was still hungry.

"I think I got a worm," he said.

Same old story. Some people bummed cigarettes. Fanelli wangled food, usually junk food. Pretending that they didn't understand his appeal, Alison Gordon and Hovde took his arms and steered him away from the fast food shop, back toward Cahuenga.

"Let's get down to business," she said.

"It's my metabolism. Burns everything up in a flash. I'm practically a walking furnace—"

"You are a charming and total neurotic, a compulsive eater, ridiculous womanizer—but you are a first-class electronics and radio man. Has Don explained the operation?"

Fanelli shook his head like a petulant child.

"He wouldn't let me," Hovde protested.

"Not on the phone. Never knows who's sitting on the line," Fanelli reminded. "I don't know if I can do it—whatever your deal is. I'm thinking of leaving town for a bit."

"How about two weeks in Vegas?"

"You need a vacation," Hovde said.

"Well . . . Yeah, Vegas might be fine. Got a little problem with some people who think I bugged their . . . Hotheads, you know? Crazy people these days take everything personally . . . Don't understand I act in a professional capacity."

They walked on as she explained the mission and the money. At the corner of Las Palmas, Fanelli tried to persuade them to "grab a bite" at a coffee shop, but most of the young patrons visible through the big window were either stoned or otherwise ravaged. The gaunt faces of these corrupted child whores disturbed and repelled her, filled her with a flush of bitterness and helplessness. She'd seen the same human decay in a dozen countries, and still the sight of doomed adolescents bothered her.

"Too crowded in there. We couldn't talk," she told Fanelli and pressed on down the street before he could argue. She let him slow down to sneak a peek at the flamboyant lingerie displayed by the Frederick of Hollywood store, a collection of gaudily colored mini-nighties, transparent robes and other boudoir items so blatantly erotic that they were, she decided, funny. Instead of laughing, she told him about the two-way radios they would need for five cars and discussed types of walkie-talkies that would not attract attention.

"Isaac Stern . . . Marie Dressler . . . Frank Sinatra," Fanelli read aloud and pointed to the metal stars and inscriptions embedded in the sidewalk to honor those celebrities.

"Knock it off," Hovde told him.

Fanelli eyed a frozen-yogurt parlor offering nine flavors but managed to control his impulse. He remembered the pizzeria on the next block, felt better and assured her that he could secure the equipment and radio operators who could be trusted.

"Right away. We're in a hurry," she said.

"Day after tomorrow okay?"

"Yesterday would be better. Give him the money, Don."

Hovde reached into his jacket and handed over a fat envelope.

"That's eight thousand dollars in fifties and one hundreds. This whole operation will be strictly cash, and there's plenty."

"Just like the good old days," Fanelli recalled.

"Be sure you count right. Agajanian likes receipts," warned Hovde.

"He would. Any other rules?"

She reached forward and gripped his shoulder.

"I don't want you chasing women in Vegas, picking up women in Vegas, getting into any kind of woman trouble at all. Is that clear, Gerry? Absolutely goddamn clear?"

"Word of honor." He made an appointment to report progress to Hovde at one P.M. the next day in Fast Fong's, the Szechuan cuisine take-out shop on West Pico.

"Strictly kosher. You'll love it," Fanelli assured.

"I'll hate it," Hovde said gloomily as they watched Fanelli hurry toward the pizzeria. She looked around at the street and shook her head.

"I hate this street, Don."

"Don't blame Hollywood," he answered. "Hundred other streets just like it in other cities—maybe a thousand."

"I hate them too. I just hate this one a little more because I used to read about it when I was a kid. Come on, let's get back to the car—fast."

She walked quickly, and when they were in the Porsche she pushed it harder than usual. Hovde sensed the impatience and the pressure. He wasn't afraid of an accident—he knew that she could handle her cars—but the police in some passing black-and-white might be less appreciative of her talents.

"Take it easy, Al. What's the rush? You got a date?"

"I've got twelve days," she replied, "twelve days to November sixth."

Then they talked about the guns.

CHAPTER 7

THOMAS ARROYO was a law-abiding man and he was not happy with what he was about to do. Too many other Navahos, defeated by third-rate educations, were dying by inches every month as cheap whiskey, inadequate medical care, bad housing and, worse, marijuana, poor diets and frustration took their toll. Thomas Arroyo wasn't one of those who succumbed to self-hatred and drifted in and out of jails and drunk tanks, who fought bar brawls with hammers and knives that left other Indians scarred or dead.

Nor was he an important man by most standards. He was not the son of a chief, and he had not even finished high school until after he came back from six years in the U.S. Army. No member of his family had ever served on the tribal council, finished college, been filmed by a TV news crew during a protest or earned more than $7,000 a year. He had been the first to earn more than that, because he had a special trade: the craft he was now about to employ. It was not steady work, but he was very skilled at this thing he had learned as a soldier, and when he was employed the pay was good. The work was dangerous. Why else would the whites pay that much to an Indian?

He did not like this job, and the thought of what he was preparing to do was distasteful. He loved this mesa, these cliffs and this valley. He had never told anyone about these feelings. He was physically strong, a stocky, muscled man of thirty-four with the body of someone a decade younger, a man who talked little except in his own family. He was private rather than silent, and he was not simple at all. He had thought long and carefully before reaching this decision.

"Keep watch," he said to his cousin as he rechecked the double-knot that bound the nylon climbing cord to the pickup truck. The Ford was seven years old, but it was not battered or dusty. The Army had trained him to take care of his tools and weapons.

"Do you think this is a good idea, Thomas?" the younger man asked uneasily.

"No, but I don't have a better one. It has to be done."

He reexamined his climbing gear and the pulley. He didn't consider the irony of the fact that the white men had taught him climbing, rapelling and demolition while he served in the military. He concentrated on lowering himself over the edge, and then he let himself down carefully. It was four hundred and thirty feet to the floor of the valley. If he fell even a fifth of that, the rocks would smash his bones like dry sticks.

The sun was closing up on the rim on the other side, and the valley was beautiful as it had been for a thousand years. The rays glinted on the multi-colored walls of rock, bouncing off pyrites, copper and molybdenum. The molybdenum was the problem, the magnet that drew the ruthless and determined men of the rich and powerful mining company. The Navaho were not rich, but Thomas Arroyo would prove to the billion-dollar company that they too were determined —and that was a kind of power. The intruders with their clever lawyers and friends in high places would not be allowed to rape this valley. The time would come when clever Navaho lawyers and doctors and geologists would return from the distant universities, and some day the Indians would be respected in high places too.

Time—that was the enemy.

It was up to Thomas Arroyo to buy some today.

Lowering himself in a series of six- to ten-foot descents, Arroyo made his way down the jagged side of the valley wall. Twice he bounced against rocky outcroppings, and he braced himself as he shielded the explosives in the faded burlap sack with one hand. He took the impact and pain with only a grunt and tried to resume his journey down.

He was stuck. The line was caught around a saw-toothed shaft of stone that thrust out like a spear. Arroyo looked up and down and off to the sides, searching for a foothold and considering the possibilities. The truth was that there were more hazards than possibilities, and there was no one near enough to help him with any of them. The most immediate threat was that the line would be severed, and he would drop to die. If his luck was bad he would die slowly. Even if the nylon held, he might remain trapped here ninety feet down the side of the wall for hours. Then he ran the risk of being discovered by the mining company people, who would find the explosives and take him to the police. After that they would desecrate this ancient valley that had belonged to the Navaho people for more generations than even the oldest medicine man could remember.

No. With great effort, he began to climb back up—trying to avoid fretting the nylon against the sharp edge of the stone. Though the sun was barely up, he was damp with perspiration. He recalled the military jargon from his past, realizing that he was again "sweating it out." This time—as it had been in the fighting north of Danang—it was literally true. His palms were sheeted with wetness, and he was breathing hard as he made his way back up the sheer face. He was only a few yards from the jagged outcropping now. He placed one foot in a fissure, eased the pressure on the line and flipped it loose.

The line was frayed—probably just a bit. The sensible

thing would be to get above the abraded section and climb back up to the rim, but that would have done nothing to save this primeval burial ground. Arroyo had chanted the prayers of his people only hours before, and he resolved to trust in them now. He started down again, finally reaching a point 140 feet down where he saw the cracks he needed. He inserted bundles of dynamite in five fissures, then set the common time-fuse for fifteen minutes—the maximum. It was bright and warming up fast, and he had to move quickly. As soon as the fuse was running, he started to climb back up.

He thought about ascending slowly to keep the line from unraveling under the pressure, but he knew that those blasts would surely kill him if he did not reach the crest in time. The climbing rope held, as it was destined to. Arroyo was not a superstitious man, not even very religious in comparison to others in his family, but he believed in destiny. When he reached safety on the rim, he got out of his climbing gear and detached the rope. He tossed the equipment into the back of the pickup, covered it with a worn remnant of a canvas top and gestured to his cousin.

"I'll drive," he said.

"Did you—?"

"Yes. Get in. When the explosions happen, we must be at least five miles from here."

They were. They heard the blast in the clear morning air of Arizona, but they did not see the many tons of rock thunder down to seal the entrance to the valley. It would take the mining company weeks to clear an access, and during that time the tribal council would have lawyers and spokesmen appeal to the judges, the press and the bureaucrats for justice. They would make the shameless men of the mining company go elsewhere for molybdenum. Arroyo was confident that right would prevail, because he knew that there were many whites who were free of prejudice, decent men and women who would oppose any further wrongs against the Navaho.

Arroyo drove back to his village by a circuitous route, one that would not suggest he had come from the site of the burial place. It was almost three hours before he reached the small general store and post office where he parked to check for his mail. There was no card from his sister, but the storekeeper-postmaster had other news.

"A man called for you, Thomas. He left a telephone number, asked me to tell you to call him back collect. He said it was important. A job."

"What was his name?"

"A hard one to say. Aganian? Abranium? It was a strange name. He was a polite man, Thomas." The postmaster handed him a slip of paper with the Beverly Hills telephone number.

A moment later, he was speaking to the accountant at A. B. Gordon Investigations on Wilshire Boulevard.

"This is Thomas . . . Yes, I'm well . . . How are you, Andrew? . . . And Miss Gordon? . . . A fine woman."

It would be rude to ask why Agajanian had called. He waited until Agajanian explained that they had need of a specialist who had experience with bombs, booby-traps and explosives. Since there was no one better at these things than Arroyo, and they all liked him, there was a job at $1,000 a week, roughly two weeks' work, waiting for the Indian if he could join them immediately. Agajanian took care to explain that Arroyo was needed for disabling explosives, not detonating them.

"If you're free, Thomas, we'd appreciate your help—right away."

Free? Some more articulate members of the tribe could speak passionately for hours on that subject. But Thomas Arroyo was a quiet person and this was no time for such talk. Moreover it would be just as well for him to be out of the area for a week or two after the explosions in the valley . . .

"Where? . . . When? . . . Assembly point? . . . I'll be there

. . . Anything else? . . . You don't know where they are? . . . Okay, there's a person who may be able to help . . . That's right . . . Thanks for calling, Andrew . . . Yes, I'll reach him today if possible. Good-by."

There was no need for the postmaster to know any more than this about his business. Thomas Arroyo made his call from an enclosed booth on the edge of Flagstaff when he stopped to eat lunch. The conversation with O. K. Littlefield was brief and unpleasant, as usual. Then Arroyo got back into the pickup and drove toward Peach Springs. If nothing went wrong, he would be in Las Vegas before the moon was up and in two weeks he would have more money for his nineteen-year-old sister. He was proud of her good grades at the Navaho Community College and her determination to wear the white hat of the registered nurse. Not just *a* nurse, a fully trained *registered* nurse.

Traffic was light, but the truck was not to be abused. He drove over the half-empty roads at a conservative forty-five miles per hour until he reached the gasoline station at Peach Springs. It was while he was paying for the ten gallons that he heard the news report of the explosion that sealed the valley blaring scratchily from a radio.

"Lots of crazies around," the attendant said as he gave Arroyo his change. The Navaho nodded ambiguously, hoped that his cousin would not speak about the incident to anyone. He had given his word, but young men sometimes could not resist the temptation to boast. Arroyo thanked the attendant politely and swung the truck back onto Route 66. The road was straight and Las Vegas was no more than 120 miles northwest. He liked Agajanian and Alison Gordon as much as they liked him, and everything would be all right, if his young cousin kept sober and silent. If not, the police would be on Arroyo's trail—hunting him everywhere within five hundred miles of the molybdenum-rich valley. The mining company would see to that.

CHAPTER 8

THE PANORAMA from the airliner window was majestic. She stared down at the beautiful vista of upthrusting mountains and oddly naked plains, a view that reminded her of those images of the moon's cold and barren surface sent back by satellite to stun earthly television viewers. But there was no sense of desolation or hostility to life in these Nevada peaks, only an impersonal grandeur that reminded her that these shapes—these *things*—were geological and she was biological. Geology outlasts biology, and all this would be here long after she was gone, just as it had been for millenia before she was born. The desert meant that her journey was almost over.

She hadn't bothered to look down during the first twenty minutes of the flight from Los Angeles. Her attention had been directed inside rather than out as she sipped the pleasant California Chablis provided by Hughes Airwest, another investment of the late tycoon. It was insane that a multimillionaire—even a paranoid one—should die of malnutrition and inadequate medical care, though no more so than the fantastic gambling craze that had been a $2.7-billion business for Nevada the previous year. Agajanian had told her that it was the second largest industry in the state, had generated almost $122 million in "gaming" taxes. She cared a lot less about numbers than her accountant did and she couldn't understand why she hadn't forgotten those statistics. She told herself that it could not be a *mere* interest in money, for wealth had never meant that much to her.

She could not wholly ignore the awesome rocks and sand of the Mohave below, but she forced herself to focus on the unequal battle that lay ahead. She didn't know who or where the foe was, and all she had—really had for sure—was a telephone number and eleven days.

"Ten days," she thought aloud.

"Please fasten your seatbelts," the blonde flight attendant said a moment later.

Some countries name their cities after saints or monarchs, and others title streets to celebrate composers, novelists or military heroes. Following a more populist American tradition, the main airport at Las Vegas—where fifteen commercial carriers deposit many of the mecca's ten million visitors each year—is named after a dead politician. Senator Pat McCarran took an active interest in civil aviation, so they dubbed the field McCarran Airport and later expanded that to McCarran International Airport as the flow of foreign pilgrims zoomed. A throng of these faithful accompanied Alison Gordon from the DC–9 into the terminal, which was —like so many other things in this dynamic community— modern, air-conditioned, efficient, bigger and busier than it had been three years earlier.

In the cool terminal she heard the buzz of scores of voices, all filled with anticipation of the fun and games that made Vegas a special place. Then there was that other sound, mechanical, metallic and full of promise. Crash! Crash! There they were—some three dozen slot machines singing their seductive chorus of coins as someone hit a jackpot. It was one of the machines that digested silver dollars, newest and most intoxicating of the one-armed bandits. Pausing to look around for Hovde, she saw a dozen of her fellow passengers pause to challenge the rows of robots with flashing lights and spinning cylinders.

She did not see Hovde. Ignoring the thump, thump, thump of slot-machine arms being pumped, she walked onto the moving belt that would carry her to the baggage-claim area. Now she heard other voices, taped messages from star performers advising her to hold on to the rail, be careful and courteous. Where the hell was Hovde? She had sent him ahead in her Porsche with the trunk filled with weapons that Los Angeles International Airport security teams would not let them take aboard planes—guns, ammunition and other hardware. He was supposed to meet her . . . here . . . now Was something already wrong?

When she reached the baggage area, she spotted him as he entered the building. He came toward her, half-smiling in apology.

"Got a phone call just as I was leaving to pick you up," he explained.

"Our office?"

"No, I don't know who he was. I did what you said, called that number and left word you'd be checking in at Caesars tonight. Then just fifteen minutes ago some guy phoned me with a funny message for you."

She saw the first cartload of suitcases being unloaded and took one of the black cigarettes from her Hermes shoulder bag.

"Ha, ha?" she said.

"Not that kind of funny," Hovde said and lit the Sobranie. "He said there'd been a call from 'those people,' promising to deliver a free sample at five o'clock this afternoon to show they're not kidding."

"That's not funny at all," she agreed. They spoke quietly about the timetable for the others to arrive, the arrangements for the command post. Then Hovde went out to move her car into position in front of the terminal, and it was only five minutes until the uniformed skycap loaded her two suitcases into the trunk and back seat of the Porsche. She slid behind the wheel. She adjusted the seat, put on her sunglasses and put the key into the ignition.

"Did he say anything else, Don?"

"He told me it would be a *double* free sample. What the hell is that?"

"Something nasty," she predicted, and started the motor, then turned to make sure that it was safe to pull out into the driveway. As she did, she spoke to Hovde over her shoulder

"What time is it?"

"Just five o'clock."

A large blue Lincoln Continental parked thirty yards away burst into flames, and at the same moment an astonishing fireball seemed to engulf a green Jaguar convertible twenty yards from the first car. People were running, shouting for the fire truck.

"*Double* free sample," she said, lowering her visor against the heat.

There it was. She'd been right. It was nasty.

To the credit of the taxi drivers, porters, tourists and a dozen other people outside the terminal, they all behaved sensibly. Five cabbies drove their vehicles away from the danger, the porters carried baggage back into the building, a uniformed policeman hurried startled travelers back into the terminal and two Hong Kong businessmen in spectacles began taking photos with the latest and most costly model Canon "electric eye" cameras. An elegantly attired "model" who could teach Masters and Johnson a few things studied the blazing cars thoughtfully.

"Son of a bitch!" she philosophized—and then looked around for the blouse manufacturer who had rented her for the next two days.

The sound of a siren was growing louder, signaling the approach of some official vehicle. An airport "emergency truck" swung around one corner of the building as a police car swooped into sight from the other direction. Alison Gordon started the Porsche, guided it away from the burning luxury cars at a prudent twenty miles per hour. It would be stupid to rush into a collision with some fire crew or hysterical gambler now. She stopped some ninety yards from the terminal and turned in her seat to survey the crisis.

She did not notice that the driver of a tan delivery van was also watching the fires professionally, and even if she had there was no reason for her to suspect that the red-haired man had any connection with the incendiary incident. A lot of other men and women on foot and in a variety of cars—one plump brunette in tight jeans on a Honda motorcycle—were staring intently too. Since the private detective could not look into either the mind of the red-haired man or the cargo compartment of his van, she ignored him.

"Probably phosphorus," Hovde calculated beside her. He was still a connoisseur of booby-traps, mines and fire weapons despite all the time that had passed since he left the C.I.A., and he made a continuing effort to keep up to date on the latest gadgets and advances. She judged that it was less than an obsession, more than a hobby and not half as sick as the private passions of a lot of the famous people who had employed A. B. Gordon Investigations Inc. during the previous year. It was—like Hovde himself—a bit odd. On the other hand, he never cheated on his taxes or abused women and that was unconventional too.

". . . 2700 degrees centigrade. It burns at 2700 degrees centigrade," he recalled.

"Phosphorus?"

"*White* phosphorus. 'Willie Peter.' Stuff the Army uses in the M–34 grenade," he specified in a lecturer's tones.

"You really dig that—" she began, and caught herself.

"What?"

"Nothing."

He opened the door beside him, started to step out of the Porsche. The emergency crew was spraying foam on the big Lincoln.

"Where are you going, Don?"

"Thought I'd take a closer look."

"You won't see anything. All you'll do is draw attention, and we don't need that. Let the cops and the fire marshals go over the mess, and we can get their reports tomorrow."

A small fire truck pulled up as Hovde reluctantly climbed into the car and a team of men in gray coveralls started to attack the blaze that was devouring the Jaguar. The driver of the tan van watched as she guided the sports car out toward the four-lane road that led to The Strip, then fell in behind the Porsche.

The road, known around the world as The Strip, is legally designated "Las Vegas Boulevard South" and runs about six miles from the southeast to the northwest. This is the newer, more fashionable and therefore more expensive part of the sprawling community. Las Vegas has more than two hundred churches, including the Full Gospel Deliverance Church, the Chapel of the Stars, the Echoes of Faith Center, the Guardian Angel Cathedral of the Viatorian Fathers, the Church of Scientology Celebrity Center, the Sunrise Congregation of Jehovah's Witnesses, the Church of Nutritional Science, two synagogues and dozens of houses of worship of the Mormons who built an adobe fort and established a temporary settlement called Bringhurt in the 1850's.

Despite this abundance of religious edifices and devotion, there are almost no churches on The Strip. It isn't that kind of a street. The Hacienda Hotel *and* Casino is the semi-official marker on the southern end and the Sahara Hotel *and* Casino stands guard at the northern limit, and in between is a wall-to-wall extravaganza of eye-catching hotels, casinos, souvenir shops, liquor stores, motels and undistinguished dining establishments offering half a dozen cuisines —including fast. Las Vegas is still more of a center for gamblers than for gourmets, and while there is plenty of hearty food at a variety of prices only a few of the largest hotels offer much more than mediocre cooking. With the prospect of a ten-day stay, Alison Gordon had carefully booked herself into the one super-hotel that tried to provide sophisticated dining.

Strip hotels are built around themes, often embodied in architecture, decor and the costumes of the buxom cocktail waitresses who circulate in the casinos that dominate every lobby. One has an Arabian Nights flavor, another a Mexican tone, a third hints at the Orient and the huge MGM Grand tries to celebrate its parent film company and the Hollywood legend. While the exterior of Caesars Palace is only modestly Mediterranean in a few arches and a squad of large marble reproductions of classic pre-Christian statues, the leaping fountains and the twin rows of imported cypress that flank the circular driveway might remind some historically minded types of Rome in the good old days when slaves did all the wet-wash and every middle-class family could afford a decent orgy once a week. Hovde pointed at a headless statue with wings as she steered the Porsche into the very grand driveway.

"That's an exact copy of the Victory of Samothrace—in Carrara marble. Cut from the same mountain where Michelangelo got his stone," he confided.

"You sound like Agajanian, or some damn brochure. I'm not sure which is worse," she said as she drove past a line of four taxis, a purple Cadillac with Arizona license plates and one of the largest station wagons in captivity. As soon as she stopped at the front doors—there were three—Hovde got out and unloaded her suitcase.

"I'll park the car," he volunteered. In the steady flow of people in and out, a uniformed bellboy reached for the bags and saw them both looking toward another large sculpture in the adjacent fountain.

"That's 'The Rape of the Sabine Women'," he identified helpfully.

"The movie was better," she replied. She gave Hovde the car keys, walked briskly into the hubbub of the vast lobby.

It was cool, softly lit and seething with the sounds of a lot of people talking and gambling and the clatter-thump-clatter of at least a battalion of slot machines. It took her eyes some moments to adjust. In that brief interval, a shapely woman in a mini-toga costume thrust into Alison Gordon's hand a card entitling her to one free pull at slot machine 109 in "the West Slot Arcade." There were two small photos of nude male statues, framing "WIN $10,000!! (maximum)." The private detective turned left past the counter where the bell captain was selling a Chicago urologist a flying tour over Grand Canyon, made her way ten yards down to an alert-looking reservations clerk. He saw the card in her hand, smiled pleasantly.

"Fat lady from Dallas won $10,000 day before yesterday," he said without a trace of pressure. Nobody *pushed* guests to gamble here.

"I'm a thin one from Beverly Hills. Gordon. A. B. Gordon."

The whole reservations and billing system was ultra-modern and computerized with visual display screens and a lot of colored buttons. The efficient reservations man tapped several, nodded.

"Ah, yes. A. B. Gordon, twelve days. You have a mini-suite in the North Tower. Lovely view. 927, very nice."

"I didn't order a suite."

"Someone did that for you. There's to be no extra charge Boy . . ."

To get to the elevators from the front desk in this hotel—and just about every other on The Strip or near the Downtown Casino Center in the older part of Las Vegas—one must walk through an appealing jungle of gambling tables and machines ringed by dozens of hopeful and determined players. Journalists with an animus toward American business have pointed out that even the pedestrian paths through this obstacle course zigzag to slow down the potential gambler, and have cynically suggested that the entire setup is designed to entice transients into assorted games of chance. Slots and keno, poker, blackjack, dice and baccarat were all in sight as she followed the bellboy on a winding course through the large room.

Money cage on the right, shops on the left. Mini-skirted change girls circulating with aprons full of coins mingled with armed men in Stetson-style hats, and Alison Gordon recalled someone telling her that the private house police in Vegas casinos had all been deputized. They could arrest trouble-makers or slot machine tamperers, or defend the million or two in the counting rooms with their revolvers if that proved necessary. There were probably a dozen guards with sidearms in the big room, and there were all kinds of alarms.

She looked up at the mirrored ceiling, pierced here and there with small round holes. There were sometimes—no one knew when—observers up there on Spy-in-the-Sky duty, looking down. Unseen television cameras peered through the holes, sweeping round the tables. Both systems were designed primarily to help The House catch cheaters—either outsiders or corrupt dealers—but they also helped watch for other kinds of criminals. There were other security devices too; no one had come close to holding up the casino in a major Las Vegas hotel in years. Gambling and non-gambling vacationers alike could feel safe here, could enjoy the luxury and surrender to the fantasy, because everyone knew that only amateurs or idiots would consider an armed robbery.

"This way, miss," the man with her baggage nudged gently.

She followed him through a stream of people to an unusual body of water. On the left of the passageway—just after a bar with only three customers on stools—was a man-made pool. In it was a strange-looking vessel, a ship that was supposed to represent Cleopatra's Barge. The executive vice president of the hotel had explained it all four years ago.

Everything in this pleasure dome had to be dramatic and exotic and memorable, something patrons would talk about when they got home. Caesar and Cleopatra had enjoyed a wonderfully romantic and legendary relationship, so what would be more logical than a version of *her* barge—with dance floor and room for a quartet—in *his* hotel? The plays about them by Shakespeare and Shaw? The *major* motion pictures, starring first Claudette Colbert and later Liz Taylor? A natural, right?

But somehow Cleopatra's Barge was one of the hotel's efforts that had never been much of a winner. The damn boat even moved realistically in the water, but it just didn't grab people the way either the Noshorium coffee shop or the Bacchanal had, she thought as she trailed the bellboy—and what the hell was a Japanese restaurant doing just across the corridor? Had commercial considerations prevailed over fidelity to the Roman theme?

There were more statues set in niches when she emerged from the elevator onto the ninth floor, and the mini-suite was exactly as the clerk had said—very nice. It was a bit flashy with a bed big enough for two couples, set on a slight platform. In the best Vegas tradition, it was too much and quite comfortable. She tipped the bellboy, and before he was out of the room she tossed her jacket on the couch and reached for a cigarette.

"The windows don't open," Hovde reminded from the doorway and jerked his thumb over his shoulder.

"Is that a code message?"

"Just telling you I'm across the hall. You sore about something?"

"Lots of things. The quality of TV programming, the lack of quality in Washington, male chauvinism, female chauvinism and architects who design buildings with sealed windows. That's for openers. I'm not sore at you, Don."

"Have a piece of chocolate," he suggested with a nod toward the coffee table.

She noticed the box for the first time, recognized it instantly. Two pounds of the European Praline Assortment from the Edelweiss Candy Kitchen, one of the great chocolate makers of North America. Every chocolate freak in Beverly Hills knew the shop on North Canon Drive, where nothing was cheap and everything was wonderful.

"You bring that?" she asked with a caution that puzzled Hovde.

"Not me. You said you were trying to kick the habit."

She studied the box, considered the possibilities.

"Maybe there's a card inside?" he suggested.

"Or something else."

Hovde reached inside his jacket, found a slim leather case and took out a five-inch piece of wood that resembled a short knitting needle. "Open the hall door, will you?" the booby-trap expert asked. That would let the blast out, and also move her beyond the immediate range of a small bomb. It was not heroics, it was standard operating procedure; the Agency had trained them that there was no point in risking *two* lives in checking unknown packages.

"It's probably candy," she said as she started for the portal.

"Sure."

When she had the door open, he inserted—slowly and cautiously—the wooden probe through the cardboard. He slid it in a quarter of an inch at a time, pausing between each advance. He pushed it in four inches, then withdrew it just as warily. He raised the probe to his lips, licked it.

"Bittersweet."

Six probes later, they were both convinced that it would be safe—and delicious—to open the box. Inside they found dozens of pieces of exotic-looking chocolate dusted with cocoa, some wounded by the probe, and a small white envelope. She popped one of the Swiss truffles into her mouth and suppressed an indecent moan of pleasure. She took the card from the envelope that was inscribed with her name in neat block letters.

"Welcome to Las Vegas, A. B. . . . Signed B. D." She read in a voice as cold as her expression. Then she reached for another piece of chocolate.

"Who's B. D.?" Hovde asked, trying to remember just what his dentist had said about candy and cavities.

"I have no idea," she replied, "but that's not what is bothering me. Whoever he—or she—is, how did the word get out that I was checking in here today and who knew in advance that I'd be in this room? . . . We seem to have a security problem and I haven't even unpacked my bags."

She replaced the lid on the chocolate box and stood up, surveying the room. "That stuff you brought in the car?" she said in deliberately ambiguous reference to the guns and other weapons.

"Less than a block away. We can get over there as soon as you hang up your clothes."

"Let's go *now,*" she said—and they went.

A few miles away in the downtown motel, Arthur Messinger looked up as Stanley Kuziw entered the room, smoking.

"Sorry," the younger man apologized in a voice devoid of sincerity. Kuziw ground the cigarette out in a repulsive green ashtray and glanced around the room.

"Lester and Gene aren't here," the ex-master sergeant answered Kuziw's unspoken question. "They're supposed to stay away from us, except when I call a meeting. I don't want anybody to see the four of us together, Stanley. There'll be a lot of people looking for a group of four men pretty soon."

"Sure. Mind if I play the radio?"

"Not the rock and roll, Stanley. That music distracts me, and you play it so loud. Did you do what I told you?"

"I always do. You got any news?"

Messinger stopped oiling his .45-caliber handgun. "Just heard some news on the radio. Radio's good for news, Stanley. Not too complete, but fast. The president has a new energy plan, there was a big flood in India and two cars caught fire right here at the airport."

"Just *caught* fire?" Kuziw asked.

"They're not sure. Maybe someone did it."

"Who?"

"I don't think they know. You're looking tense. Pour yourself a drink. Relax."

Kuziw found the Seagram's Seven, sloshed three fingers of it into a bathroom tumbler and downed half in a single gulp. It would be a pleasure to be rid of this thug in a few days, Arthur Messinger thought. Tomorrow they would recheck the timers on the bombs; two days later Gene and Lester would begin to hide them in the places that Messinger had selected with such care. He'd made a point of not telling Kuziw where the explosive devices were to be concealed. If he were caught by the police—with someone like him one couldn't rule out a bar fight or even an argument with some hooker—he might blurt out anything. Or everything.

It might even be necessary to get rid of the wheelman after the job; there was no telling what the younger man might say in an outburst of alcoholic braggadocio three weeks or four months hence. It might well come to that, as a question of survival. The security of the unit always came first, and there were times when one man had to be sacrificed to that principle if he proved himself unfit to adhere to it. That was the reason Messinger was prepared to kill Stanley Kuziw. The extra money that they'd divide from the dead man's share had nothing to do with it, Messinger thought, and considered his plan for an auto accident at least two hundred miles from Las Vegas. It would be best if fire charred the corpse so badly that it could never be identified—a fierce blaze such as the ones that had destroyed those cars at the airport less than an hour earlier.

CHAPTER 9

ALISON GORDON walked with Hovde out of Caesars Palace, squinting as her eyes adjusted to the late afternoon sun and shivering as her body dealt with the temperature change from the air-conditioned lobby. The hideous birds—at least seven feet tall—made her wince. Everything in Las Vegas had to be larger than life, but these monstrous pink flamingos seemed particularly grotesque. Man-made of glowing fluorescent tubes, they were bizarre beyond mere garishness. There was a certain lunatic logic in adorning the hotel across The Strip with these caricatures, for this was the famed old Flamingo, founded in 1946 by Mr. Benjamin Siegel. A man with a dream and many armed friends who assisted in the financing, Siegel was among the first progressives to erect a hotel and casino on The Strip, away from the already crowded area downtown. There had been many changes since then. The Flamingo itself is now much larger and part of the Hilton chain, while Ben Siegel—the Brooklyn boy who made bad—is not around at all. Siegel, who never appreciated the nickname "Bugsy" the journalists gave him, was shot to pieces in Beverly Hills more than a quarter of a century ago.

"Our stuff isn't *there,* is it?" she asked Hovde.

"No, *there.*"

He nodded diagonally across the intersection of The Strip and Flamingo Road to the twenty-six-story MGM Grand, which has, if no flamingos, then almost everything else, as befits a 2,100-room hostelry claiming to be the largest resort hotel on the planet. After copying with two sets of traffic lights, they made their way into the immense lobby and found themselves facing a 140-yard-long casino—a football field lit by a platoon of massive crystal chandeliers and echoing with the sounds of almost one thousand slot machines. Half a dozen other types of games of chance were occupying a few hundred men and women as Hovde guided her along the near perimeter past the check-in desk, cashier and a lounge where a score of thirsty gamblers were sipping complimentary cocktails as they rested for another bout with the crap and blackjack tables, roulette and Big Six wheels and other diversions. The young trio of musicians and the smiling brunette singer offering a respectable version of "Rhinestone Cowboy" were barely audible in the noisy room and nobody seemed to mind. Activity was what counted, for without it there could be no fun and that's what people came to Vegas for.

When they entered the room on the fifteenth floor, Hovde put up the chain and opened a closet door to expose three hard-sided plastic suitcases. He pulled one out, found his key ring and unlocked it. She saw a dozen objects of varying sizes, each wrapped in towel and sealed with black tire tape. He took out several, felt them and put two on the king-sized bed.

"I think those are yours," he reported.

She opened the smaller one, found her .357 and the belly holster. She picked up the weapon, turned to Hovde.

"Here's the ammo," he volunteered. He took from his jacket pocket a Zip-Loc plastic bag—the kind used to keep food fresh in the refrigerator—and placed it in her hand. She could see three clips inside. She put on the holster, loaded the Magnum and sheathed it. She placed the other clips in her shoulder bag and pointed at the other package.

"It's no bigger than a bread basket."

"And weighs just over seven pounds."

"You're crazy, Don."

She removed the wrapping, looked at the eleven-and-a-half-inch-long Ingraham 10. Half a foot shorter than the Israeli Uzi it resembled, this nine-millimeter submachine gun had been Hovde's Yuletide gift to her two years earlier.

"Merry Christmas," she said harshly.

"I thought you might need it."

"You bring bulletproof vests too?"

"As a matter of fact I did. Fourteen, if anybody's counting. I brought sniper guns with night 'scopes, gas grenades, a dozen handguns—all kinds of hardware."

"No flame throwers? Don, this is an investigation by a private detective agency in an American resort—not a search and destroy mission in Vietnam. You're geared up for World War III, damn it."

He glared at her silently.

"Don, this *isn't* World War III."

"Not *yet.* I'm thirsty. You want a drink?"

He was defiantly changing the subject, and when Hovde was in this state he could not be reached. Maybe he wasn't to blame for the fact that sixteen years in the Agency had left him with a permanent "war" mentality.

"I want *two* drinks," she answered and helped him replace the suitcase. On the way to one of the street-level bars they talked about plans for their command post and getting all the weapons there as soon as possible. They were finishing their first drinks when she saw him sneak a glance at his wristwatch.

"I gather we've got to go somewhere?"

"Downstairs. He'll be there in five minutes."

The Navaho was on time, as usual. A small group of tourists clustered nearby, but Thomas Arroyo stood alone. All the others were animated, fascinated and a bit uneasy in the presence of a very live lion. Though he was no longer young and appeared to be securely restrained by a chain, this was the King of Beasts, the powerful animal that killed weaker animals in real life as well as in MGM movies. The chatter of the tourists signaled their fear and delight, just as Arroyo's sober appraisal signaled his rejection of both the people and the photo-taking.

"Get your picture with the MGM lion," invited an almost pretty young hotel employee who smiled splendidly. Vacationers shuffled forward, with one giggling woman in a colorful Suzy Creemcheese creation from The Boutique of the Stars leading the pack. The Navaho did not move. He would have no part of this thing. His face showed indifference—until he saw Alison Gordon. Then his eyes widened in greeting.

"Thank you for coming, Thomas. How are you?"

He hesitated for just a second, and she sensed that something was troubling him. She knew enough not to ask; he would speak of it only when he was ready. He had his rhythms and reasons, and she had learned to respect them.

"All right. And you, Miss Gordon?"

After she assured him that she and the rest of A. B. Gordon Investigations were well, there was a short silence; Arroyo had never shown much interest in small talk. He was a man who accepted time as a fundamental thing like weather, but he did not waste it. The notion of "passing" or "killing" it was not only foreign to him; it was repugnant. He cleared his throat, spoke softly.

"Is it here?"

"What?" she answered.

"The . . . thing they sent you. Andy said you wanted me to look at it. I'm ready now."

They found a telephone booth, and she dialed the number that Spinoza had given her.

"Yes?"

The voice of a man under forty. Strong. Direct.

"My name is Gordon."

"Been expecting your call."

"I'm in the MGM Grand with two of my associates, and we'd like to see the sample."

"When?"

"Now. Have you got it?"

"Outside the Convention Center . . . Paradise Road . . . behind the Landmark . . . fifteen minutes."

He had not said whether he had the bomb.

"Brown seventy-eight Cutlass," he added before she could repeat the question and hung up the telephone.

As Alison Gordon and the two men walked out of the hotel, a woman in the uniform of a maid was finishing her work in Room 927 at Caesars Palace a block away. Making beds was not her business, but she was used to working in strange costumes and places. She looked at the tiny transmitter in the open phone, screwed the base of the instrument back on and left Room 927. What Alison Gordon might do or say here was of no interest to this woman. Her job was done, and the rest was up to someone else.

CHAPTER 10

IT WAS easy to find the Convention Center. The thirty-one-story Landmark Hotel nearby thrusts boldly into the sky and the round disk of the top six floors cantilevers out of the $20,000,000 Hughes-built edifice like an oversize hat. The nearby Hilton is said to be nineteen feet taller and the loftiest spire in the state, but the Landmark has a six-sided tower and a swimming pool shaped like a whale so there is no possibility of confusion. Using the Landmark as her navigation point like a planet in the heavens, Alison Gordon located the Convention Center, drove into the enormous Center's very large parking lot and looked around cautiously.

The Center was a low domed structure, and the parking area was nearly empty. Only a dozen cars dotted an expanse that could accommodate hundreds. There was no brown Cutlass, but she was five minutes early. This was intentional, routine. It gave time to examine the rendezvous area, to look for traps and escape routes. She circled the parking lot slowly, eyed the Convention Center that was the foundation of Las Vegas' second biggest industry. She wondered about the man who would meet her. What sort of person went with that voice? He didn't sound like another hoodlum in a blue silk suit, but if he wasn't one of The Syndicate's button men, who was he?

"Brown Cutlass," Hovde announced.

She watched the sedan pull to a stop in front of the huge hall, then drove the Porsche slowly toward it.

"Nevada plates. Can't see anyone but the guy at the wheel," he rasped a few moments later.

"Wave to him."

Hovde did. The Cutlass swung in a tight turn, halted ten yards away. The man who got out moved and looked like an athlete, and he was handsome enough to do television commercials. Curly-haired, at least six feet tall and no older than thirty, this man with the wide brown eyes resembled those interchangeable young actors who pursue criminals in interchangeable TV series. No, his eyes were a bit different and his smile not quite that professional, and his clothes weren't nearly as expensive-cool as those of the smooth "gentlemen" of Malibu and Bel Air. Maybe he just couldn't afford the cashmere and the Guccis, or maybe he had a different notion of laid-back taste.

"Miss Gordon?"

He looked her squarely in the eye, spoke in that direct voice and didn't flash his teeth at her. There was nothing visibly clever, guarded or intentionally charming about his manner.

"Yes," she acknowledged.

"I don't mean to be rude, but . . . could I please see some ID?"

He wasn't going to deliver the bomb to the wrong person. He was being careful, and that made sense. She didn't like him at all. When she moved to take the driver's license from her bag, he caught a glimpse of the .357 and said nothing. She wasn't surprised. If he worked for Spinoza's people, he was no stranger to firearms. He studied the color photo, returned the license.

"Thank you, Miss Gordon. My name's Ben Prince. I'm supposed to help you, and if—"

"Could I see *your* ID?" she interrupted.

She thought he might argue or force a smile. Instead he nodded calmly and handed her a plastic-laminated card with a picture taken at least a year earlier. The head in that picture had much shorter hair.

"Benjamin D. Prince, Kublai Khan Hotel," she read aloud.

" 'In Xanadu did Kublai Khan a mighty pleasure dome decree,' " he recited.

"Aside from quoting Samuel T. Coleridge, what else do you do?"

"Would you prefer some T. S. Eliot, or Yeats?"

"I'd prefer you just answer my question," she replied in a voice thirty degrees colder than the temperature in the parking lot.

"Right. The Kublai Khan is a tidy little nine-hundred-room hotel and casino down The Strip, and I'm the Assistant Chief of Security. I guess I'm on detached duty right now though."

The phrase "detached duty" signaled military service, and his unruffled air of authority suggested that he'd been an officer.

"What outfit were you with, mister?" she asked.

"I was Deputy Security Officer down the road at Nellis till nineteen months ago, ma'am. Couldn't tear myself away from sunny Las Vegas."

He probably hadn't tried. After a couple of years at Nellis as a captain or major—more likely captain since he seemed too young to win oak leaves in the peacetime Air Force—the easy life among the high rollers, show girls and money men must have been irresistible.

"I asked for someone who knew the town from top to bottom," she said.

"Well, Mr. Mintzer picked me. I'm a walking encyclopaedia, ma'am. You need a drive-in liquor store open twenty-four hours a day, try Friendly Fergie's. A rabbi who makes house calls, an indoor range for that three-fifty-seven in your belly holster, a restaurant with live Maine lobsters or hookers—male or female—who take either Master Charge or Visa, just ask Ben Prince."

She ignored his jive. "Who's Mintzer?"

"Sanford Mintzer is the president of the Kublai Khan, a noted philanthropist and pillar of the community."

And front for the Syndicate owners of the hotel.

"Sandy Mintzer's a big man in Vegas, and he pays me very well. I do what he says, and the last thing he said was to do whatever you said."

How much did Prince know?

"He tell you anything else?" Hovde asked.

"Not to ask questions, just answer them. Who are *you?*"

Hovde stared, yawned.

"His name is Don, and he works with me. Now where's the package?"

Very impatient, very pretty, very determined and analytical. It wasn't going to be easy with this woman. She wasn't going to give an inch, waste a moment, flirt at all. Prince caught a whiff of her perfume and appreciated the subtle herbal scent. She was fierce and feminine, or was it firm and feminine? It might be interesting to find out . . .

"Follow me," he said.

They were beyond the city limits, past the signs heralding North Las Vegas, when she saw the Cutlass make a right turn off the interstate highway. Now there was a billboard celebrating Valley of Fire State Park—eighteen miles ahead, but Prince pulled off onto a side road shortly after they passed it and five minutes later he stopped in front of a gray cinderblock structure with an odd hipped roof that came to a point. Much of the paint on the sign over the door had peeled, but Prince read it aloud from memory.

"Injun Joe's Pizza Parlor. That's supposed to look like a sort of wigwam."

"Doesn't," Hovde said hoarsely.

"You've sure got a terrible cold," Prince observed sympathetically. Then he saw Arroyo drive up in the truck, puzzled as the Indian disembarked to join them.

"This is private property," Prince announced.

"He's with us," she explained. "I guess you didn't notice him back at the parking lot. It's all right, Mr. Prince. Thomas is a friend."

Arroyo eyed the fake wigwam with open contempt; the Kublai Khan's security specialist wondered whether all of the beautiful woman's associates shared her short temper.

"Anything else I ought to know?" he asked warily.

"Don't call him Chief."

"Nice to meet you, Thomas. My name's Ben." Prince wondered what was in the tool box the Navaho held. Uncertain as to what kind of Indian this man was, and hoping that Arroyo would not be offended, Prince extended his hand in greeting and Arroyo shook it firmly.

"May I see the bomb, please?" Arroyo said.

Prince unlocked the door, led them into the abandoned restaurant and explained that an acquaintance of Mr. Mintzer was planning to reopen it as a natural-food establishment next month.

"Gonna call it Sprouts 'n' Stuff," he announced as he flicked on another light. He guided them back to the kitchen, opened the door of a big restaurant refrigerator.

"All yours," he told them.

They looked at the wooden box, a neat cube of pine boards.

"It's eighteen inches on a side," Prince said, "and the top is loose. They tell me that two of the wires to the timer were not connected, so it's supposed to be safe."

Arroyo reached in, pulled the small crate out and carried it to a butcher-block countertop beside a double sink. He studied it for a few seconds and lifted the lid.

"Dynamite." He took rubber-handled cutters from his

tool box, snipped the other wires to the timer and removed it from the crate. Then he carefully separated a pair of detonators, put them down—eight inches apart. He found a visor in his kit, slipped it down onto his head and lowered the optically ground glass that provided eight-power magnification.

He shook his head. He wasn't satisfied. He took a powerful three-cell flashlight from his box, played the beam slowly over the bomb. Then he reexamined the timer and the detonators.

"Army," he said.

"What do you mean?" she asked.

"The detonators . . . they're U.S. Army. Stamped right on them. The timer is professional too, and it didn't come from any surplus store or electronics hobby shop. Look at this, Don."

Hovde stepped forward, took the flashlight and peered at the bomb parts. He grunted in recognition. "That timer didn't even exist three years ago . . . and the detonators are just as new . . . Big bomb."

"Forty-eight sticks," Prince told them.

She looked at him appraisingly.

"Whose idea was it to store it here, Mr. Prince?"

"Mine. Had to get it away from town, out of the heat too, I figured, and I thought the walls of the fridge could contain it—well, take some of the blast—if anything went wrong. Was it a bad idea?"

"Good idea," Arroyo said, "but this whole place wouldn't contain it."

"Good bomb too," Hovde said—and then he saw the look in her eyes.

"If you like bombs," Alison Gordon added. "Anything special about this dynamite? Thomas? Don?"

They shook their heads, explained that it was a common brand used in every state each day on a broad variety of construction and demolition projects. Almost anyone could buy or steal a case without enormous effort.

"We can't leave it here, Mr. Prince. Some drifter or petty thief might break in, and there's always the risk of fire, short circuit in the wiring, anything. Suggestions?"

Prince found himself noticing her body for the first time, intrigued that he hadn't been conscious of her sleek figure before. Whether it was intentional or not, she had managed to keep his attention fixed on the bomb until now.

"Not the police," Prince decided.

"*Not* the police," she agreed. "How much do you know about this business, Mr. Prince?"

He shrugged boyishly. "Just enough to understand nobody wants any questions. Of course, if you ever want to fill me in on the deal I might be able to help more."

"Bury it," Hovde said.

They found a shovel, buried the sticks of dynamite in a hole behind the restaurant and covered it with two feet of earth. Arroyo tamped the soil down hard and heaped some rocks on top so no rooting animal could uncover the cache. Then they walked to their cars. It was getting dark, and the horizon was blurring into a red and purple glow. She realized that she had forgotten how beautiful this state, these mountains and this desert and the lakes could be. Suddenly she remembered something. She put her head out the window of the Porsche.

"Mr. Prince?"

"Just follow me. I'll lead you right to Caesars," he promised as he opened the door of the Cutlass.

"Thanks. And thanks for the chocolate."

He thought about blowing her a cheery kiss but guessed that might be a mistake. He gave her a mock-gallant quarter-bow instead and got into his car. No doubt about it. She was as sharp as they'd said, a real challenge. He put the Olds into drive, and smiled as he considered the battle of wits ahead. Women who were lazy, simple or easy had never interested him for more than a weekend. It looked as if

Alison Gordon was going to be very goddamn fascinating.

"He sent the candy?" Hovde asked a few seconds later.

"The signature on the card—B. D.," she answered. "I must be tired. Should have spotted it the minute I saw his hotel employee's card. Benjamin D. Prince. B. D. to A. B.—that was supposed to be cute."

"Don't let it bother you."

"That's not what's bothering me," she snapped. "How did he know about my favorite candy store in Beverly Hills? How did he know where I was staying—the exact room—if he knows so little about anything else? What's this pretty boy trying to tell me?"

Hovde pondered the reference to Prince's good looks, wondered why she was automatically lumping him in with the handsome-selfish Hollywood men who played women as adroitly as they did tennis. It was entirely logical that Prince should know a couple of hundred people in the Los Angeles entertainment community; many dealt with or visited Vegas regularly and five or ten thousand Angelinos came here to frolic every weekend. What was so suspicious about Prince phoning someone in southern California to find out more about her? Hovde would hardly expect less of a trained security specialist. Hell, it was what he'd do himself.

"Could be he's showing you he's on the ball," Hovde offered.

"No, he's been letting us think he's *not* on the ball, but Mr. Prince isn't dumb. You saw the way he took care of the bomb. He's smart. I'm glad he is. We're going to need some smart help here, and this is his town."

"He doesn't look like a typical mob guy to me. What do you think?"

She shrugged, edged the Porsche to the side of the two-lane road to let an approaching mobile home roll past.

"They come in all shapes and sizes these days, Don. It's not just hoods in blue silk suits, especially here. It's all neat and camouflaged. There are probably two Luxembourg holding companies and three Panamanian corporations between Spinoza and the Kublai Khan. The F.B.I.'s been trying to track these connections for twenty years, and the I.R.S. has been looking for that unreported skim money even longer. I'd bet that Prince has never *seen* Spinoza, and that Sandy Mintzer hasn't either. Top people like Spinoza don't even show their faces in this state. Why risk stirring up an investigation by the Gaming Control Board? The Board's got undercover agents in Vegas and every other Nevada town where there's gambling."

"And they don't know about the mob?" Hovde asked cynically.

"They're looking for *proof*. Lots of secret wheeling and dealing. It's the Cold War without the violence. It's covert action with triple bookkeeping instead of double-barreled shotguns. If somebody has to be hit, the job is handled by an out-of-state pro and usually not in Nevada. This state's as safe as a kindergarten."

Hovde sighed.

"Got the message, Don. Back to the practical world of dynamite and detonators, and Mr. Prince. He can find out what torched those cars at the airport. He knows the cops."

"You said he's working for the mob. Are you telling me the Vegas cops are on the take?"

She lit a cigarette. "No more than anywhere else. This is a big law-and-order center. Terrific rate of convictions for littering, and double parkers don't dare show their fenders anywhere in town. With Prince, it's his job to be friendly with the local law. Maybe there's a suicide attempt at his hotel he wants to keep out of the papers, or some dumb gambler gets juiced and tries to rape a maid. He's good at handling those things quietly."

"Think he knows the fire marshals too?"

"Knows everybody, and they all must like him. Handsome young guy like that, nice manners, great after-shave, gives people presents—who could resist him?"

"You hate him, Al."

She shook her head as she saw the turnoff for the wide interstate.

"I find him interesting, and you might too. Suppose we split the duty. I'll take the first shift, and you're on tomorrow."

"If that's what you want."

She saw his alarm and laughed.

"No, Don. I'm not going to shack up with Ben Prince. Not to get information, not to win his loyalty and not for . . . the physical satisfaction either. He wouldn't be that good, although he's sure that he's dy-no-mite in bed. My shift ends before midnight, sometime after a four- or five-course meal with a lot of fine wine."

"So the plan is you invite him to dinner?"

"He invites *me.* Slick young stud like that has to prove himself twice a week. Wouldn't be anything personal. A few laughs, a roll in the hay and a pat on the ass after breakfast—that's the way I figure Ben Prince. Just an old-fashioned guy."

"A smart one," Hovde reminded.

"I'm *always* careful," she answered and realized that she was lying. There were three, maybe four times since the death of her husband eight years ago when she'd been something else. On each occasion a man had been involved—an extraordinary man. The most recent had been the very special bomber pilot named Logan, a stubborn and authentic *good* man whom Hovde still admired. He had the sense not to mention Logan, the grace to avoid the hurtful confrontation by asking whether he might turn on the car radio. He was not surprised when she welcomed the change of subject.

Alison Gordon found a soothing soft-rock program on some station that was bold enough to do its own programming. Indifferent to the call-in concept of participatory democracy, it blessed the last sixteen minutes of the ride back to Caesars Palace with a stream of excellent records introduced by the articulate woman who had selected them. By the time the three vehicles swung into the tree-lined driveway of the hotel, she was humming softly.

Hidden spotlights were turning the fountains into geysers of gold and the whole front of the building was bathed in an exotic green glow. The usual mob of cabs and cars choked the road directly in front of the entrance. She told Hovde to help Arroyo check in, then make the calls to Beverly Hills to find out when Agajanian and the radio unit would arrive.

"Here he comes," Hovde whispered as Ben Prince got out of his sedan and walked toward them. She half turned to speak to the man seated beside her.

"So it's breakfast at nine in the coffee shop," she said.

"How about dinner at eight anywhere you like?" Prince suggested. "That should give you time to unpack and wash up, and I'll shoot myself if you say no . . ."

Now he flashed the 1,000-watt smile. She hesitated for a few seconds to let Hovde offer to take care of the car "and those other things."

". . . And I'll get fired if my boss hears that I left you alone on your first night," Prince added.

"I doubt that—but it might be helpful if you told me more about the local scene. Palace Court all right?"

"I'd say, since it's one of the two or three best dining spots in Clark County. Don't be late."

Three minutes later, she was naked and wet. Stretched out in the ample tub, she enjoyed the warm water and the hypnotic drone of the television set in the adjacent bedroom. The unwinding, the hot liquid that covered most of her, the vaguely amniotic quality of the experience made her drowsy. And sensual. Definitely erotic and sensual—from the tips of her long toes to the curve of her flanks, from navel to breasts to her very scalp, she felt animal and carnal and open for skin-to-skin connection and affection and communication. The affection and communication were important to Alison Gordon, who couldn't share the view that sex was a pleasant form of physiotherapy—like jogging or roller disco. One third asleep, she reached for the handle to let in more of that soothing hot water.

The TV news announcer was reporting the usual terrible events. A hundred and ninety-two people drowned when a Japanese ferry capsized, a St. Louis nursing home burned with the loss of eighty-seven senior citizens, a locust plague in eastern Africa, a chemical plant destroyed by explosion near Birmingham, another prostitute disemboweled by "the new Jack the Ripper" in London and the failure of the French police to capture a notorious international terrorist in a raid that left three dead in northeastern Paris. The teenage V.D. rate was up and the value of the dollar down. She didn't hear any of it. She floated, and—for the moment—she let herself forget. Not to think about where she was, and why, was an indulgence, one that many other women could afford more often. Perhaps not much more, but she envied them for it.

There was no sound of a bell and no clock in sight, but she knew that it was time to get dressed. She had cultivated this inner time sense years ago when she was at college, reinforced it during her training at the place the C.I.A. had called The Farm. She opened her eyes, gripped the handle of the soap dish in the wall and pulled herself to her feet. After opening the drain, she stood under the pulsing shower briefly before she stepped out to face the mirror. As she rubbed her body dry, her mind returned reluctantly to the realities and tensions and the guerrilla warfare she could expect at dinner. She looked at her reflection as she toweled under her breasts, even approved what she saw. It was a fine body for a woman of thirty-five, one that many women a decade younger might envy. Men of any age would admire, desire, it if they saw it like this. Ben Prince would never have that experience.

She considered a piece of chocolate, eyed her figure and

rejected the idea. She turned her attention to the atomizer on the sink stand, carefully sprayed tiny clouds of Aromatique at half a dozen places on her body. The whole bathroom smelled delicately, femininely floral and she enjoyed the scent as she began the process of "putting on" her face. She pursed her lips as if to kiss—remembered a lover who had told her that she looked like a pouting goldfish when she prepared to apply lipstick. He'd been her first sculpture teacher eight years ago when she was working to recover from the shock of her husband's disappearance and the impact of leaving the cloak-and-dagger world to start over.

"Clem," she said to the mirror as she recalled his name. He was an "important" figure in the New York art scene now, far from her in more ways than one. She completed the makeup process, wiggled into candy-striped bikini panties, decided that she wouldn't wear a brassiere—her breasts were still firm enough so she didn't need one—and pulled the black spaghetti-strap dress over her head.

"Not bad." She surveyed the way the bare-shoulder dress looked on her. Then she put on the spike-heeled shoes, the simple gold Omega and a one-of-a-kind necklace handmade by jewelry artist Louise Parrish, gold-capped beads of blue lapis linked by twenty-two-carat tubing. The effect was just right—the elegance without ostentation that chic critics called "drop dead" fashion because of its understated sexiness. She looked at herself in the mirror again and grinned.

"Vanity, vanity, thy name is woman," she quoted and tried to identify the Shakespearean play. She frowned, failed and hummed softly as she left the room at five minutes after eight. She was still humming three minutes later when she crossed the crowded casino to the glass-walled elevator that would lift her to her rendezvous at the Palace Court. It was as she emerged from the elevator that Thomas Arroyo began knocking on the door of her mini-suite. He rapped again, and when there was no reply he turned to Hovde.

"You're sure about this?" Hovde asked.

"Yes, I counted the dynamite as we buried it. Forty-seven sticks, *not* forty-eight."

"Maybe he miscounted, Thomas."

"Maybe he didn't. It didn't seem important, but I should have told her," the Navaho said as they started down the corridor.

"You think it means something? One stick?"

"I do now. I think I should have told her."

Hovde knew that the Indian was right, even though the odds were that either Arroyo or Prince was guilty of poor addition. A lot more explosives than a single stick were involved in this operation, but Alison Gordon would want every scrap of information.

"No sweat, Thomas," he reassured. "Tell her in the morning. You like Spanish food? There's supposed to be a good Spanish restaurant right here in the hotel."

"Sure," Arroyo said. He didn't say anything more as they walked to the elevator. He listened to Hovde's talk about the colorful and extravagant oddities of Las Vegas, a place the Navaho had never visited before. Hovde did his best to divert and cheer him up with a string of anecdotes—with no visible effect. Finally, after they disembarked at the street floor and made their way down the corridor lined with gift shops, Hovde became silent too. Then he brightened as he saw the restaurant sign ahead.

"The Spanish Steps!" he pointed out with exaggerated enthusiasm.

"I should have told her," Arroyo replied, and thought about his young cousin back on the reservation.

CHAPTER II

THERE WAS a tree in the middle of the room. There was a leaded glass dome overhead, several marble statues of Roman women on pedestals and the tree—right in the center of the Palace Court. The waiters were all in tuxedos, and Alison Gordon noticed that Prince was now wearing a fresh white shirt and Liberty floral print tie. Attire for visitors to Las Vegas is generally casual, and she knew from earlier visits that it is usually the hotel and casino executives—not the tourists or gamblers—who wear ties and jackets. All of the men at the tables in this room were wearing jackets and ties tonight, and only two of the woman diners were in slacks. As the gourmet French restaurant in town, the Palace Court invited that sort of propriety.

"Magnifique!"

She knew that Ben Prince was doing his charming number. There were other attractive females nearby, some of them, such as the Italian starlet, quite dramatic, others such as the television producer's consort delicate and youthful and a few who had great smiles, astonishing busts with revealing gowns and a gift for listening and shopping. There were several good-looking women of a certain age, past forty and handling it better than their husbands. There was an extremely pretty blonde who happened to be five feet ten, cheery and available for $100 an hour if you were polite. Still, the eyes of half the men in the room—including the waiters—signaled that Alison Gordon was the brightest star shining in this galaxy tonight.

"You mean the necklace?" she evaded.

"The necklace is a Parrish, and it's terrific. The lady wearing it is even more so."

So he knew about jewelry. He was probably something of an authority on women's clothes, too, which she suspected wasn't a common trait in Las Vegas men. The female diners were dressed expensively but not in high fashion. Good figures, diamonds and pearls were much more in evidence than sophisticated clothes. Prince seemed a bit more cultivated than most of the men she'd met on earlier trips to this city. She wondered whether he'd come from the east. It was difficult to tell from his speech, which was oddly free of regional accent and as smooth as he was.

"Thank you, Mr. Prince. I appreciate the compliment from an authority."

Now why the hell had she said *that?*

"Your table's ready, Mr. Prince," the maitre d'hotel announced in a voice tinged with the Mediterranean, and guided them to a banquette. As she sat down, she saw the framed portraits on the wall.

"There are a dozen," Prince told her affably. "The various Caesars who ruled Rome. Used to hang in the Forum of the Twelve Caesars in New York. If you have any questions, just ask your faithful Ben. I took four years of Latin."

Few U.S. high schools still offered Latin. It didn't add up right; he didn't fit her image of the assistant security chief of a mob-owned hotel. Had the world changed so much that cool young operators in slick commercial enterprises such as the Kublai Khan studied the classics? Perhaps he was lying, or joking?

"Question," she said.

"Yes, ma'am?"

"May we order drinks?"

That was when the waiter put the bottle of Dom Perignon on the table.

"How did you know that I like champagne?"

"I didn't order this."

"With Mr. Berg's compliments," the waiter announced.

She felt relieved and pleased. It wasn't threatening that the executive vice president of Caesars Palace remembered Dom Perignon was her favorite—he was one of the smartest and most efficient hotel executives in town. It would have been disturbing if this man seated beside her—a person she'd never met until this afternoon—knew that much about her.

"You've got important friends," Prince said.

"He's a very good host. We met a couple of years ago," she told him—and wondered why she felt she had to explain. It really wasn't Prince's business who her friends were in Vegas, or anywhere else.

She told the waiter to transmit her thanks and waited alertly for prying questions. Prince didn't ask any. He told a relatively clean joke, commented on an Albee play he'd seen when last in Los Angeles and recommended the pâté as a first course.

"The smoked salmon's good too," he added.

"Scotch?"

"What else would be fit for Caesar—belly lox?"

Prince spoke authoritatively about the eastern and western curings of smoked salmon, agreed with her judgment on Sweden's *gravlax* and refilled the champagne glasses.

"Do you miss New York?" she ventured.

"Now and then . . . Say, you're as good as your reputation, Miss Gordon. Most people tell me there's hardly any Manhattan left in my speech at all, but you nailed me. I know you're from California."

"*My* speech?"

"No, I'm not one tenth as good a detective as you are, I

read the article about you in *Time.*"

Probably within the past thirty-six hours in the local library. Prince was the sort who would do his homework. It would be a mistake to underestimate the pleasant men who ran and protected these hotels, she reminded herself, for they were totally professional and they took no chances. They left the gambling to others who were more romantic or neurotic.

'Tell me about the gambling business here," she invited.

He sipped at his champagne.

"Sure. First, I hope you won't be offended if I say you're right—and you're wrong. It is a carefully planned, efficiently operated business with total cost control . . . clearly defined profit centers . . . the works. Computerized, automated, and amortized. Only restaurants and gaming spots in the world operating twenty-four hours a day, year round. No waste. The people in charge know exactly how many rooms are occupied, what it costs to serve you a glass of orange juice and what the average take is on each kind of slot machine every month. Last year, the dollar slots in the 115 major casinos in this state generated 13.8 percent of the total gambling revenue, twice as much as the year before and more than all the nickel machines."

"So they're putting in more dollar slots?"

"Brass ring for the smart lady. Exactly. You were right. It's a large business. The top hundred fifteen outfits—the ones that grossed a million or more from gambling—have assets of two billion bucks and eighty-three thousand employees. That's more than a quarter of Nevada's entire industrial working force."

He paused to drain his glass.

"You said I was also wrong?"

"Only in an external, but externals are important here. You asked about *gambling.* No *gambling* here. Vegas and Reno are the Middle American Dream. *Gambling* takes money from suckers, ruins careers and families. It's a sickness, a sin. Criminals often run *gambling.* They corrupt public officials, work with mobs handling drugs and prostitutes, hurt or sometimes kill people. None of that stuff here. No, this is *gaming.*"

"And *gaming* is just fun, I suppose."

"Give that lady a cigar, or at least a complimentary cocktail—the kind they hand out to people busy at the slots or tables."

"So the people will continue gamb—excuse me, gaming."

"Think of it as merchandising. Your diagnosis is correct, but what's wrong in making the customers comfortable? Sure, the free drinks are to keep them in the casinos and those very cheap all-you-can-eat buffets at two-seventy-five a crack are to keep the beloved guests in the building, near the casinos. Lordy, Miss Gordon, that's just good business. Nobody's trying to fool anyone."

She shrugged.

"Okay, it isn't evil."

"And there's all that big-time entertainment—the top stars bunched together in one town. Next week Sinatra will be here, Dean Martin at the MGM, and a bunch of other major acts at the other hotels. Stardust is doing a terrific show with dozens of showgirls, lions and tigers, a swarm of dancers and a digest musical impression of *War and Peace.*"

"*War and Peace* with *topless* showgirls?"

"Tolstoi wouldn't mind. They're doing it in good taste, no big boobs. Men bring their wives and girlfriends to these shows. Large boobs would be *vulgar,* might make guests nervous. This market is not only middle-America, but middle-class. We give them a fabulous show with revolving stages, fountains, acts descending from the ceiling—and a lot of skin. Look but don't touch. It's practically family entertainment."

"I don't want to argue with you, but Tolstoi would mind," she said.

"Let's not tell him about it."

"We'd better not mention that other fun show down The Strip with all the boys in drag," she said, taking the large menu from the captain. To his credit, Prince did not try to ply her with another bottle of champagne. The smoked salmon, rack of lamb and '72 Margaux were all delicious, and the rich chocolate dessert was appropriately excessive. There was no more general economic or sociological commentary. It was strictly Q. & A., with Alison Gordon doing the questioning.

How and when had the bomb arrived? Did the owner of the Kublai Khan have any personal enemies? Any financial problems? Were there any recently discharged employees who might be bitter enough or technically equipped to assemble such a powerful device? What had Sandy Mintzer done before buying the hotel? She noticed that Prince tensed before he answered that question.

"I heard he ran a hotel in Miami Beach. Maybe he owned it. The State Gaming Control Board would know. They require a complete bio, and they check it out pretty conscientiously before granting a gaming license. Sandy's been licensed for a couple of years, before I was hired."

"Who are the other investors or owners?" she inquired.

"Not a clue. Never heard there were any. None of my business," Prince replied casually. "You know, middle-level employees like me aren't encouraged to ask questions about confidential financial matters in Las Vegas—or anywhere else."

"I know. How about threats? Any previous bombs or other threats in the past year or two? At your hotel or the others?"

Ben Prince took several seconds to consider.

"No . . . no bombs," he responded softly. "We haven't had anything like that since I've been at the Khan, and I haven't heard about any real problems at the other hotels. I think I would have. Security people here tend to share information. If a new scam comes up at one hotel, or if a crooked gambler is spotted at another, we spread the word."

She looked down at the last ruins of the bittersweet temptation, succumbed and cleaned the plate. Prince had the decency not to comment, but something like amusement glittered in his large brown eyes.

"These gambling cheats," she said. "Some of them use fairly sophisticated hardware, don't they?"

"Very elaborate stuff, but they usually work with an inside man, or woman. The scam generally requires the cooperation of a dealer who'll sell out the house for half the ripoff. It's a dumb deal. They score ten or twenty grand . . . sometimes a few more . . . and we nail them."

"Is that a figure of speech?" she asked as she poured more espresso.

"Miss Gordon, this is not ancient Rome, the trappings here notwithstanding. We don't crucify people. Maybe some of the casinos were rough on cheaters thirty years ago, but nobody gets hurt anymore. The mob era is gone. Hell, we've even got a chapter of the Civil Liberties Union over on Jackson Avenue."

"And Sandy Mintzer sent them two hundred dollars last year . . ."

"Five hundred. And he gave the United Way a thousand. Good guy."

She patted her lips with the napkin, resolved to eat a spartan breakfast. Yes, this was as good a time as any.

"That box you showed us came with a note, Mr. Prince. Did you see it?"

"No."

"The note asked for a lot of money, but it wasn't signed. Any idea as to who might send such a demand, or why it came to your hotel rather than one of the larger operations?"

He shook his head. "Can't help you."

Was that an answer or an evasion?

"I want the note."

"I've never seen it. I could ask Mr. Mintzer about it in the morning. He'll be in at ten."

"Good. At nine, you can check in with the cops about those cars that burned up this afternoon at the airport. Try your chums in the fire department too."

Prince took a cigar from within his jacket, and she froze for a moment as she recognized the brand. The dead bomber pilot had smoked Don Diegos too. Prince saw her flinch, misunderstood and started to put the corona back in his pocket.

"Smoke it. I don't mind," she said.

He lit the cigar, puffed.

"What do you want to know about those cars?"

"Everything. Who owned them, how they caught fire and anything else. *Anything.* I'm a fire freak. See if you can get the note and the information about the cars, and I'll call you at the Kublai Khan at half past ten. That would be helpful." She glanced at her wristwatch. He gestured to the waiter for the bill, speculated on the outcome of next week's heavyweight fight at Caesars' own sports arena and noted that the odds on the reelection of the Clark County sheriff were being quoted at 50–50.

"Good sheriff?" she asked.

"Mr. Clean himself . . . some people say."

"What do you say?"

His smile was genuinely boyish.

"I'm like Will Rogers. Never met a sheriff I didn't like. You think I'm gullible?"

When they stepped out of the glass elevator at the street floor, she declined his invitation to drive through the glitter of the massive electric signs that lined The Strip "to catch the show at the Khan" and see some extraordinary Chinese magicians.

"Tomorrow night?" he countered.

"Hope so," she answered and wondered precisely how old he was and how much he could be trusted. Four minutes after they said good night, he was speaking into a telephone at a booth a mile down The Strip.

"You're gonna love this," he said. "The lady is smart and sexy, her explosives expert is some kind of an Indian—*American* Indian—named Thomas and she's got another guy who calls himself Don and seems to have a terrible sore throat."

"What do you think?" said the voice on the phone.

"They're all pros," Prince responded. "That Indian knows bombs from top to bottom, and the way both he and Don forgot to mention their last names was sensible. Oh yeah, she carries a three-fifty-seven magnum and doesn't mind cigars. Great body. I'd have to rate her jugs as outstanding, and there's a definite possibility she's the smartest female I ever met, very sharp and classy. She could really turn me on, Tony. Too bad she's working for the other side."

"Remember that, and keep in mind all that money we're after. That's the name of the game, kid—not tits. Does she trust you?"

Prince laughed. "Hell, no. Much too clever for that, too experienced. She wants to see the note, and she told me to find out about those two cars that went up at the airport."

"Let *us* know what you find out too."

"What else are friends for? *Ciaio,* baby."

Prince relit his corona as he walked back to his car, looked up The Strip at the incredible display of flashing lights on a score of dazzling hotel and casino signs. He thought about the sophisticated and lovely woman he'd left at Caesars Palace, sighed. Too bad she worked for the other side, people who would probably kill him if they knew. They would make it look like an accident, of course; they were good at accidents too . . .

He started the Cutlass and swung out into the late-night traffic to return to the Kublai Khan. Sherri would be finishing her second show soon, looking splendid in her peacock feathers and belting out that big closing number in the powerful voice that had once dominated the largest church choir in Altoona, Pennsylvania. A clean and affectionate person who read a great deal instead of wasting her time on television, Sherri was currently studying Indian culture, and was halfway through the Kama Sutra which she had described to Prince as "a gas and a challenge." She had shared her new insights from the vantage point of her water bed, and the security man felt confident that they could sail the seas together again tonight. Inspired by the knowledge that reading and singing were not the only things at which versatile Sherri excelled, Prince began to whistle.

CHAPTER 12

SOME TWENTY-THREE miles north of the District of Columbia line, The Gettinger Institute sits on a nine-acre plot of green and gracious Maryland countryside. People in the area know that the huge house built by a long-deceased millionaire is now a treatment center for affluent alcoholics, and some joke that the stone walls that once kept the lower class out now keep the upper class in. There is talk that famous folk come here to dry out at astronomical rates, but those rumors remain unconfirmed. No local residents work here, and truckers delivering food or other supplies are obliged to unload them on a concrete ramp *outside* the kitchen at the rear of the thirty-one-room mansion.

People here rarely speak about the Institute anymore, for it does nothing to distress the community. It has never claimed immunity from taxes, and none of the drunks have escaped to cause trouble. Bills are paid within ten days, proof enough that the group that took over after Dr. Gettinger died in 1974 is making lots of money. Yet all of this is untrue, a deliberate falsehood created by professional deceivers. No one earns a penny of profit from this institute, which is neither a commercial venture nor treatment center for alcoholics. Gunshot wounds, not cirrhosis of the liver or delirium tremens, are the most common ailments here.

"Nice country," the black man driving the Chevrolet approved. He had an M.A. in African History from the University of Michigan, a gray pin-striped suit from Brooks Brothers and the good humor of a thirty-two-year-old civil servant who has just received a four-thousand-dollar "merit" increase in his annual salary.

The man beside him was a quarter of a century older, and a lot less cheery than he had been when he joined the Office of Strategic Services in 1942. Now the fourth most powerful man in the Central Intelligence Agency, he had stomach trouble and eye problems, caused by something terrible done to him in Berlin in the 1950's that condemned him to dark spectacles. These sun glasses were his trademark in the cloak and dagger establishment, where he was known as The Man With the Shades.

"Very nice, Lou," he agreed in a tone that said his mind was elsewhere. Louis Jefferson guessed that it might be the operation code-named Calendar turning sour in Singapore, but didn't ask. They drove on in silence until they faced the guard at the gate house of The Gettinger Institute.

"We're here to visit Mrs. Kelleran," Jefferson announced, offering his ID.

This week's password was "Mrs. Kelleran." The guard swung open the heavy metal gate, and a few minutes later the two men were speaking to a plump woman at the reception desk in the front hall of this unique hospital . . . the secret place where the C.I.A. takes care of its physically or mentally wounded. Despite the recently publicized view that most C.I.A. employees are idiots or assassins, this private healing facility is logical and necessary. The wire grills covering the windows, the concealed TV cameras, the carefully screened doctors and nurses and the strong woman in white at the reception desk are all part of the security program. Although the ten-bed hospital is not large, the importance of guarding these patients and their secrets is.

"Yes?" the receptionist asked.

They produced their official ID cards again, and she moved her foot away from the hidden alarm.

"Mr. Bob White," Jefferson said. Neither patients nor hospital staff used their real names. Colors were functional designations; when Mr. Bob White left, a future arrival would be signed in as Mr. Fred White or Howard Black or Norman Brown. For some reason no one remembered, female patients were all registered as Miss Gray or Mrs. Green.

"Room six," the woman in white responded. She pointed to a quilted door whose exterior leatherette masked an inch of steel, and signaled. The guard watching the TV monitor threw the switch to unlock the barrier at 9:55 A.M., correctly noting the time in his log book. When the steel door swung shut behind them, they saw a security agent in the uniform of a hospital orderly halfway up the corridor. He watched them until they entered Room 6.

"Hey, Lou." The tall man in the bed greeted them in that soft Floridian drawl.

"Hey. Owen, this is—"

"The Man With the Shades," Albion finished knowingly.

Aware that the deputy director did not favor this nickname, Jefferson winced and tensed for the eruption. The older man stalked to the window and stared out for several seconds. Having won control of his temper, he turned to speak.

"How are you coming along?"

"Not bad. If that slug had been an inch higher, you'd be talking to an urn. You wouldn't have a cigar, would you?"

The deputy director sat down and sighed as he crossed his legs. His eyes hurt, and in a few hours the Director of Central Intelligence was going to be unreasonable with him about the mess in Singapore.

"No cigar, Owen," he announced, "but the Director told me to give you his best wishes. Hopes you'll be out soon."

That was a lie. The Director had never heard of Owen T.

Albion, and was much too busy with budgets, administrative reorganizations and keeping the President happy to send kind words to wounded field agents.

"Thank him a heap," Albion replied—not fooled a bit—and waited for the questions.

"I will. We're all bothered by the . . . just what happened at Casa?"

Albion noted that neither of them carried a pad or tape recorder; he smiled.

"Room's wired, right? Okay, I'll talk loud."

"Don't push your luck, Owen," Jefferson advised. "Of course the room is wired. What happened at that airport?"

"Start from the beginning," The Man With the Shades said, "and don't leave out *anything*—not the tiniest detail. Don't assume that we know one bit about this thing. Is that clear?"

He wasn't shouting, but the gloves were off now and he spoke in tones of icy command. The amenities were finished. Talking slowly and pausing often to recall exact events, the field agent reported very carefully on everything that had occurred from the moment he reached Morocco—except the sex.

"Do you remember anything else? Anything at all?"

"Just the screwing. You need that?"

Jefferson turned to his superior, who shook his head.

"She was a nice woman," the wounded agent said defensively.

"She still is," the deputy director announced, "and so is her widowed mother who works in the export china section at Harrod's. You wouldn't like her boyfriend though. He drinks too damn much. Reuters just fired him."

"She didn't mention a boyfriend, sir . . . Wait a second. The hardware. The bastard who shot me used a French P–15. Sure, a fifteen-round magazine. It was a P–15, wasn't it?"

The two visitors nodded.

"Tillie's people stole a crate of those seven or eight

months ago!" Albion recalled excitedly.

"I don't believe this. *Tillie's* people?"

"Some of the field personnel refer to Attila as Tillie," Jefferson apologized.

The Man With the Shades stabbed his index finger at Albion. "We code-named this son of a bitch Attila because he's the most vicious creep in the whole jungle of terrorists—a crazy barbarian like his goddamn namesake. He blew up a plane full of nuns last year, torched a Jewish children's hospital—and you're calling this animal Tillie? You think he's cute?"

"I didn't mean—" Albion began, stopped. "I'm sorry, sir."

After several moments, the deputy director lowered his finger and took several deep breaths before he spoke again.

"You did a good job, Albion. Fast reaction, professional, probably saved some lives. They weren't blasting at you, you'll be relieved to know. Looks like the Moroccan cop spooked them and you waded into it. As far as we can tell, they thought he'd recognized them."

"Is he okay, sir?"

"Dead. So are the two shooters. If it makes you feel better, they *were* part of Attila's group. Had tickets to London and a one-night booking at a hotel near Russell Square. We'd like to know what they were doing in Casa, and where they were going from that London hotel."

He glanced at his wristwatch, thought about the mess in Singapore. It was getting more difficult to manage all these messes, to maintain control. Was it age and the fatigue that came with it, or something else? "Lou," he said to signal that it was time to go. They both thanked the man in bed, wished him a full and speedy recovery.

"I'll be okay," Albion predicted. "Had a great time in Morocco anyway. Ever been there?"

"Lincoln," replied The Man With the Shades. "I was in Casa in '42 with an O.S.S. team, working a black transmitter code-named Lincoln. You weren't even born then, were you?"

Albion tried to figure out why U.S. Intelligence might have been operating a clandestine radio in Morocco in that almost prehistoric era.

"I didn't check in till '49," he confessed.

"Vichy French were in charge," the older man explained, "and the town was crawling with Abwehr. We were getting set to invade North Africa . . . to drive out the Nazis."

Nazis. Was it going to be another of those boring sessions with the graybeards reliving their hoary World War II adventures? Even when the tales were not exaggerated, they seemed embarrassing.

"Morocco's changed a lot since then," Albion announced cheerily. "Modern hotels, fine restaurants, air conditioning —all up to date. Credit cards and everything. You ought to get back."

Although underwhelmed with respect for the field agent, the deputy director succeeded in masking his contempt with a vague grunt. "Take it easy, Owen," Jefferson smoothed hastily as he saw the older man start for the door. It wasn't until the Chevrolet was nearly a mile from the hospital that the senior executive spoke.

"He's a thug! A week in Morocco, and he never went to Volubilis!"

"Maybe Roman ruins aren't his thing . . ."

The deputy director took off his dark glasses to rub his eyes for a few seconds before putting them on again.

"No goddamn sense of history," he said. "You see that blank look when I mentioned the Abwehr? One of this century's major intelligence organizations, and that Yahoo never heard of it."

"I'm sure he knows about the Abwehr," Jefferson said earnestly. "There's a three hour unit on German espionage in World War II in the basic training, and I think there's an hour on the O.S.S. North African operation. I'll check on that tomorrow."

"Don't humor me, Lou. Can't blame Albion. Whole damn generation doesn't give a crap about . . . the past. As far as they're concerned, it all began when God created The Beatles. Liverpool was the Garden of Eden!"

Jefferson chuckled courteously, slowed the sedan to avoid colliding with a delivery van.

"The way he picked up on the P–15 wasn't bad," he reminded.

"It was damn good, and the way he coped in an emergency was excellent. He's not incompetent, Lou, just uncivilized. *Tillie?* That's the worst!"

At that moment, the radio telephone on the dashboard buzzed and The Man With the Shades scooped up the instrument.

"George?" the controller at C.I.A. headquarters tested and waited for the countersign.

"Patton . . . What is it? . . . 11:30? Yes, tell him I'll be there."

There was plenty of time to reach Langley for the meeting with the testy Director. It was only 10:20 A.M. here . . . 3:20 P.M. in London and 6:20 P.M. at K.G.B. headquarters in Moscow. What time was it where Attila was preparing his next attack? And where would it be?

CHAPTER 13

"ONE STICK?" she asked as she turned the Porsche off Route 15 onto Flamingo Road.

"One," Arroyo confirmed.

"What the hell does it mean?" she wondered aloud. Then she answered her own question.

"Taggants?" she speculated.

"That's what I was thinking," he answered, "but that means a sophisticated laboratory and organization that could analyze the unique composition of this particular batch of dynamite and trace it."

"This is the *new* Mob, Thomas. No more tommy guns and mustache Petes talking with funny accents. The lawyers and accountants and security experts are the most sophisticated money can buy. That goes for the hotels that the Syndicate doesn't own too."

Arroyo squinted into the glare of the midmorning sun. "These people could handle taggants?"

"Probably. Maybe nuclear weapons, for all we know. Modern town. To bend an Oscar Hammerstein lyric, everything's up to date in Vegas city. You can find hookers in the Yellow Pages of the phone book. They come to your room, they take credit cards. Next year they'll be drip-dry and transistorized."

Something was annoying her, and Arroyo doubted it could be anything as unimportant as prostitutes or the technological capacities of organized crime here. When she knew and wanted to discuss the matter, she would speak of it. She was easily the most honest and intelligent leader under whom Arroyo had worked, beautiful and considerate. That made her vulnerable, of course. He saw the sign, pointed.

"Pot of Gold Mobile Home Park," she read.

There are mobile homes that are on wheels and readily mobile, and there are other things called mobile homes that are actually compact prefabricated houses that sit on cinder blocks or other supports. This park was half filled at the moment with forty mobile homes of the truly mobile variety plus some smaller campers and a few customized vans. One of the vans sported black zebra stripes like the vehicles that take tourists on photo-safaris in Kenya, another's odd-blot design suggested a Rorschach test, and a third was painted to resemble a Day-glo sunset. She studied the more garish vehicles intently for aerials and was relieved to find none that might indicate a powerful radio transmitter. Perhaps Fanelli wasn't as weird as they thought. She parked the sports car, and they both emerged to continue the search on foot.

"Jee-sus Christ!" she said.

"Not exactly," Fanelli replied affably, "but one of his servants."

Wearing a black shirt with matching pants that implied clerical garb, Fanelli stood in the doorway of a large blue trailer. Alison Gordon looked at the white Byzantine cross painted on the side of the vehicle, and the words lettered beside it.

"Children of the Lord?" she read incredulously.

"We're all children of the Lord, aren't we?"

"Right on!" the Asian woman emerging from the trailer agreed.

"Sister Maxine," the communications specialist identified.

She was in her mid-twenties, and the dark T-shirt and skirt in the same color as Fanelli's outfit did little to disguise an arresting figure. With no trace of accent in her speech, she had to be U.S. born.

"You're not weird, Gerry. You're crazy," the detective said. Fanelli looked around, leaned forward confidentially.

"You told me not to come here prowling for women," he reminded, "so I brought my own. She's a first-class radio op, you know."

Fanelli nodded inquiringly toward the Navaho.

"Brother Gerry," A. B. Gordon introduced, "meet Brother Thomas. He's here all alone . . . doing his own missionary work. Too bad you didn't bring another sister for him to . . . pray with."

Alison grimaced, afraid she'd made a bad Japanese joke, but the woman in the doorway grinned, turned and spoke to someone inside. As Fanelli and Arroyo shook hands, a second Asian woman—perhaps a year or so older—appeared in identical costume. The family connection was obvious.

"This is my sister, Kate. She really *is* my sister, Miss Gordon. She was a communications technician for the San Diego P.D. for two years . . . and very religious too."

Alison Gordon studied the two attractive women, shook her head.

"What the hell did you tell these people?" she asked.

"That the money was good and the guys we were after are bad. That's what Hovde told me, and *I* bought it."

She shook her head again.

"You think anybody's going to buy you and these . . . sisters . . . as religious types? Chinese nuns in Vegas?"

"Chinese-American," Fanelli corrected. "Who said they're nuns? And in Las Vegas, why couldn't they be nuns? Stardust has a couple of Kraut lion tamers, so why not Chinese-American nuns? You a bigot?"

Arroyo stepped forward silently. He made no threat, but his entire muscular body showed unmistakable menace.

Five inches shorter and more than forty pounds lighter, Fanelli flinched—and apologized.

"Just kidding," he concluded. "You know me, Al. Listen, they're not exactly nuns. We're not sacrilegious, goddamn it. No, the outfits just suggest we're into some kind of religious number."

"Think of the effect as an impressionist painting," Sister Maxine suggested.

Alison Gordon led them all inside the air-conditioned trailer, which had a compact but fully equipped "galley" and fold-out sleeping facilities for three, and a bookshelf crammed with Bibles and religious tracts. Small framed paintings of Moses, Mohammed, Buddha and Jesus of Nazareth hung on one wall beside a banner embroidered with the message that "God Understands."

"Their mother did that," Fanelli said; the Wu sisters smiled proudly.

"It's splendid," Alison Gordon said with as much sincerity as she could muster, and asked about the radio gear. A smiling Fanelli pressed a button; one of the Formica wall panels opened to reveal a transmitter.

"Strictly legit," he announced. "Licensed by the Federal Communications Commission, with only a few hundred hours of wear. Bill of sale from the legal owner, no outstanding traffic tickets or tax liens. Not bad, huh?"

"Only used on Sundays by a little old lady?"

"No, a kid who was a ham operator. I think he did some dealing too—coke. Feds grabbed this rig down near the Mex border six months ago, sold it at public auction to a mobile-home dealer whose daughter I know. A little kinky, wonderful dancer."

Arroyo stood up suddenly.

"Have you a shovel?" he asked.

"That's an excellent idea, Thomas," she said and gave him the keys to the Porsche.

"Is something wrong?" the senior Ms. Wu asked.

"How would I know?" Fanelli replied. He'd learned to obey without raising questions during his years with the C.I.A., and working with A. B. Gordon Investigations wasn't much different. It was still "need to know" and "mind your own business." Even when it was over, they never told you the whole story. It was worse than his first marriage. Fanelli gave Arroyo a small spade, bade him a courteous farewell and began to tell Alison Gordon about the rest of the special radio equipment. . . .

It was after 11 A.M. when Arroyo parked the sports car in front of the abandoned pizza parlor. Ignoring the "wig-wam" roof, he took the shovel and walked to the rear of the building. If there was something unique or distinctive about this dynamite, laboratory tests might show it now. He was half a dozen yards from the spot where they had buried the explosives when he stopped, stared.

There was a hole in the ground. It was a ragged-edged and messy excavation, one that somebody had tried to make look like the work of an animal. Arroyo knew the ways of the animals of the desert, the coyotes and other creatures. A human had done this. When and why were not clear, but the forty-seven sticks of dynamite were gone.

CHAPTER 14

"MIND IF I ask a question?" Fanelli said as he guided his sedan out of The Strip traffic to the curb.

"Of course," Alison Gordon replied.

"You're bailing out here because you don't want Prince to know about me and the radio, right?"

"One free question a day is all you get," she announced and opened the car door.

"Watch your ass, Al."

"You do that for me," she told him.

He studied her swaying rear as she started down The Strip toward the fourteen-story Kublai Khan a block and a half away; so did several other men along the way. The hotel's six-and-a-half-foot-tall doorman, rather dashing in his historically accurate copy of Mongol warrior attire, nodded admiringly as she approached the building.

The Kublai Khan lobby was a dimly lit maze of gaming, with a high level of babble and air-conditioning, floral carpeting and voluptuous cocktail waitresses bulging green leotards and pink-straw coolie hats. There was the smell of money and the latest after-shave cologne in the air.

The Charlie Chan Coffee Shop occupied one corner of the vast room, the Orient Express Bar another and Fu Manchu's Gourmet Paradise a third. A twice-life-sized statue of karate film star Bruce Lee loomed in spotlit splendor near the gift shoppe. During the minute that it took Alison Gordon's eyes to adjust to the man-made gloom, her eyes roamed over the vast room as she worked to absorb the impact of this lavish display.

"Glorious, isn't it?" Prince said.

She turned to face him, pointed to the ceiling.

"Yes, I saw you on our overhead TV cameras," he admitted, "and rushed right down to welcome you on behalf of the entire staff—including Mr. Mintzer. Give him a big smile."

She looked up at the ceiling, spotted the cameras and waved at her unseen audience. It was wholly routine for the operating heads of local hotels to have television sets in their offices, with remote-control devices to zoom in on a single gambling table or person in the casino below.

"You'll like him, Miss Gordon. He's got a great smile too."

Sanford Myron Mintzer had a splendid all-purpose smile, about one-sixteenth of a millimeter deep and resting on some $6,500' worth of capped teeth. He had a large office done in unobtrusive, light-colored costly modern furniture, with the obligatory photos of S. Mintzer with assorted superstars, U.S. Presidents, world-class athletes, astronauts and the late Golda Meir covering the walls nicely. There was also a picture of a much younger Mintzer in an Air Force lieutenant's uniform, receiving a medal.

"That's the Distinguished Flying Cross," Prince told her loyally.

"Long time ago," Mintzer said with a shrug. He was a husky man in his late fifties, appropriately executive-looking in a three-hundred-and-seventy-five-dollar custom-made suit from Hong Kong, Italian loafers, gold-rimmed glasses and white shirt with multicolor tie. The tie wasn't too bold, actually, but the smile wasn't that sincere, so it all balanced out nicely.

"Glad you'll be able to help us. Really appreciate that, Miss Gordon," he announced. "Not that we don't have plenty of confidence in our own security folks. Outstanding group, but they've never dealt with this kind of thing before. It's . . . it's *unusual.*"

"Happens once in a blue moon," she agreed.

"Please . . . please sit down," Mintzer urged.

She settled into an armchair, scanned the big room and noticed the closed-circuit TV set. There was no audio, but the hidden camera was focussed on a high-stakes poker game below. The heaps of red and blue chips indicated that a lot of money was changing hands—the reds were worth fifty dollars and the blues one hundred. Prince wasn't looking at the set. He was studying her legs, seriously but discreetly. She couldn't tell whether this was part of his act or genuine interest, and she had no reason to care, of course . . .

After she declined Mintzer's offer of coffee, he used the desk intercom to tell his secretary to hold all his calls—and he sighed. She suggested that he start at the beginning, so he began with the arrival of the extortion letter five days ago in an envelope marked PERSONAL, ended with yesterday's telephone call about the "free samples." Then he shook his head.

"You think those cars at the airport were the samples?" he wondered.

"Let you know. I assume that you've kept this whole situation confidential. Who's been told?"

"Almost no one. Not even my secretary, and she's been with me for six years. With all this money around, we check out our people pretty carefully before we hire them. Most of them are bonded. I trust our people."

"No, you don't. You've got TV cameras and spy-in-the-sky peepholes and half a dozen other systems to catch your employees screwing you. I don't blame you for not trusting them, but let's be candid with each other—or I'll leave now."

Mintzer swallowed. He didn't like being forced to do

things, and he resented it even more because she was a woman. Women with real power—not just the kind they got in bed—were still unfamiliar to him and uncomfortable to accept. He had no choice, nowhere to maneuver. Her own reputation as a tough and independent operator was bad enough, but *they* had chosen her and one call from her to *them* could cost his $180,000-a-year job. He strained, forced out a sheepish smile.

"You're right, of course. Sorry. If you've got any questions, I'll try to answer them fully . . . candidly. We're on the same team, right?"

"Who else besides you and Prince knew that the bomb was stored at that abandoned pizza joint, Mr. Mintzer?"

"Call me Sandy."

"Sandy, who knew?"

The two men exchanged glances.

"Only Pat Baird," Mintzer answered, and Prince nodded. "Pat is our security chief, Ben's boss. Joined us about two years ago. Used to handle security for Harrah's in Reno. Good man."

"Top-notch," the younger man said. "Knows all the tricks and keeps his mouth shut."

"Ben's right. Pat Baird's a real pro. He and I and our lawyer in L.A. who approached you are the only ones who have looked at the note. You want to see it?"

"Can I see Pat first?" she asked. That reference to the non-existent "attorney" in Los Angeles was well done, but no surprise. He certainly wasn't going to mention Spinoza or mob people.

" 'Fraid not," Mintzer replied as he unlocked the lower left drawer of his imposing teak desk. "Pat's out of town until Friday afternoon. Flew to Minnesota yesterday to see his mother in the hospital . . . Here's the note."

He handed her an eight-by-ten-inch envelope and explained that the single-sheet extortion note and the smaller envelope in which it had arrived were inside. As a knowledgeable ex-police lieutenant, Baird had insisted that the threat document be handled carefully to avoid contaminating any clues.

"Pat had it dusted for prints," Mintzer told her, "and his friend found a couple. Two and a partial, he said. No matches in the F.B.I. files in Washington, though, and that's about as far as you can go."

Short of Cyclops. It probably hadn't been hard for Baird to bribe—the British would say "bend"—a detective in Nevada or some other state to teletype the fingerprint specifications to the F.B.I. on some pretext, but tapping into Cyclops would be much more difficult. She was outside the so-called intelligence community now, and for outsiders access was almost impossible. It hadn't been easy for those inside, she remembered, since the "community" had actually been a bureaucratic jungle. She thought about the years with the Agency and her dead husband whose body had never been found, and she stood up to go.

"Thanks for the candor," she said as she accepted the envelope. The squawk-box on the desk sounded abruptly.

"I know you said to hold all calls, but this man said to tell you it's a matter of life and death and five million dollars. He insisted that I repeat it just that way. He says you don't know him but his name is Mr. November."

Alison Gordon pointed at the speaker-phone. The head of the Kublai Khan pressed the button to turn it on, told his secretary to put through the call.

"Mintzer?"

"Yes. Who's this?"

"No time for jokes. Here are your instructions. We want two million dollars in fifty-dollar bills, the rest in hundreds. All used, non-sequential serial numbers. Get the money ready. We'll let you know about delivery. You got that, Four Eyes?"

"I'm not sure we can raise that kind of cash," the hotel executive protested. His tone suggested that he was ready to start bargaining, but he never got the chance. A nasty-tinny laugh from the phone's speaker unit stopped him abruptly.

"It won't be a couple of cars next time," the voice promised, and hung up. The sound of the telephone's dial tone humming from the speaker chilled all three in the office with its soulless electronic menace. Mintzer shrugged and shut off the speaker phone to end the noise. He looked across his desk at Alison Gordon.

"That man is crazy," he blustered.

"Not about cars. Maybe not about hotels either. You intend to pay him?" she asked.

"That's an enormous amount of money, and then there's the principle. The precedent. I'm counting on you to stop these people, Miss Gordon."

Something in his tone reminded her of the former U.S. President who had assured the world that he was "not a crook." She tucked the envelope with the threatening letter under her left arm, flashed a "thumbs up" salute of encouragement with her right hand.

"You really think you can catch them?"

He didn't believe in her at all. He was humoring her because the underworld chiefs had sent her, but he was just going through the motions of cooperating. Polite but patronizing, the chief executive officer of Kublai Khan Resorts, Inc. still nurtured the conviction that women were equipped to type and titillate. Period. He was puzzled that this difficult and dangerous job had been assigned to a female; women were to be given chores and some courtesy, not power or responsibility. This pretty and ambitious woman from Beverly Hills had to be the mistress of one of the top racketeers, someone not to be confronted. There was some kind of strategy involved, some novel and complex game being played. After all, *they* were no fools. *They* must have another plan, another team—run by men.

"Why not?" she replied. "My people are the best in the

business, and you're going to help us a great deal. You're going to cooperate *fully,* aren't you, *Sandy?* Your *lawyer* promised you would."

"Whatever you need, just ask. Day or night, call me or Ben and you'll get everything," Mintzer said hastily. This woman made him uneasy. She wasn't like the showgirls or cocktail waitresses who understood the sex-money-power realities and smiled, danced or laid down when appropriate. She wasn't like the ordinary female guests either. A million-dollar nightclub show, the chance of hitting a fifty-thousand-dollar jackpot or receiving a mink cape wouldn't turn her on at all. She had her own rules, probably had her own tastes and methods too. Mintzer showed her to the door, then sat down at his desk and adjusted the camera control on his TV set to scan the lobby, waiting uncomfortably until he saw them pass through the casino toward the street exit.

When he had watched them leave the building, he left the hotel himself by a route that took him through the kitchen at the rear. It galled him that the chief executive officer of a thirty-million-dollar firm had to conduct certain key aspects of his business over outside pay phones, but his instructions were quite clear. He was to assume that the lines from the hotel were tapped. Calls on confidential matters could only be made from telephone booths at least two blocks from the Kublai Khan, and he was not to use the same pay phone more than twice in a month.

Perhaps They were right, and somebody was listening . . . Even if They were wrong, one had to humor Them and report any significant problems or developments promptly by calling the phone number that he had memorized. The orders against writing it down anywhere had been very specific. He reached the booth just as a buxom brunette woman emerged from it. Fifty-dollar hooker, he identified. The Kublai Khan and other better hotels excluded such action and tolerated only the one-hundred-dollar prostitutes who had more class. The question of "class" was as important in the world of Vegas whores as in the clubs of British gentlemen. She looked at him and turned away. She knew the rules. Hookers did not solicit in the Vegas streets. That would be tacky, incompatible with the city's image as a family entertainment resort.

Mintzer dialed the number, recited the extortionists' latest demands and reported the reference linking it all to the cars blown up at the airport. "The woman from Beverly Hills was in my office when the call came in," the president of the Kublai Khan concluded.

"Who?"

"The woman you sent. She took the note. She insisted."

"Give her whatever she wants, aside from financial information."

The man at the other end of the wire didn't ask what Mintzer thought of her, or the situation. He didn't care, and he made no effort to hide it. This was no way to treat a one-hundred-and-eighty-thousand-dollar-a-year executive, but he and Mintzer both knew that the men who ran the Waldorf in New York, the Dorchester in London or the Georges V in Paris didn't earn half Mintzer's salary.

"Just as you say," Mintzer said, and wondered who gave the man at the other end *his* orders. As he left the booth a few moments later, he had to stop suddenly at the curb to avoid being pulped by a passing Ford. Although he knew that the near accident was his own fault, Sandy Mintzer shook his fist at the sedan as it turned the corner, vanished from his sight.

The Ford drew up at the Kublai Khan's parking lot at nine minutes before noon. Both Lester Wyatt and Gene Hance checked their watches as they stepped out of the car, nodded.

"Practically on time. Just two minutes behind schedule," Hance said.

"He isn't going to like that," Wyatt predicted. It was no

mere guess. They were both familiar with Arthur Messinger's passion for precision and punctuality. It was part of his personality, like the thing about hand washing. He had planned the routes, the timetable and the hiding places where they would conceal the bombs.

"Maybe we can catch up," Hance said and patted the United Air Lines flight bag slung over his shoulder. Muscular, in their thirties and dressed in sports clothes, they started for the front entrance of the hotel. They strolled into the casino, removed their sun glasses and looked around at the action. After ten seconds, they made their way to a row of slot machines that took quarters, and lost $2.75.

Nothing to attract attention, Arthur Messinger had specified. Just blend right in and you won't be noticed in the flow of tourists and gamblers. They separated now, each clear as to what he had to do. They sauntered through the casino to peer into shop windows, and gradually wandered onto the elevators. Wyatt, who was the heavier and shrewder, went up first and Hance followed in another car almost immediately. At three minutes after noon, they faced each other in a carpeted corridor on the second floor. Hance unzipped the flight bag, took out a screwdriver and deftly removed the metal access plate over the emergency air-conditioning repair duct. Then he took out the bomb.

"What are you guys doing?"

They turned, saw a sharp-featured man in his early forties. The pair of binoculars hanging from his neck didn't mean anything to these out-of-towners, who didn't recognize the high-powered glasses as the tool and trademark of hotel security men who watch gambling from the spy-in-the-sky observation posts hidden above the casino ceiling. Whoever he was, he had seen them and he was a threat to the entire operation.

"What is that thing?" the security specialist asked.

Hance hesitated for a second until Wyatt nodded. The man with the screwdriver raised it, stepped forward swiftly.

Wyatt slammed his hand over the man's mouth. There was a thump as the long thin blade pierced his chest, a muffled cough followed by a faint groan. The stare of shock in his eyes faded slowly as if someone were manipulating an internal rheostat to dim out his life.

"Again?" Hance asked.

"Not here. We can't afford to have any blood near the duct. Be better if we got him to another floor and unloaded him there."

The mortally wounded man could still *hear* them. He tried, very feebly, to cry out, but Wyatt easily silenced him.

"Stairs?"

"Stairs," the older man agreed and pointed down the corridor, "but be careful. Keep one hand on that screwdriver. If it comes out, there'll be a mess all over the rug. You cover his mouth while I put this thing in place."

With both hands free, Wyatt concentrated on the delicate task of setting the timer and inserting the bomb in the duct. As the older man rescrewed the duct cover with his Swiss army knife, Hance felt tremors in the man impaled on his screwdriver. He shoved it in an inch deeper, saw the man's eyes glow again in helpless suffering.

"Hurry up, Lester," Hance hissed. . . .

Some five minutes later, Debbie Hoffinger—Mrs. Jack Hoffinger to her friends in Portland—stepped from the elevator onto the fourth floor of the Kublai Khan Hotel. Her lecture on "New Trends in Vitamin-Packs for the Mature Face" had received a standing ovation at the beauticians and cosmetologists convention, and she was still thinking about it when she tripped and fell. She stood up, looked at what had caused her to stumble. Her mouth opened at the sight of the corpse, but no sound came out. When she noticed that the whole front of her $185 white silk, mid-knee, semi-formal dress was smeared with red, it took a moment to accept the fact that it was *his* blood.

She began to scream.

CHAPTER 15

"WHATEVER YOU say," Prince said as he stopped the Dodge at the traffic light.

"That's what Mr. Mintzer said," Alison Gordon replied coldly.

"Sandy," he corrected.

"Screw Sandy."

"You don't like Sandy Mintzer?" he asked as the light changed.

"I don't *trust* him."

Prince smiled, nodded toward the huge sign for the Circus Circus hotel and casino ahead on the right.

"Great show if you love animals," he volunteered.

She refused to be deflected.

"And *he* doesn't trust me either. He started it."

Prince laughed affably. "You noticed? Don't let it bother you. Why should he trust a total stranger? Listen, 99 percent of the folks who come here are good people—but we got goniffs and bad dudes too. Don't be hard on him, Miss Gordon."

"That son of a bitch patronized me," she said, and wondered why she was annoyed that Prince was so reasonable.

"Maybe he's afraid of you, Miss Gordon. I only had one

year of psych at college, but it might be . . . just a guess . . . your reputation intimidates him."

She had run into that before. Middle-aged men who could not cope comfortably with intelligent, independent, effective women who thought and decided for themselves . . . nothing new. They had been more numerous seven years ago when she started the detective agency. They were no longer quite that common, but still around. She turned her attention to the big hotel sign.

"Why Circus Circus? Why did they have to say it twice?"

"That's for the hard of hearing, and it makes the point. No harm in a little razzle-dazzle and bugle blowing, is there? Swell family show with a gang of acrobats and all sorts of animals. It's different. Nice change after all the topless showgirls and wall-to-wall superstars."

She glanced at her watch, calculated that Arroyo should be waiting at Caesars Palace by now. She looked down the gaudy Strip and suddenly understood.

"The whole town is a circus! They've switched in $2.89 buffets in place of the pink cotton candy, but it's all still colored sugar and hot air. It's a circus for kids of all ages. Acrobats for the younger, boobs and slot machines for the others."

"And elephants. Circus Circus has elephants, and I think the MGM show has one too."

There were dogs—not elephants—in the parking area at Caesars Palace. A tall man with a semi-military crewcut stood beside a trailer, holding leashes attached to a pair of big German shepherds. Another dog was barking from inside the trailer, not fiercely but loud enough to summon one of the uniformed bellboys from the front door.

"We don't take pets, sir," he announced politely.

"These aren't pets," the big man in the neatly pressed denim suit responded—and turned his back.

"It isn't up to me, sir. They're fine dogs, but it's a house rule. There are some motels that accept dogs—across town."

"Get lost, sonny. I'm waiting for somebody, so don't bug me. Push off."

Alison pointed, and when Prince pulled the Olds up nearby she saw the "O. K. L. Services" sign on the side of the trailer.

"Littlefield?" she asked.

The tall man ignored her, raised a big hand to menace the bellboy.

"Get your fat ass out of here, or I'll bust you one!" he threatened.

"O. K. Littlefield? Are you O. K. Littlefield?"

"Who wants to know, lady?"

"My name is Gordon, and you work for me. You might go on working for me if you clean up your act. I don't employ goons, Littlefield."

"I'm a dog handler, the best there is. That dumb-ass Indian never said A. B. Gordon was a fee-male."

She was a foot shorter, but she looked down on him icily.

"Did he say what the money was?"

"Top dollar."

"For dog handling, not creating a scene with bellboys. If I want monsters, I call Central Casting. You'd better apologize. I'm staying at this place and I don't want the staff to think I associate with thugs."

"How do I know you're A. B. Gordon?"

She slipped open her jacket, exposing the .357 in the silk-lined belly holster.

"You want to see the permit?"

Prince stifled a grin as O. K. Littlefield shook his head.

"No. No offense meant. Just drove six hundred fu— . . frigging miles, and I'm a mite tired. Dogs are kinda worn and hungry too. We could all use some sleep and eats."

"After you apologize."

"It's all right, miss. He didn't bother me," the bellboy soothed. The sight of the heavy magnum had made him nervous.

She glared at him.

"Don't be silly. Be quiet, and Mr. Littlefield will express his regrets."

The six-foot-four-inch dog handler took a deep breath.

"I regret . . . Sorry if I gave you a bad time, boy . . . Only one I'm truly sore at is that numbskull Navaho. Okay?"

She assured the bellboy that the dogs and trailer would be gone within a few minutes, watched as he returned to his post.

"Where's the Indian? What the hell is this all about?"

"Thomas is doing a job for me, Mr. Littlefield. I'll explain the assignment later. Now I want you to drive your dogs over to the Pot of Gold Mobile Home Park on Flamingo Road. Space has been reserved for you, and you'll get further orders this afternoon."

"Okay."

He uttered a soft command, and the sharp-eared dogs obeyed at once. They trotted to the trailer, waited as he unhooked their leads and jumped inside.

"Mr. Littlefield?"

He locked the trailer door, turned to face her.

"Yes?"

"Exactly what *is* top dollar in your business?" She took out one of the gold-tipped Sobranies. Prince lit it instantly with the inevitable Dunhill, but to her surprise it was a simple silver model—not the heavy gold status symbol favored by every twenty-three-year-old boy wonder producer.

"Eight hundred a week . . . and expenses . . . ma'am."

"You'll get nine hundred, and expenses." There was no chance that she'd pay this unpleasant man as much as Thomas Arroyo was getting. She took a sheaf of currency from her purse, gave the dog handler half a dozen $50 bills.

"Expenses. Good-by, Mr. Littlefield."

Wondering what to say, he looked over at Prince as if seeking support or guidance.

"Ben Prince. Glad to meet you," Prince volunteered cheerfully.

"What do you do?"

"Whatever she says."

Unable to decide whether Prince was serious, Littlefield grunted and walked to his car with as much dignity as he could manage. They watched him drive away into The Strip traffic.

"Dogs?" Prince asked.

She glanced at her watch, wondered what was delaying Arroyo.

"Why dogs?" the security man pressed.

"Why not?"

"Sniffers," he guessed with a large boyish smile. "Bet you four-fifty—that's two pounds sterling—that those bloody bow-wows are here to sniff out something. They can't just be guard dogs, because we ain't got nothing to guard. Want to bet?"

"Never gamble."

He shook his head, waggled his index finger at her.

"With all due respect, *ma'am,*" he replied in parody of the dog handler, "you're funning me. I'd wager as much as thirteen dollars that you're a gambling lady. A terribly intelligent and sophisticated gambling lady, of course, which is why you win so much of the time."

"You read tea leaves too?" She waved at Arroyo in her Porsche. He stopped the sports car ten yards away from her, and she understood that he had news he didn't want Prince to hear. She walked to him quickly.

"Littlefield's arrived with the dogs, Thomas."

"They're trained to smell out explosives?"

"Yes."

"We don't have any explosives. The forty-seven sticks of dynamite are gone," Arroyo said and looked over at Ben Prince in the Cutlass. Only four people had known where the explosives were buried, and neither A. B. Gordon,

Hovde nor the Navaho had discussed the cache with strangers. The odds against a transient outsider stumbling on the dynamite were overwhelming. That was why Arroyo was staring at the cheery young security man ten yards away.

"Him?" she thought aloud.

"Or someone he spoke to."

"Or maybe your room is wired. Thomas, did you discuss this with Don after you got back to the hotel last night?"

He nodded.

"You going to tell Mr. Prince?" he asked.

"Later. Let's go check on what burned up those two cars. Follow us, please."

She walked to the Cutlass, slid in beside Prince and pointed toward the "downtown" area of Las Vegas.

"I'm lousy on riddles," he confessed.

"I want to talk to the cops down at headquarters about those cars that went up at the airport yesterday, the cops and the fire marshals."

"I already did that. I phoned a buddy at ten this morning and got the score—just the way you told me to. Both cars were torched . . . delayed-action gear with precision timers. Tell you about it at lunch."

"Who's your buddy?" she asked.

"Lieutenant Barrett . . . Charlie Barrett . . . runs the bomb squad. The cars were stolen and the bombs were professional. That's the whole bit. Where do you want to eat?"

"At police headquarters. Move out, Mr. Prince."

He complied, and some ten minutes later they were only two blocks from the ten-story half moon of a building that housed City Hall and the main police facilities when a traffic light stopped them. The vehicle halted beside the Cutlass was a tan van, and the hair of the driver was as red as the traffic light itself. When the light changed, the van made a sharp left turn.

By the time that A. B. Gordon, Prince and Arroyo were entering the third-floor offices of the police bomb squad, the red-headed man was parking outside a liquor store half a mile away. He wasn't blowing up cars today. He adjusted his sun glasses and walked in and went straight to the clerk at the cash register.

"Vodka, please. Smirnoff."

"Quart or fifth?"

"Quart . . . Better make it two."

"Getting kind of thirsty out there," the clerk joked mechanically as he put the two bottles in a plastic shopping bag.

"Usually does, doesn't it?"

Matching inanity with inanity was always safe, the red-headed man thought as he left the store. No one ever remembered people who uttered brainless clichés like that. He unlocked the rear door of the van, put the bag down on the floor beside the other two. Each of those held another quart of Smirnoff. The orders had been—as usual—brief and specific. He was to spread the purchases over fifteen days, not to buy more than two bottles at any store and never to return to the same shop. He'd already been to Calamity Jane's on West Charleston Boulevard, Atomic Liquor on Fremont, King of Clubs on North Decatur and Lucky Ducky Liquors between the Dunes and Tropicana hotels. It had to be quarts, and it had to be Smirnoff vodka.

The plan was clever, Eric Adler reflected as he relocked the cargo compartment and started back to the driver's seat. Too bad he wasn't more fond of vodka. It would all be over soon, he reminded himself as he turned on the engine, and then there would be enough money to drink anything he pleased.

"Five million dollars," he celebrated in the privacy of the van. He was grinning exuberantly as he drove east into the mid-morning glare on his way to the house near the cemetery. It was appropriate that he had rented the aging three-bedroom home near the resting place for the dead.

Before Eric Adler and his friends left town, a lot of people were going to perish.

CHAPTER 16

THE CHIEF of the bomb squad of the Las Vegas P.D. did not resemble Telly Savalas, Clint Eastwood, Sherlock Holmes, J. Edgar Hoover or any other legendary law-enforcement officer. He certainly bore no resemblance to any of those famous sheriffs, marshals or film stars who rid the West of the criminal element. He seemed to be sensible, alert, about forty years old and no more than fifteen pounds overweight. He was all those things. There were the first touches of gray at his temples, and a serious look in his eyes. He was either impossible to bribe, underpaid or buying clothes from some mail-order catalogue. With the exception of the silver-tipped leather thong tie looped around his neck, everything he wore appeared to be at least a size too large.

"You're doing fine, Charlie," Prince commended.

"Just twelve more to lose," Barrett replied and automatically patted his stomach as he rose. He was a polite and classical sort of cop, the kind who still stood up when women entered a room. He'd been in charge of the bomb squad for three years, and enjoyed it even if there wasn't an enormous amount of work. This was a prestige assignment, plainly superior to the vice squad where he'd spent twenty-nine months. The memories of those smirky taunts about the "twat team" still rankled.

"Miss Gordon, this is Lieutenant Barrett—number-one bomb expert in the sovereign State of Nevada, which entered the Union on October 31, 1864."

"Ben loves to read up on things, Miss Gordon," the policeman explained as he put out his hand. She shook it, found it strong, dry.

"Just following the ancient traditions of my people," Prince said deadpan.

"Welcome to Las Vegas, Miss Gordon," Barrett said and glanced at Arroyo.

"Thank you, lieutenant. This is my associate, Mr. Arroyo."

"Nice to have you visiting, Mr. Arroyo." The lieutenant always made a point of dealing correctly and formally with Indians, even if they weren't local Paiutes. A number of these "Native Americans" were terribly sensitive, quick to complain to the federal government (which owned more than 85 percent of the land in Nevada) or to the media. After nineteen years of conscientious law enforcement, Barrett knew that the goddamn media would screw you any chance they got. Of course, private detectives weren't much better.

Barrett invited them to sit down in the straight-backed chairs, offered to order coffee from the vending machine or the cafeteria and confided that it was only mediocre.

"It was worse last year, Charlie," Prince recalled.

"Lot worse. Sorry to crowd you all up like this, but we don't get great big offices. Taxpayers want us lean and mean."

"You don't seem mean to me," she assured him, "and Mr. Prince says you're one of the nicest and most helpful people in town."

"Do my best," Barrett replied. She was even more attractive than people said, and not pushy. Most of the Beverly Hills women came on a lot stronger.

"Be helpful if you tell Miss Gordon about those cars at the airport yesterday," Prince suggested.

They were doing a number on him, the bomb squad chief

realized, but what kind and why? A high-powered-priced private eye like A. B. Gordon didn't screw around with routine insurance claims. Barrett decided to play it cool, to hold his questions till later.

"I can give it to you in one sentence," Barrett announced. "The cars were hot, and the bombs were good."

She nodded.

"Thank you," she answered. "We don't care much about the cars. Let's talk about the bombs."

So it wasn't insurance—not on the vehicles anyway.

What the hell was it?

"How much do you know about timers and detonators?" Barrett tested.

"Not as much as I used to, lieutenant, and I never knew half as much as Mr. Arroyo knows now. Why don't you tell him all about the hardware, and I'll try to keep up."

Arroyo began to ask questions—the pointed questions of a technician. Hovde had been right. It had been white phosphorus burning at 2700 centigrade, 425 grams of it with a small tetryl burster charge.

"That's an M–34," Arroyo identified.

"Right. An M–34 rigged with a delayed-action timer. Timer had a twenty-four-hour capacity, but we figure that it was set for two hours. Maybe you know it. TD–7."

"The British TD–7? That doesn't make any sense."

"No, a U.S. Army incendiary grenade hooked to a British timer to torch cars in Vegas doesn't make any sense at all," Barrett agreed.

"Is there anything special about the owners of the cars?" she asked.

"The green Jag was a rental job, taken out two days ago by a hotshot lawyer from New York. Shulman. Allen Shulman, heavy in the music business. Very smart. Good tennis, bad jokes, clean as the proverbial whistle. No mob clients, no woman troubles, no loan sharks out to muscle him. Pays his taxes, watches his weight and tans good. You know twenty guys like him . . . this guy's a copyright expert."

"I don't go in for that kinky stuff. What about the blue Lincoln, lieutenant?"

"Heisted late the night before, just like the Jag. Belonged to one of our top orthodontists. Highly respectable, loves kids, spends a day and a half a week doing free work for the patients who can't pay. Sixty-six years old, still living happily with the little lady he married forty-one years ago. She's a jogger and a member of the Democratic State Committee. Maybe you've heard of her, Felicity Northshield."

"That's her real name," Prince said.

"So the cars don't mean anything?"

"Nothing I can see as of now. But even if the ownership of the vehicles doesn't tell us anything, somebody stole them and blew them up for a reason," Barrett said.

"Thomas?"

"Nothing that unusual about the components used," Arroyo said. "Mass-produced timer issued to British demolition and commando units around the world for at least five years, and the standard U.S. Army M–34 grenade. There are probably a million of them spread from here to Ho Chi Minh City. The North Vietnamese must have captured one hundred and fifty thousand of them in warehouses when we pulled out."

"*Somebody* was sending *somebody* a message," the bomb-squad chief insisted. He looked at her, silently demanding that she answer the unspoken questions.

"Wouldn't be surprised. It'll all come out sooner or later," she said blandly.

"*Sooner* would be better."

That was when the fountain-pen-shaped device in Prince's shirt pocket began to vibrate, signaling that he was to call his office at the Kublai Khan.

"Crisis at the O. K. Corral. Mind if I use your horn, Charlie?"

Scant seconds later, while Prince was hearing about the bloody corpse found on the fourth floor, the two murderers were circling a parked tour bus toward the rear entrance of the Union Plaza Hotel downtown on Mainstreet. The yellow plastic bag that Hance carried concealed a bomb that looked identical to the weapon they had planted at the Kublai Khan, but the other device had been filled with C–4 plastic explosive. This one was a fire bomb.

"Six more to go," Hance said uneasily.

"Seven," Wyatt corrected, "and it's going to work. I laid out the whole thing to Arthur on the phone . . . the guy, the screwdriver and where we parked the stiff . . . and he told me we handled it perfectly. 'No reason to panic'—that's a quote."

"I trust Arthur's judgment. Okay, let's go to work."

Six minutes later, they walked out of the twenty-one-story Union Plaza's front door and stared at the signs of nearby Fremont Street. Wyatt took out his notebook, carefully inked out the name of the hotel and studied the next item on the schedule.

"Lunch at the Chuck Wagon Buffet at the Frontier, three-twenty-five for all you can eat," he said.

"That's back on The Strip. Why can't we eat here?"

"Arthur says it's the best value in town, and it fits his schedule. Trust Arthur," the older man urged.

The food was far better than that featured at most of the "all you can eat" rooms in Vegas hotels, and they were in excellent spirits when they resumed their appointed rounds in accord with the schedule. When they drove past the Kublai Khan, Hance smiled and pointed.

"No black-and-whites. Maybe they haven't even called the cops yet."

He was wrong. While none of the clearly designated ninety-five uniform cars of the Las Vegas Metropolitan Police Department were visible in front of the hotel, three unmarked vehicles used by detectives were parked behind the Kublai Khan and a hearse was en route. Homicide investigators were already at work on the fourth floor. The hunt was on.

CHAPTER 17

THE TIME was 1:40 P.M. and the place was the Pot of Gold Mobile Home Park, and the argument erupted as soon as Alison Gordon explained the plan.

"Don't like it," the dog handler announced.

"It's a good scheme," she said reassuringly. Littlefield glared at her. "It isn't my idea, you know. Your friend, Thomas, came up with it."

"No friend of mine. Don't like the idea, and don't like the Indian either." Littlefield leaned against the dog trailer. One of the shepherds barked, subsided swiftly when the handler called out a curt command.

"You got a better plan?"

"This one is . . . creepy. The glasses and the Navaho pretending to be my . . . this playacting ain't for me. There's gotta be *five* better plans, ma'am."

"All we've got is this one, and very little time. No time for a referendum on it either. We're a very old-fashioned outfit. No chaplain, no personnel department, not even a consulting psychologist or group therapy setup. You'll play this part exactly as written. How else can we get those dogs inside hotels that don't admit dogs? For God's sake, the idea's brilliant."

She was right, and that made the dog handler even angrier.

"This isn't my way of doing things—"

"No, it's mine. Now get those dogs and remember the instructions. Bombs are likely to be near the casinos because that's where the concentrations of people are, so work the lower three floors first."

Littlefield's bitter glance went to Arroyo, then back to her as he pointed at her navel.

"Dogs are tired. I'm not promising a thing, hear?"

"Do what you can, and remember, you're the best in the business and we're counting on you."

O. K. Littlefield's answer was not exactly what most trial lawyers would call "responsive." He muttered something that sounded a good deal like "goddamn Indians" just before he entered the trailer, and A. B. Gordon was puzzled as she turned to Arroyo.

"What's the matter with him, Thomas?"

"Hates Indians. Nothing personal. Hates old, young, men, women, all tribes. Parents raised him that way in Oklahoma. It's funny. I know some nice people from Oklahoma."

"He's not one of them."

Arroyo considered this, nodded.

"Hates Mexicans and Chicanos too. He told me that in 'Nam."

" 'Nam?"

"That's where I saved his life. Last week of the war. That's what he's angry about—owing his life to an Indian. Can't stand it. He wants to pay the debt, but something crazy inside tells him that whatever he does won't square it. What would you call a man like that, Miss Gordon?"

"A racist son of a bitch . . . with problems," she said and waved to Fanelli emerging from the nearby communications van. He responded with a "V" for victory gesture that said the two-way radio had been installed in Littlefield's vehicle.

"Lot of problems," Arroyo agreed, "but excellent with those dogs. We're lucky to have him with us."

"You don't *like* him, do you?"

"Miss Gordon, I'm a Navaho—not a saint. I accept him for what he is, and I call on him when I need him."

She knew men who had built major careers in television, advertising and politics on that same basis, and there was the president of a famed university whose principles were identical. Suddenly she thought about The Man With the Shades, and she wondered whether he was any more successful now in his efforts to reconcile Cold War reality with personal morality . . .

The dog handler came out of his trailer, spoke to Fanelli about the frequencies and controls on the radio. When the details were all clearly understood, Littlefield grunted and eyed Fanelli's garb.

"You a priest or something?"

"I'm a Leo and a tail-hound," Fanelli confided. It is difficult to predict what Littlefield might have answered if he had not seen the Wu sisters beside the radio van.

"Gooks," he sneered loudly and gestured toward Arroyo.

The Navaho sat beside him twenty seconds later as he drove off toward the Sahara Hotel, first stop on the route Alison Gordon had laid out for them. Maxine Wu walked slowly to Fanelli, who put his arm around her and kissed her affectionately.

"I heard what *he* said," she announced.

"A weirdo," Fanelli minimized.

"He called us *gooks.* Where does he come off with that crap?"

Fanelli rubbed his chin, pondered the weighty question and finally found the answer.

"Probably comes natural for him, Max. Way I figure it, he's at least half an asshole."

She looked to A. B. Gordon for confirmation.

"There's one on every flight," the private detective acknowledged. "Friend of mine's sister is a stewardess for American Airlines, and that's what she told me—at least one on every flight. We're lucky."

"Lucky?" Maxine Wu asked.

"Some flights have two."

At that moment, the mobile telephone in her nearby Porsche sounded and she walked quickly to answer it.

"It's Don," Hovde announced. "Andy's just checked in with a load of gear, and I finally got some feedback on that guy you asked me to check. It's interesting. Tell you when I see you."

But not now.

Not over a radio-telephone so easy to monitor. The odds were that he was calling from a public booth somewhere half a mile from Caesars Palace, for Hovde was compulsive about security routines.

"You at the hotel, Don?"

"No, but I can be at the mini-mall in twenty minutes." . . .

He was. Directly across The Strip from the Stardust's immense sign—188 feet high and 40,000 light bulbs, 10,000 fluorescent tubes wild—is a miniature shopping mall catering to tourists, souvenir hunters and honeymooners. Hovde stood waiting near stairs leading to the second floor boutique of a trendy woman known as Suzy Creamcheese. There was one rumor that a witty rock star had given her that name, another that her father had run a non-kosher delicatessen in Philadelphia. It was obvious that Hovde didn't care which was true. The look on his face said that he had something more urgent on his mind.

"I think Mr. Prince is connected," Hovde told her.

"I'm listening."

"You ever hear of Mendy Schwartz? Very big, very bad."

She ignored two women in polyester suits of puce, closed her eyes for a moment and remembered.

"Cleveland. Mendy the Shtarker?"

"That's him, one of the top guys in the Cleveland combine. Owned half a hotel here till the Gaming Board pushed him out in '72. He had a sister named Ida."

She lit a Sobranie.

"Ida Schwartz got married, and moved to New York," Hovde continued dramatically.

"Let me know when you get to the good part, Don."

"She's Ben Prince's mother. Your boy is all mobbed up. The word is that he associates with some damned unpleasant people."

"Most of us do these days. Who are his?"

"Friends of his uncle, top mob guys from Detroit, New York, Cleveland and Miami."

She remembered that Mintzer had come from Miami.

"Find out anything else?"

"Your boy's got a sister who's a surgeon, no arrest record and a reputation for keeping his mouth shut. Doesn't do much dope aside from a Thai stick now and then. Pays his bills, and doesn't chase women."

"They chase him."

"And they catch him. One lady at a time, but there's always a lady."

"Does he need money?"

Hovde's attention was diverted by a passing shopper with a wonderful walk; it was the tall and shapely English woman who paraded topless in the Stardust's twice-nightly Lido de Paris show. When he refocussed on Alison Gordon's question, he shrugged.

"Don't know. You can't get an accurate fix on anybody's finances in sixteen hours."

"How does he live?"

"Bunks alone in a furnished flat in a decent building, but nobody thinks he's rich. His women get flowers, not furs. Supposed to be a good shot. Number Two pistol marksman in the Air Force couple of years ago, and in June he won the Clark County fast-draw competition."

"Politics or hobbies?"

Hovde shook his head emphatically before answering.

"Zero, unless you can read something into tennis and contraception. He seems keen on both."

"Thanks, Don," she said, and found herself wondering who Prince's current lover might be. She was about to ask Hovde, but decided not to because he might misunderstand. She'd get all those details later after she turned over the extortion note to Agajanian. The accountant's analytical and meticulous mind might detect some clue, some lead, some signpost to the identification of the bombers. That was the essential first step.

"Maybe the dogs will find them."

"You want me to get more information about Prince's money situation?"

She nodded unenthusiastically, thought about the corpse at the Kublai Khan and the $5,000,000 and Benjamin Prince. She had never credited Hovde with telepathic powers, but he must have been reading her mind.

"How do you figure this Prince guy? Whose side is he on?"

"He's on *his* side, just like everybody else. *His* side might match up with *our* side—at least till November sixth. At least those dogs are on our side. Hell, they may have already found something at the Sahara."

Three quarters of a mile away, the doorman at the Sahara held open the hotel portal for two men and a dog. One of the men was bronzed and muscular with the features of an American Indian, and the taller man whom he hovered beside protectively was blind. The dark glasses were standard Vegas attire, but the large "seeing eye" shepherd signaled that the man who held the lead was sightless.

They had found nothing in the Sahara but a pleasant reception based on the facts that (1) the management was affable and humane; (2) the casino crew knew that the blind gambled just like other people; (3) the hotel's lawyers and the city's tourism staff didn't want any of that ugly trouble generated by charges of discriminating against the handicapped. This blind man was lucky to have his Indian friend with him, for the shepherd seemed to be new to the "seeing eye" routine and his master appeared annoyed by the clumsiness.

"New dog?" the doorman wondered softly.

The Navaho replied with a smile, and wondered what was happening back home in the war against the mining conglomerate. He helped Littlefield into the car, and it wasn't until they were safe in the noise of traffic that the dog handler began to curse. He swore at Arroyo bitterly, scourged the entire idea until they turned off at the Aladdin.

The theme at the Aladdin was sort of Arabian Nights, as conceived by a Hollywood set designer. The staff here was equally cooperative, and the bomb-hunters made their way through the first three floors without difficulty. They even managed to "stumble" into service areas and food preparation rooms "by accident," with the trained dog pausing again and again to sniff. The shepherd was a female, spayed to avoid "distracting" male dogs on the team with her scent. The animal worked with her mouth shut, a standard technique to concentrate on nasal identification of the explosive's distinctive "odor profile."

"One more pass around the casino perimeter?" Arroyo said.

"Okay," Littlefield said, "but it's damn near hopeless. So much perfume, after-shave, whiskey breath and scented powder that ol' Greta won't have much of a chance. Damn fine animal. Seven months at the Research Institute in San Antonio before I got her. Smart, loyal, well trained. If she wasn't worn out by the trip out here, Greta might find something if there's anything to find. This takes a helluva lot out of a dog. Total damn concentration . . . exhausting."

"Maybe we'll get lucky." They circled the large gambling area again, hardly noticed by the busy players who were so totally involved in pumping the slot-machine levers, invoking the deities of craps and other ancient faiths and wondering whether they might do better at cards or keno.

Their luck was no better than that of Thomas Arroyo, O. K. Littlefield and a seventy-pound shepherd named Greta. "The dog needs a rest," Littlefield insisted when they drove away from the Aladdin, "and I do too. What makes this Gordon woman push so hard?"

"She pushes herself even harder," Arroyo said.

Littlefield patted the shepherd, rubbed the animal's head until it made a low rumble of appreciation.

"What's the rush? Does she know something we don't?"

Arroyo didn't answer. There would be no point in telling the Oklahoman that she knew a lot that they didn't—about this operation and more.

"I don't mean to take any crap from that woman," Littlefield announced abruptly. "Humored her a bit earlier, but I'm not gonna be hu-mili-ated by some California princess. This country boy 'preciates a fine set of tits—and hers are definitely *outstanding,* but your grand lady can't lord it over me. Nobody dee-grades ol' O. K.—"

"I've seen her kill people."

Littlefield sat bolt upright in shock.

"She carries a .357 magnum. Actually she's a very nice person if you don't provoke her. Might even be a bonus for all of us if this mission works out right. Put your mind on that."

O. K. Littlefield thought about the money and the .357 all the way back to the Pot of Gold Mobile Home Park, and he was still brooding about those matters when he fed and watered his dogs and dozed off in his bunk. By the time Littlefield fell asleep, Thomas Arroyo was in the communications trailer finishing a cup of Kate Wu's excellent oolong tea. When he drained the last drop and thanked her again, she put him in radio contact with the command post where

'anelli had just installed a compact but powerful transceiv-
er-scrambler unit.

"Nothing so far," Arroyo reported, "but there are a lot nore casinos to check."

"How soon?" A. B. Gordon pressed. It was largely visceral, feeling that there was not a moment to waste even though he deadline was more than a week away.

"Littlefield's sleeping. I guess he might go out with a fresh log in a couple of hours."

"Two fresh dogs, and he can work them in forty-minute hifts. You can tell him that when he wakes up. You should e back by then."

"From where?"

"Sky Harbor on Highway 41. Six miles south of McCarran. 'ake the freeway to the Henderson turnoff. This is a high-evel mission. We're expecting you in twenty minutes."

"On my way," the Navaho replied and stood up to leave. He could see that Kate Wu wanted him to stay, but she nderstood.

"I'll see you later," he said. It was more than a polite emark. It was a commitment, one that made her smile. She ent him her sky-blue Ford. Minutes later as he drove down he freeway looking for the Henderson sign in the afternoon lare, he thought about the older Wu sister. It had been a ong time since he had met an attractive woman with such warming smile. For some moments he wondered what the 'high-level" mission might be, but then his focus returned o Kate Wu's smile. It did not leave until he saw the Sky Harbor sign, and by that time he had accepted the fact that his might be the woman to end his months of isolation. He lid not think that she was merely being considerate or riendly. There had been something more in her woman ook than that.

Perhaps he was being naive about this. Maybe it was a onely man's fantasy, but he did not think so. He would find out in due course. Long ago, he had learned that these things with women were not to be rushed. It was so easy to offend or frighten them, and each one was so completely different from the others. He thought of his years in the military, recalled how impatient and baffled men had roared and boasted and angrily chosen to buy women rather than understand these special qualities. He wondered how long it might take—if he were lucky—to find the special aspects of Kate Wu, and whether it could be done in the few days they had. He would return to her this night, and the next and the next. He had survived a difficult year without complaining. Now it was time for Thomas Arroyo to be lucky.

He saw Alison Gordon's Porsche, parked beside it and found her inside the low building nearby. She looked up, gestured and smiled in greeting. Her expression was in part automatic reaction. She put out her cigarette in a free-standing ashtray, gestured toward the swinging doors at the other side of the building.

"Bird's waiting. Let's go," she said.

CHAPTER 18

IT WAS a high-level mission as A. B. Gordon had said, some nineteen minutes long and 3,000 feet high. The black pilot of the chartered craft had learned to fly helicopters in the U.S. Army, and he remembered how to obey orders without asking too many questions. He had the additional emotional callouses built up in four years of coping with diverse Vegas tourists and sensation seekers, including two blonde members of a female rock group who made love to each other in the nude at 1,000 feet over scenic Lake Mead—at dawn. There had been a half-page obituary in *Rolling Stone* when the one with the livid appendectomy scar overdosed in '78.

He'd also been hired by an Arab petro-prince who rented the chopper for a full week—and never used it, an albino photographer taking aerial shots for a new hotel brochure—a witty man whose clothes smelled of marijuana, three Japanese executives who sought privacy and safety to talk out some secret deal and a gaunt Swedish movie director who wanted to be shown "the slums." The three men and the woman now in the rotorcraft seemed bland by comparison. They were neatly dressed, calm and sober and involved in some business project.

The fact that they didn't explain it was hardly unusual, for customers rarely told the pilot much besides the route or region they had chosen. The good-looking woman seemed to be in charge of this group, and she was clearly the sort who didn't explain her affairs to hired aviators or other strangers. In fact, she had hardly spoken to the pilot at all. Just before the quartet boarded the Sikorsky, she had opened an elegant briefcase of black leather and taken out five maps. She passed one to each of her companions, retained a copy for herself and gave one marked "P" to the pilot.

"The route is marked," she said, and climbed up into the helicopter. The others followed her, and the machine was airborn a few minutes later. The man at the controls flew the course that she had selected, skirting the southern perimeter of McCarran International Airport, then north over The Strip with all its hotels, flashing signs and calculated splendor. She was speaking to her colleagues and pointing at the map with a silver ballpoint, but the flier concentrated on his job and only caught occasional phrases.

Some of them were familiar to the ex-captain, but didn't fit this time and place. Strategic reconnaissance? Primary targets? Mobile security units? Tactical diversion? These were all military terms, with no possible connection to this resort in fun-loving Nevada. Now the route took the machine over the downtown casino and hotel area, and then through the skies above City Hall, the main power plant, the key gas and water-processing installations and a "farm" of huge oil tanks.

Swinging back, the pilot pointed at the perfect wedge of military jets silhouetted against the sun. One of the passengers—a bronze bulky man who looked Indian—turned his head to observe the superb formation flying.

"Thunderbirds," the flier shouted as he jabbed his index finger toward the crack Air Force show team.

The Indian nodded politely, but turned back immediately to the map on his lap. At that moment, one of the other men leaned over to ask the woman something and the pilot saw the heavy automatic in Agajanian's holster. The aviator blinked because men that well-dressed infrequently carried weapons. He said nothing. Though 98 percent of the males in Las Vegas violate very few statutes, ordinances or minors, the pilot had met enough of the other 2 percent so that he was good at not noticing guns. This policy and annual check-ups by his physician were sensible health precautions.

As the helicopter neared its home base, the pilot realized how silly he had been. Their clothes, their manner, their talk and their discipline all contradicted his initial judgment. He laughed as he told the woman about this after they had all disembarked at Sky Harbor.

"You won't believe this," he confided with a chuckle, "but I thought you might be . . . uh . . . mob people. Wasn't that dumb?"

She smiled beautifully, benignly.

"You're federal, right? This is a government deal, isn't it?"

"It's classified. Afraid we can't talk about it, and we have to appeal to you to do the same. National-security matter."

He told her that he was an ex-captain, assured her that she could rely upon his understanding and discretion. After all, he was still flying for Uncle Sam in the reserves once a month and he was not about to compromise a secret project.

"Thank you, captain," she said crisply—and nobody laughed until the Porsche swung around the curve and out of sight and earshot of anyone at the Sky Harbor building.

"That was super," Agajanian said. "Well played, as our Limey cousins would say."

"You were quick, and good," Hovde added.

Her eyes flicked to the rear-view mirror, saw Arroyo in the Ford coupe and returned to the road ahead. There had not been a second's rest since she met the Navaho for breakfast more than seven hours earlier, and the nonstop concentration was beginning to take its toll. She was not quite weary, but she could feel it coming—somewhere back behind her eyeballs. She sighed. Agajanian recognized the sound and the sign.

"Double espresso, anyone—or is it cocktail time?" he suggested.

"What about the conventions?" she asked.

"Full briefing on the conventions, sporting events, police patrol schedules, fire department radio frequencies—everything—*after* we absorb some liquid refreshment," the accountant promised.

"I'll drink to that," Hovde agreed, and began looking for a roadside bar.

Some twelve miles away, Eric Adler did not face that problem. What the red-headed man faced in his kitchen closet was seventeen quarts of Smirnoff vodka. It was a dangerous error to keep so many, for if anyone should stumble on the cache there could be questions. There was only one thing to do, and it had to be done now.

He picked up four bottles, carried them to the sideboard next to the sink. Then he brought out another quartet, going back and forth until all the glass containers stood lined up like soldiers. When the comparison struck him, he straightened the row.

"Attention! Present . . . arms!"

He half-filled a tall glass with ice cubes and tonic water, opened a bottle and added a healthy dose of vodka. He found a cluster of plastic cocktail stirrers, selected one pilfered from the Desert Inn and used it to mix the drink. He put on the television set, turned off the sound and watched a horde of Hollywood's finest Sioux attack a wagon train—in total silence. It was eerie and unreal without the sound, he thought as he sipped his vodka and tonic.

He did not finish the drink. Instead he opened another bottle and fashioned a Bloody Mary with tomato juice and then lemon juice, and he only consumed half of that. Next he mixed a vodka Martini on the rocks, using liquor from a third quart. He took three sips before the game began to pall. He had had enough of the Smirnoff and the lark, so he rose and dumped the contents of the three glasses into the sink. Then he began to pour the contents of the bottles—one by one, according to their place in the military formation he'd shaped—down the drain.

He looked over at the television set, was pleased to find that two of the wagons were burning and that the Sioux were charging again—right into the camera. When all the bottles were empty, he began to wash them in lukewarm water. He did not use detergent or soap, for the plan said to pour the Smirnoff down the drains when no one else was present and to wash the bottles out carefully with tepid water—and nothing else. Adler knew that he had to follow the plan in every minute detail, or he might be decapitated or set on fire like certain other people who had deviated.

After he had finished nine bottles, the battle was interrupted by a commercial for a "feminine-hygiene deordorant"—a change which caused Adler to switch channels. When he found a monstrous creature walking out of the sea toward a scale-model of Tokyo, he relaxed again and returned to the washing. Now there was another hideous creature on the screen, and a third was flying into view. Adler completed the rinsing chore, tilted the bottles upside down to drain and leaned back to enjoy the war of the monsters. He was resigned to the fact that he would not see the conclusion of this epic . . . he had to go out again soon to purchase more quarts of Smirnoff.

That was the plan, and nothing else mattered. He glanced at his calendar watch, saw that it was 5:13 on the 27th. They were on their way.

CHAPTER 19

HE HAD no doubt that the plan was good, but common sense and his combat experience told Arthur Messinger that the components of the scheme should be pre-tested. That was why the ex-sergeant was driving up U.S. Route 95 toward Rhyolite, at the turn of the century a booming mining camp with a population of ten thousand and now a quaint tourist stop with only half a dozen permanent residents.

"Nobody smarter than the advertising crowd," he had told Kuziw, "and they pre-test everything before they commit to a product or campaign. What's good enough for Madison Avenue ought to be good enough for us, Stanley."

"Screw Madison Avenue," the wheelman had replied—but he had obeyed the orders and three times during the past five days he had driven the planned escape route. Messinger had done the same himself to check traffic conditions and to clock and chart the red lights. Being short, bellicose and devious, Stanley had a tendency to resent and rebel; one had to keep an eye on his adolescent arrogance. He did not respect the plan or the man who made it; for that matter he could not accept anyone's authority. Messinger believed that the runty wheelman was out stealing the two vehicles that they would need, but he could not be quite *sure.* That was the infuriating thing about Stanley, worse than his vulgar clothes or bad taste in women . . .

"RHYOLITE—40," the sign said. It was too bad that Messinger wasn't going all the way to the historic town, because he had heard of its old bank, abandoned mines, vintage buildings and the railroad terminal once known as the "Dearborn Street Station of the West." It was too bad that he didn't have the time to see it all or visit the other old mining centers such as Searchlight and Pioche. Former Master Sergeant Messinger had always appreciated Americana, always done well in history at school too.

This was a business trip. He had scouted the area for an isolated spot where he might test the launchers. He found the turnoff again, and after three miles on the blacktop he spotted the even smaller road that twisted up into the hills. He reached the isolated valley just after six P.M., drove warily up the rutted route that led to the abandoned cabin. He nodded contentedly when he saw the rusted-out truck beside a ruined lodge—the vehicle that would be his target.

He parked his car, took out the two golf bags and unzipped them, removing from one a pair of M–72 disposable missile launchers. He estimated the distance to the truck to be less than forty yards. That was all right, he meant to use the weapon at a range of no more than twenty. He removed the protective caps before moving the inner tube to the locked position. He lay down in ground-firing position, squinting through the rear peep sight, aimed and shot. The fin-stabilized 66-millimeter rocket flew straight and true, and the M-412 impact-detonating fuse did not fail. The truck chassis was blown up with a loud explosion. Pieces of metal flew through the air, and acrid smoke drifted back from the wreck. Very good. Now he would test-fire the other M-72, just to make certain. His eyes wandered over the adjacent hills and ridges in a 360-degree circle as he loaded the second launcher, finding no other habitation or sign of life. He was about to shoot again when a flicker of motion caught his eye.

A young man stood framed in the cabin door. It was impossible, but there he was, dressed in jeans, plaid shirt, hiking boots and some kind of a cowboy hat—probably a nature lover or environmentalist out on a trek. He was in his early twenties. He was looking at the wreckage and at Arthur Messinger and the M-72. He had no business here, damn it. Destroying this itinerant idiot was not part of the plan.

"Hey, what the hell's going on here? What are you doing?"

The former noncommissioned officer dropped to the earth, pointed the launcher and squeezed the trigger. The young man screamed something, turned to run—the rocket blasted his head off, throwing it and one arm over beyond Messinger's car. The ex-sergeant was rather pleased. It was logical that an anti-tank missile that could penetrate 260 millimeters of armor plate would dismember a two-legged animal, and encouraging that he could still fire that accurately that fast.

"Not bad for an old soldier," he complimented himself. He was delighted that he still had his reflexes. When they went, you were in trouble. He dragged the body into the cabin by one foot, being careful not to be splashed by the blood coming from the neck and shoulder. There was the dead man's backpack, and Messinger knew that he must rifle it. If this lump of flesh were to be found in the next day or two, the clues had to point to robbery. Messinger coolly took the corpse's wallet and watch, scattered the contents of the pack as a thief might.

He decided not to burn the cabin. The smoke and fire might be seen miles away. And time was as important as deception. He walked outside, picked up the empty M-72 firing tubes and put them back into the golf bag. He placed both bags in the trunk, neatly laid the watch and wallet on the front seat and went out to collect the severed pieces. He had picked up pieces of people before in Viet Nam, but that did not make it easier. He found the arm first, left it in the scrub while he wandered on searching for the head.

There it was. He put them both on the plank floor beside the corpse.

He drove some thirty miles back toward Las Vegas before he examined the contents of the wallet. Forty-four dollars in bills, a California driver's license, membership card in some hikers' organization and a pass that entitled Harper Preston to use the library research facilities of the University of Santa Clara. He tore the papers into bits, let them stream out the window beside him in short bursts several moments apart. Some twenty-three miles closer to the resort city he spotted a roadside trash basket. He shoved the empty wallet under a tangle of pizza crusts, sandwich wrappers, cigarette packs and soft-drink cans.

Now he felt both virtuous and safe. Littering was unclean. Killing was nothing new to Arthur Messinger, and this incident had not been part of his plan. There was no way to anticipate that some transient would be unfortunate enough to be in the wrong place at the wrong time. The imminent execution of noxious Stanley Kuziw after they escaped with the money would be an entirely different matter. The former NCO was willing to accept the responsibility for that killing. After all, it was part of the plan.

Now the towers of Las Vegas were on the horizon, rising incongruously in the desert like surrealistic phallic mirages. This city that offered everything to everyone meant nothing to Messinger, had no appeal at all. It was simply a place where he could apply his military training, intelligence and will to take possession of millions of dollars. He drove more slowly now, staying at least five miles an hour below the speed limit to avoid attracting the attention of the police—another part of the plan.

When he locked the door of his motel room behind him, the former master sergeant went first to the bathroom to wash his hands. Even before he took off his jacket, he carefully soaped and scrubbed them. It had nothing to do with what he had been handling. Arthur Messinger simply preferred to be clean and neat. An Army doctor had once suggested that Messinger had a deeply buried sense that he was somehow dirty, but the former NCO knew that this was nonsense. A man with clean hands did his job better, felt better too.

He hung up his jacket, drank a glass of low-fat skim milk from the carton in the refrigerator and wondered when Stanley Kuziw would return. After a few minutes, he began to grow impatient, and uneasy. That was when he went in to wash his hands again so he could recheck the fuses. A clean mind in a clean body, he thought cheerfully as he lathered his fingers. It was a pleasant and comforting sensation, and he began to sing. This day's deaths of two people who blundered into his plan would not be connected to his operation, and everything was proceeding on schedule.

He started to sing even louder, and was halfway through the romantic Johnny Mercer lyric to Mancini's lilting "Moon River" when the telephone rang.

CHAPTER 20

EVERYONE—INCLUDING the commandant of Special Branch—afterward agreed that what happened had not been the fault of Sergeant Harrington. Harrington had been in charge of the surveillance team watching the Vogelsang man in the cheap hotel near the British Museum since receipt of the Interpol alert, but there was no way that he could have anticipated the bloody disaster. After all, such savage incidents rarely transpire in London and this one was over in less than a minute, obviously the work of persons unknown who had been planning it for days.

When the phone rang in Room 304, the man whose Austrian passport said he was Johann Vogelsang of Salzburg picked up the instrument. Detective Rodney, who was manning the wire-tap equipment in the basement, did not have to do anything but look at the voice-activated recorder and watch the tape roll.

"It's me. I'm at the airport. Ready for Freddie, as the Americans say," a woman with some sort of Dutch or German accent announced.

"When does your plane take off?" Vogelsang asked.

"Eine halbe Stunde. We board immediately. Are you all set?"

"I'm picking up my Pan Am ticket in twenty minutes; 747,

isn't that amusing?" he said with an odd laugh.

"It is *appropriate.* We'll see you there on the second if all goes well."

"It will. Nothing will stop the 747's."

They exchanged farewells, and Detective Rodney wondered whether the new computerized gear had traced the call.

Some moments later Vogelsang locked the door of Room 304 behind him and started down the corridor toward the lift. In America he would have to call it the elevator, he thought, and made a mental note to remember that. Foreign usages would draw undesirable attention. Some such blunder had probably caused the Casablanca airport disaster, he reflected.

Treading the rug worn shabby by the footsteps of platoons of budget-minded Asians who dominated this hotel's guest list, he barely noticed the round-faced nun as she emerged from Room 312. She drew an odd-looking pistol from a Marks & Spencer shopping bag and shot him six times in the face and throat. The bulbous device on the end of the gun reduced the sounds to the pops of champagne corks being pulled, but there was nothing festive about this occasion.

The "nun" left the hotel, smiling benignly as she blended into the flow of pedestrians. Nobody paid attention to the good sister, who had checked in two days earlier on an Italian passport. That document later proved to be an excellent forgery, and authorities in Rome telexed that the religious order in Turin to which "Sister Rosealba" belonged had never heard of her. Who was she . . . ?

"Somebody bloody good with a .22 pistol," Inspector Cuthbert was saying after he had read the report. "A professional with a high-penetration .22-caliber weapon. Remind you of anything?"

"The Israeli security types who ride their transport aircraft, sir," Harrington replied.

"Precisely. Let's suppose for a moment that we're looking for an Israeli lass in nun's clothes. Why would a professional agent who isn't Sister Rosealba execute this fellow you tell me is not Johann Vogelsang?"

"I don't know, sir. The Vogelsang passport was pinched from the luggage of Herr Vogelsang four months ago after he died in that Ankara . . . well, truth is it was a brothel, they say."

Inspector Cuthbert looked across his office at the framed portrait of Her Majesty, thought how attractive his wife would look in the peekaboo black negligee he'd bought for her birthday. Being a dedicated and patriotic policeman as well as a good one, he refocussed on the murder.

"A nun who isn't shoots a man who isn't. What do you think, sergeant?" It never hurt to show interest in the men's ideas. Good for morale, and sometimes the chaps came up with fine stuff.

"We were watching him because S.I. thought he might be hooked up with that terrorist mob, sir. Perhaps the Israelis had the same notion. They've been looking for those bastards, sir."

"Everybody's looking for that lot," the inspector agreed. "You say the call came from Gatwick, and that a Laker DC-10 left for New York at the time the woman on the phone tap announced she was due to take off. Yes, that would mesh with her remark that she was ready for Freddie. Good thinking, Harrington."

The sergeant beamed. It was a distinct pleasure to work with a supervisor who didn't look down on the staff as lower-class dolts.

"Thank you, sir."

Cuthbert glanced at the handsome wristwatch his portly brother-in-law had given him for Christmas. "Our message should be in Washington."

"Oh yes, sir. It was Red Flash, Priority One. I don't know whether it arrived in time for the Yanks to spot her at

Kennedy, but it's surely there by this time."

"Good. The Yanks are mad keen on the Attila group. Wouldn't do any harm to have them owe us one."

"They're probably out searching for her right now," the sergeant said.

He was right.

CHAPTER 21

"THAT'S CRAZY!" Hovde protested as he stared at the device in Agajanian's hand.

"Crazies were last week," the accountant corrected. "Four thousand shrinks in for the psychiatrists convention, but they left yesterday. A real cheap bunch, according to the hookers."

"Why is he talking about hookers?" Hovde wondered.

"Sexual obsession," Alison Gordon replied and picked up one of the gadgets herself. Agajanian got her message to stick to the subject, nodded and complied.

"Okay. Day after tomorrow, the teachers of the deaf start their national get-together. Hordes of them, some with hearing problems of their own," he reported.

"That's why we won't attract attention wearing these," she explained. The small plastic box she held had one wire to a transparent earplug, another to a flat little microphone.

"Looks like a hearing instrument," Agajanian pointed out, "but it's an efficient walkie-talkie with a throat mike you wear under a scarf or foulard. Neat, huh?"

"I don't wear foulards," Hovde objected hoarsely, "and Littlefield will hate it. First the blind man's glasses, and now hearing instruments. What's next—wheelchairs?"

"Next is getting these to all our people right away," she

answered. She turned her back to the men in the command post, unbuttoned her silk blouse and slipped it down from her shapely shoulders. Her large brown nipples were visible through the flesh-tone, barely-there-at-all John Kloss brassiere. Agajanian caught a glimpse reflected in the mirror before he swung his glance to the large map of the city on the nearby wall, and he was startled by the impact of her erotic beauty after all these years.

She carefully placed the microphone against the base of her throat, shivered as the cold plastic touched her skin and wondered what Prince was doing. After she gingerly inserted the plastic piece in her left ear, she fluffed out her hair and reached for the volume control on the walkie-talkie. Then she turned, saw Agajanian and Hovde adjusting their sets too. There was a knock at the door. Hovde opened it to admit Fanelli, who stared at her and nodded twice.

"Yeah, you were right," he said curtly.

"You got anything else to tell me?" she asked.

"It's a lovely bra."

She buttoned her blouse, pointed at the transmitter on the large table and asked Fanelli to take the next shift while she went to deliver walkie-talkies to Arroyo and Littlefield.

"I don't understand why we have to use a bigot like Littlefield," Agajanian complained.

"He gives a good dog," Fanelli answered. He saw her wince, watched her scribble a note and hand it to the accountant who absorbed the concise message and automatically tore the sheet of Caesars Palace notepaper into strips. Following security procedure, he heaped the pieces in an ashtray and set them ablaze. When they were consumed, he crushed the ashes into gray powder with the blade of his throwing knife and dumped the powder into the toilet bowl. He flushed it twice.

"It's past seven," she said. "Why don't you and Andy eat, and you can relieve Gerry in an hour or so? He's got some other chores to clean up before he leaves."

"I don't like this," Hovde announced, and they all knew what he meant. She led the two men from the suite that had been converted into their command post, talking casually about the ways the dogs were trained and how they signaled the presence of explosives by abruptly sitting down. There had been a mini-documentary about it on the *Today* show only a month earlier.

The sun had not quite set as they walked out of the building. Las Vegas looked rosy, imaginary and not at all unattractive. Even the horrid neon birds on the sign across The Strip were almost acceptable in this light . . .

"Who do you think—" Agajanian began, stopped. There might be sensitive parabolic microphones aimed at them at this moment. She asked them to let Fanelli know where they were dining, walked to her car and tested the powerful radio installed earlier. It was much stronger than the walkie-talkies, with a range of some thirty miles. Fanelli responded to her call to Blue Moon Central immediately, and she felt some reassurance as she started toward the Versailles. According to the schedule, the dog unit should be leaving that pseudo-French pseudo-palace in about ten minutes. She parked her car beside that hotel five minutes later, waited for them to emerge. She lit one of the gold-tipped cigarettes, considered the results of Fanelli's electronic sweep.

Who the hell was it?

She finished the Sobranie, then lit another. She was halfway through a third and Arroyo and Littlefield still had not emerged from the Versailles. Could they have found something inside? Was that the reason for the delay? Had something gone wrong, or perhaps right for a change?

There they were—entering, not leaving. She scooped up the pouch containing the walkie-talkies, hurried after them past the bewigged doorman in the costume of an eighteenth-century French dragoon officer. A cluster of some twenty Japanese blocked her way, all listening earnestly as their tour guide described their evening schedule in their native tongue. Unable to pierce the wall of flesh, concentration and cameras, A. B. Gordon had to circle around them in her effort to catch up with the dog unit.

They were gone. The lobby—large and crammed with gaming tables and players—was an obstacle course just like the other casinos. She walked swiftly up one twisting aisle, then turned to another opening in the maze. Where the hell could they be? Her eyes swept the room. This was stupid and infuriating. Limited by the pace of the shepherd, they couldn't move very fast. They had to be somewhere within forty or fifty yards of her. She heard the clatter-crash of a nearby jackpot at one of the dollar machines—and then she saw them.

They were walking toward the bank of elevators at the back—over beside the Plexiglas-fronted booths where cash clerks were exchanging chips for currency. Brushing past one of the large-bosomed change girls and avoiding a trio of motorcycle distributors in for the Western Honda Dealers Supersales Rodeo, she zigzagged through the crowd and reached them just as the door of the elevator directly in front of them opened.

Before she could say a word, Littlefield, Arroyo and the dog entered. Two other men—one carrying a United Air Lines shoulder bag—followed them in, and Alison Gordon barely joined them before the door closed. Now the Navaho saw her, but his face showed no flicker of recognition. He'd wait until the pair of strangers were gone before he spoke. The younger of the duo pressed the button for a stop at the second floor, and the Indian pushed the button for the floor above. That was hardly surprising, for she had instructed them to search the bottom three floors. She would hand over the walkie-talkies in a few moments when they were alone.

It happened—just like that. No warning, no reason to expect that the case was about to tear wide open. There was no gunfire, no explosion, no meaningful comment or dramatic confrontation. The dog sat down. It didn't bark or snarl, tug at its lead or hurl itself forward in snarling attack. Three of the five people in that elevator knew what it meant: one of the two strangers was carrying some type of explosive, one of the kind that this shepherd had been trained to detect. Either the dog was wrong, or these ordinary-looking men in the rather typical Vegas-visitor sports attire were the bombers.

There could be a bomb in that shoulder bag, or was it hidden somewhere in the elevator itself? Her eyes began to rove across the compartment. Littlewood's head was tilting back, and she realized that he was looking up at the roof of the moving unit. The elevator stopped. The door opened, and Wyatt and Hance stepped out onto the second floor.

She had a split-second to decide. Take them or follow them? If she signaled her team to take them there could be a shootout or, worse, an explosion. If she followed them they might well spot the tail and get away. Maybe they had already recognized the shepherd as specially trained and were about to open fire.

She calculated, gestured, indicating that Littlefield was to follow the men and that Arroyo should ride up to the next floor in a moment. The dog handler and the Navaho left the elevator, stopped abruptly.

"This is two," Arroyo said. "Why don't you wait here with Tarzan while I go up and get the car keys? I won't be a moment."

"I'll be all right here," Littlefield said.

Hance and Wyatt cautiously looked back as they turned the corner at the end of the corridor, seeing that Arroyo was gone and that the blind man was alone. *He* certainly wouldn't see where they went with the bomb. . . .

She threw the "emergency stop" switch, halting the elevator just above the third floor. She thrust the pouch at Arroyo, told him to rejoin Littlefield and report by walkie-talkie after the dog had sniff-searched the second floor. Arroyo noticed that she looked confident, stimulated by the action. It agreed with her. She was one of those women who excelled in challenge situations, but there was something restless in her too. He didn't know exactly what it was, but he sensed it was there.

"I'll be outside to follow them when they leave," she said and turned on the power. She descended by another elevator, returned to the Porsche and made radio contact with the command post.

"We may have found our friends," she said guardedly.

"Fan-*tas*tic. Gonna have a party?" Fanelli asked.

"Depends on whether we can get a good crowd together. This could be an all-night number, the kind Don and Andy enjoy. I'll get back to you."

Some eight minutes later she did. Wyatt and Hance had strolled from the hotel's front door to their station wagon and driven off toward downtown. They did not appear to be aware that they were being followed. She described their vehicle and recited the license-plate number to Fanelli, saying that she hoped that the accountant had finished dinner. "You can have dessert with us in twenty minutes."

"Fifteen," Fanelli assured, "if you let us know where."

She drove on down The Strip, tracking them warily with the skills she'd honed in the years with the Agency. Sometimes she deliberately let other vehicles come between the Porsche and the station wagon, falling back and then moving up again. There was a lot of traffic out now. Good and bad. The good was that the other cars masked her from the view of the men in the wagon, the bad the risk that she'd lose them in the traffic. Arroyo should have reported by now, damn it. Had the dog found a bomb or hadn't he? Now she heard his voice in her ear, and she swallowed hard as her throat tensed.

"Blue Moon Two to Blue Moon One."

"Go ahead, Blue Moon Two."

"Bingo. Do you read me? Bingo."

They had found the bomb. No, *a* bomb; there were probably others, perhaps booby-trapped to make disarming dangerous.

"Is it clean? Have you examined it, Blue Moon Two?"

"Affirmative. No problem. We should have it out in a few minutes. Awaiting your instructions on where to deliver the package," Arroyo said.

He must have already disconnected the detonating mechanism.

"Get it out of the building and continue search pattern. Check with Central every half-hour. Tell your friend he did a good job, a *very* good job," she instructed Arroyo.

"He'll appreciate that, and so will Tarzan."

She didn't mind when the radio conversation ended. The stalking had just begun. Within minutes she would have two other cars for the tracking, two more pieces in the game She had told herself many times that this was not for healthy adults, that it was a thing for adolescents, a no-win lark that she should have outgrown years ago. But there was something about this game that absorbed her, challenged her mind and instincts . . .

They were heading for the Downtown Casino Center, the original heart of the city and still an active attraction for the less affluent and/or sophisticated. The names of the hotels in the Fremont Street area were less exotic, more directly related to gambling. There was much less of the superstar or big-budget entertainment in these hotels, which sported such names as The Four Queens, the Horseshoe, Golden Nugget and The Mint. The bets were smaller here, but the glittering electric signs even larger and more frenetic in their efforts to win attention. The flashing of the masses of bulbs almost dazzled her as she trailed the station wagon into the heart of the Fremont Street cluster of casinos. It was one gambling house after another, some offering *free* cocktails or *free* computerized character analyses—and budget slots that could be played with a nickel.

She saw the station wagon stop, watched the younger man

step out with the airline bag and enter The Mint. She stayed with the car; still the driver seemed to have no thought that he might be under surveillance. He had not looked back since leaving the Versailles. When he parked on a side street three blocks from The Mint, she reached for her radio again. As she turned on the switch, she heard Agajanian speak first.

"Blue Moon One. Blue Moon One. We're ready for the bingo party," the accountant said. She asked him to tell Thomas that "his friends" were "having a drink at The Mint," instructed Agajanian to meet her across the street from where the station wagon sat. "Separate vehicles," she specified, and leaned back to wait.

They arrived in nine minutes. She smiled when she saw that the accountant had half of a large Hershey bar in one hand.

"Dinner," he explained. "We were midway through our first course when we got the flash."

"We'll all eat later—maybe a lot later. Could be a long night—but I think we've got 'em." Hovde dug into his pocket and handed her another bar of chocolate.

"Brought one for you. Not fancy like that Swiss stuff, but I thought you might be hungry too."

She thanked him, described the two men and pointed out the station wagon. Then she established the pattern for the mobile surveillance, a familiar leapfrog schedule in which the three vehicles would rotate being closest to the bombers.

"Don't crowd them," she ordered. "They don't seem to be too bright—not about security, anyway—but we can't take any chances. I don't want to spook them. We've got to be very careful. More than usual, Don. This is our first break. Let's not blow it."

There was one danger, one possible flaw. The logical accountant put it into words.

"What if they don't come back to the wagon?"

"They will. I know they will—any minute now. Get

ready," she said with a bit more confidence than she could justify.

Ten minutes. Twenty. A half-hour. It shouldn't take them this long to hide a bomb. Something was wrong—maybe her own instincts. Maybe they had abandoned the wagon, walked out of a side door of The Mint to vanish into the crowds of gamblers. Forty minutes.

Where were they? How could she find them again among the tens of thousands of tourists in the scores of hotels, casinos and motels in this crowded city? Now it was forty-five minutes, and there was no sign of them. What was happening?

"I'm going in," she announced. She walked toward the hotel, making a conscious effort not to hurry and wondering how and where she might locate two men in a building that size. She *couldn't* lose them now. It had been a mistake not to follow the driver, wrong to hang back so far to minimize the risk of being noticed. This mess would never have been if she'd had more people with her. Goddamn it, she had told Spinoza that this was a job for a big law-enforcement group with plenty of personnel.

She reminded herself as she walked into The Mint that it was too early to panic. She made her way through and around the dice games, slot machines, card tables. Nothing. She crossed and crisscrossed the large chamber, searching. Zero. They were gone.

They could be miles away by now.

They might be at McCarran Airport already, buying tickets for L.A., Vancouver or Mexico City.

They could be out poisoning the water system, or setting charges to blow the roof off the Hilton in twenty minutes. She didn't know who they were, or how many others might be involved. Even if Prince's police friends went over the station wagon meticulously, it might be days before they found any solid leads, if they found any at all. Somebody bumped into her from behind. Frustrated and furious, she turned in a rage.

She saw Hance. He was wiping his mouth with the back of his hand, just two steps beyond the white-haired grandmother who had collided with A. B. Gordon in a rush for a "lucky" 25-cents machine.

"C'mon, Gladys," the bespectacled senior citizen sang out to a colleague carrying a paper cup filled with coins—trademark of the slot addict. Alison Gordon saw Wyatt too now and retreated so that he wouldn't notice her. He might remember her, might not believe in coincidences. She took refuge behind a pillar, stifling an impulse to shout in relief. The bombers had been enjoying The Mint's $2.85 special unlimited buffet—with coffee.

Suddenly she felt hungry too. She trailed them out onto Fremont and radioed warning that they were on their way. When the station wagon started, Agajanian was in the number-one position, nearest to the suspects. Hovde was second, and she followed at the rear. They would not get out of sight again. She sighed, tore open the candy bar and sank her teeth into the mass-produced milk chocolate and almonds. It tasted mass-produced, undistinguished and—absolutely delicious.

There were still a great many questions, hardly any answers so far. Most of the pieces were missing from the puzzle, and one of the nagging blanks was why these strangers were placing bombs now when the deadline for payment was days ahead. It had to be preparation for more violent "preview" explosions.

Although Alison Gordon didn't believe in reading palms, the knobs on people's skulls or character as expressed in eyes or faces, she felt reasonably sure that the two men in the station wagon were merely soldiers carrying out orders; they did not have the air of leaders. These were the Indians who would lead her to the chiefs who had masterminded this extortion scheme. There had to be a base, perhaps more than one, and there was an inside man too, someone who had penetrated the secrets of the Kublai Khan and other Mob-financed operations here. There had to be.

"Central to Blue Moon One, Central to Blue Moon One," broke into her train of thought.

"Go ahead, Central."

"Thomas has just found another bingo game. He'll be late for dinner. Over."

They all would, she realized as she finished the candy bar. It might be hours before she or her colleagues had any chance to eat a proper meal.

"Do you read me, Blue Moon One?" Fanelli pressed.

"Roger, second bingo game, and the night is young. Out." She wondered how many bombs the dogs might find tonight. The station wagon rolled on through the balmy October night, stopped in the shadows near the chemistry building of the University of Las Vegas. She sat in the darkness eighty yards away. She was the nearest now, in the number-one position.

Why place a bomb here? It didn't add up. The chemicals would fuel impressive fires and secondary explosions, true, but this was a state school, not a gangster-controlled business.

The question still gnawed at her at a quarter to ten when she saw Wyatt and Hance enter their room at a motel neaı the Hacienda Hotel. She was not aware, of course, that their names were Hance and Wyatt, or that another man named Arthur Messinger had chosen this site for them because it was far from where he resided with a fourth conspirator. They were still anonymous but important "subjects" in the stilted argot of law enforcement.

"You hungry?" Hovde asked the moment he walked to the Porsche.

"Intensely, but I'll take the first—"

"No, first watch is mine," he insisted. "Go get some food, and bring me a couple of rare cheeseburgers with a carton of tea. Never mind, Andy can deliver it. He's got the two-to-eight A.M. shift anyway."

"But—"

"You get your beauty sleep," he told her, "and don't argue with me. Remember who's the boss."

"I'm the boss—"

"Then please stop bothering the help," Agajanian urged from behind her. "You good-looking women think you can get away with anything."

She smiled. "Thanks—and be careful. I don't want either of you guys to take any chances. There could be more of these creeps, maybe nearby. No heroics, please. Just watch them from a distance. Anything strange or fancy happens, use your head and your radio, not your guns."

Both nodded, and Hovde reminded the accountant that he liked kosher pickles with the burgers. Extra napkins, of course. She was almost at Caesars when she heard that a third bomb had been removed, and that the dogs' fatigue was forcing that team to return to the mobile-home park for rest. She found herself thinking about the unfinished business as she swung into the hotel's long driveway, the devices planted at the Versailles, The Mint, the chemistry lab and the almost finished casino on The Strip.

As she parked and locked the Porsche next to a silver Rolls, she felt more pangs of hunger sweep her empty stomach, fought them down. Her mind moved on to scheduling a wiretap on the phone at the bombers' motel. The enigma of the inside man bubbled to the surface again. Avoiding a cart loaded with Louis Vuitton luggage and two leather golf bags, she reached the front door of the hotel.

There he was.

She was tired, hungry and sure that her clothes were as rumpled as her hair; Ben Prince looked immaculate and handsome—in a rather obvious way. There was something very warm in his eyes as he smiled, something that reminded her of a man who had failed her three years earlier.

In this weary state, how could she judge? She was not going to trust him, but she wanted to learn what the police had discovered about the corpse at the Kublai Khan.

Prince seemed to sense her fatigue and reached out to take her arm. Without being quite sure why, she felt a need to accept, not to resist his touch.

"We've got a lot to talk about," he said.

"After we eat."

"A small ox?"

"Two."

He guided her into the hotel. He was really quite attractive for a young man of this sort. As they made their way through the slightly too cool and too dim casino, she hoped that he would not turn out to be on the wrong side of the developing situation. It would be nice if he were simply a more civilized hedonist with greater compassion and intelligence than the usual run of handsome gentlemen so in love with themselves, their after-shave lotions and gold chains . . .

After letting Fanelli know that she was dining at The Spanish Steps, she settled down with Prince in the copper-and-wood restaurant with a sigh of letting go and a strong thirst. Two drinks later, the idea that Ben Prince might be an ally of bombers and murderers seemed almost remote. He obviously lacked the hard-edged toughness it would take to challenge Spinoza's organization.

After he had ordered the suckling pig and roast lamb, he apologized that there was no ox on the menu and began to report what the homicide detectives had found. She listened carefully, alert for any link to the extortion plot.

"There doesn't seem to be any connection to the notes," she said. "Your Eye-in-the-Sky security man could have been killed by any one of a thousand people for any one of a hundred reasons. Did Barrett say anything else?"

"He wanted to know what was going on between you and

me. I told him that it was purely physical," he said with a straight face.

"You got any ideas about why this fellow was stabbed, Ben?" she asked as the hors d'oeuvres arrived.

"Negative. He was just a typical Vegas guy with one and a half wives, two and a third children and four sets of good cuff links. What about *your* afternoon and evening."

Part of it was gut instinct, and part her C.I.A. training. The old need-to-know rule was the safest. There didn't appear to be any way in which telling Prince about the bombs and the men Hovde was watching would help, not at the moment anyway. Perhaps she would let Prince see them tomorrow. Right now—tonight—he did not need to know. It might be safer if he didn't. There were still too many questions to which the answer might be Benjamin Prince. So she lied. As adroitly and without hesitation as most delegates to the U.N. and your legendary used-car salesmen.

"We've been walking the dogs and getting organized," she replied. "Hasn't been easy checking out these hotels, Ben. The wall-to-wall tourists are a problem."

He refilled her wine glass, warned that the casinos might be even more crowded soon as Sinatra and other superstars were about to open and a whole new group of conventions would bring in fresh hordes. In addition to the teachers of the deaf, there would be an army of insurance salesmen, major-appliance dealers, antique collectors and assorted boxing and model-aircraft fans for world-championship competitions.

"Poor George," Prince concluded. "He was dying to see that fight, and now he's dead. Crazy freak thing. Damn rare for a security man to be totalled in Vegas. I had to tell his wife. Hope I never pull that kind of duty again."

So he had feelings as well as a line? It hardly mattered, because she was here to save lives and not to make friends, she reminded herself. She guided the conversation to the security setups and directors of several other major hotels—

groping for some kind of defense pattern just as the bombers would. He offered a lot of facts and candid opinions, with some colorful anecdotes about burglars, counterfeiters, con persons of all ages and sexes, crooked employees, greedy tarts, teams of pickpockets and assorted mental cases. Aware that she had to be up before seven A.M. to take the morning watch, she looked at the Omega on her wrist, and he saw her.

No fuss, no muss, not even a comment. He didn't press when she declined his offer of an after-dinner liqueur, and when they rose to leave she could see that the statuesque waitress was as charmed by Ben Prince as by his generous tip. The nephew of the Shtarker from Cleveland had style, and some manners too.

"Good food, good room, good company. Thank you, Mr. Prince," she said as they reached the door of her room.

"I had a terrific time myself, with a terrific lady."

She recognized the look in his eyes, braced to cope. He moved toward her—just an inch or two, stopped. It surprised her.

"Call you in the morning," she promised.

"A terrific lady," he repeated, and walked to the elevator.

She double-locked the door before she put down her purse and stripped. She looked at herself in the full-length mirror, naked except for the walkie-talkie still hanging around her neck. She had taken the earplug from her ear just before reaching the hotel and pushed it into her high-necked dress. It was a relief to take the rig off now, and she rubbed the slight soreness above her breasts. The line cut into her middle by the elastic top of the pantyhose looked like some strange belt, she thought, as she reached for the phone to leave the "wake up" call.

That done, she turned off the last lights and pulled aside the covers. The clean crisp sheets were cool, the pillow soft and accepting. She thought first about Hovde's patience and discomfort on the surveillance, then about Littlefield and

Arroyo going out with fresh dogs at six in the morning. It was degenerating into a battle of time again, for there were surely several more explosive devices to be found and a number of buildings to search. What was the schedule for the blasts? What was the bombers' plan? How long did she have to find them?

Drowsy from the day and the drink, she yawned as she wondered again about the missing dynamite and the equally provocative "bug" that Fanelli had found in her phone. Who was listening? Where and why? Questions that could not be ignored, but she would get to them in the morning. They had made a start today. Finding the two men with the station wagon was a big step. What was that game she'd played in the fifth grade? What did they say? Oh, yes—take a giant step. They had taken a giant step toward identifying the extortionists this evening—down a road that might prove long. It would no doubt be twisting. It always was.

Another yawn, and then an odd thought from nowhere. Ben Prince might not be fierce or shrewd, but he was *sexy.* Sliding toward sleep, she thought that he *might* be foolish enough to betray his family and Spinoza's group for a piece of that $5,000,000—but he was *definitely* sexy. It was more than charm. There was a physical attraction. Animal, she identified with an amused sigh-groan. *Very sexy,* she concluded, and drifted off into slumber.

She would not have slept nearly that well if she had known how soon the bombs were set to go off.

CHAPTER 22

IT WAS not the late-morning sun that was making Alison Gordon perspire. The Porsche was parked in the shade, half hidden in the alley from which she could watch the motel diagonally across the road. If a film of wetness was coating her back, it was due to the messages that Arroyo had radioed during the past two hours.

What the hell was happening today? It was set for today, all right. She didn't even know who the two men in the motel were. They were registered as out-of-state tourists, but they had navigated through Las Vegas in the dark as if they knew it well. Now she saw Prince in her rear-view mirror, watched him advance up the alley and nodded in silent greeting as he opened the far door. He lifted her shoulder bag from the other seat, handed it to her and settled down beside her.

"What have you got in that—a tire iron?"

She ignored his question, pointed at the motel.

"There are two men over there we have to identify," she told him, "and they could be locals you know."

"Local whats?"

"Guns."

"So it's getting to that time?"

"That time, and there isn't much of it. Last night one of

O. K.'s dogs spotted two men—those two—with explosives at the Versailles. We found three bombs last night, four more this morning."

"Jesus."

"I ought to tell you that one was in the Kublai Khan," she said as she adjusted her sun glasses.

"There's probably a lot you ought to tell me, but I don't hold grudges. Go ahead."

"There may be more bombs. All those discovered so far have been removed and deactivated. All were set to detonate at twenty minutes before one this afternoon, and I don't know why. That's a hundred minutes from now. While we're waiting for those two to come out so you can look at them, do you have any suggestions?"

"I'd call the fire department, Clint Eastwood and the Air National Guard, and I might ask the bomb squad in too. Charlie Barrett could have some ideas, you know, and he's got his own dogs."

She thought about this, wondered whether it might be necessary to do something to lever the two bombers out of their room. What could it be that would not warn them?

"We *could* give the lieutenant a list of the places our dogs have already covered," she reasoned, "and tell him what little we know about the two men. That's their wagon, rented from Budget three days ago by a middle-aged man whose driver's license identified him as Dr. Moses Siegenthaler of Murfreesboro, Tennessee. They're registered as Rex Bayless and John Leonard of Boston."

"John Leonard writes for *The New York Times,* I believe."

"I figure this is another John Leonard—Go ahead, this is Blue Moon One."

"What?" Prince said.

"Got it. The Horseshoe Drive end of the parking lot in twenty-five minutes . . . Right . . . Over and out."

"Who the hell are you talking to?"

She brushed back the hair over her right ear, exposed the

colorless hearing device. "Walkie-talkie. Comes with a throat mike. Somebody just phoned the bombers and set up a rendezvous at a parking lot."

"Sunrise Shopping Center backs onto Horseshoe Drive," he offered. She patted his cheek.

"Knew you were going to be helpful . . . Blue Moon One to Blue Moon Two and Three. The parade starts from the motel in about ten minutes, with Three up front. Please confirm . . . very good . . . don't be late."

Prince shook his head, took a cigar from his jacket.

"Sniffer dogs, fancy radios and the way you got the court order for that wiretap so fast—I'm impressed."

"Don't be a smart-ass, we don't have the time. The question right now is whether these guys planted any other bombs, and whether the bomb squad could find even one of them in the next hour and a half."

"You don't want to bring in the cops?"

"Promised I wouldn't. But if I was sure that there really were more—hell, here they come."

She handed him the binoculars that had been resting on her lap, and he took them up quickly. The older man had emerged from the room first. He stood there as if enjoying the 80-degree temperature, soaking up the sun and showing no tension at all as he looked right, then left, slowly.

"Don't know him," Prince said. They watched as Lester Wyatt said something into the open door behind him, then strolled to the office of the Happy Dollar Motel. As he entered, a younger man carried a suitcase from the room Wyatt had just left.

"That's his partner. Looks like they're checking out," she said, "but why?"

"Never seen him either," Prince said.

"Why are they leaving now without a penny of that five million? Are they simply changing motels, or is it going down? And what the hell is *it,* anyway?"

The security man puffed on his cigar. "Seven bombs is

more than an intimidating gesture, ma'am. Seven bombs is hea-*vee.* Big bombs?"

"Dozen sticks of dynamite each. Big enough." The expression on her face as she took back the binoculars said it all. She had calculated the odds, applied her experience and instincts to the threat of mass murder. She was going to tough it out.

They watched Hance put the suitcase in the back of the station wagon, go back to collect a second large piece of luggage and two shoulder bags. One bore the name and logo of United Air Lines.

"That's the one they used to carry the bombs into the building last night," she said, "and we've got eighty-three minutes to make sense out of this."

Lester Wyatt emerged from the office. She was certain that he had paid the bill in cash. No checks, no credit cards, no documents to be traced by meticulous detectives. The older man reentered the room. When he came out he held a pair of identical overnight bags. Products of Taiwan, black nylon, not built for long wear. She noticed the way he closed the door.

"Fingers didn't touch the knob. Bet there's not a print left inside the room either. Probably Dr. Siegenthaler's bright idea."

"Ask him at the parking lot," Prince suggested and tapped the ash off his corona.

"Yeah, he could be there," she agreed. They saw Wyatt examine the way that the bags were stacked in the rear, watched him circle the vehicle and check the tires. Then he spoke to Hance, and the two men got into the wagon. They looked around again, a bit less casually this time. Hance started the motor—

"Damn it, they're moving out."

Where the hell were the other two cars with Agajanian and Hovde?

"They're jitterbugging," she noted.

"Jitterbugging?"

"Fooling around to draw out into the open anyone following. They didn't do this number last night—things must be more serious today. What's the time?"

"Sixty-eight minutes. Sure you don't want to call Barrett?"

"Not sure at all," she replied and radioed to the dog unit for an up-to-the-second report. This time it was O. K. Littlefield whose voice sounded in her ear. Two more hotels had been patrolled by a fresh dog. No bombs. She thanked him, urged him to continue the searches and drove on in silence for a minute.

"Barrett will get nasty," Prince warned, "and if anybody gets killed by one of these gadgets you could buy twenty years in the slammer. When he hears that you knew about these birds last night—"

"You going to tell him, Ben? *I* won't."

"Not me. I can't afford to get involved in this kind of mess. No way. Sandy Mintzer would rip my butt if I did that to you, Miss Gordon."

He was, she was sure now, lying about something . . . If he were allied with these bombers, he'd have to make his move soon. Within minutes he'd try to warn them—if he could do it without exposing himself. But if the risk was too great, Prince might abandon the others for his own survival.

"What's *your* hunch, Ben? Any more bombs?" she tested.

He hesitated as he relit the Don Diego.

"No idea. Guessing's not my game, and I've got no female intuition at all—hey, there's the shopping center."

She instructed Hovde to take up a position on one street parallel to the large parking lot, ordered Agajanian to watch in readiness from another at right angles. "We're going in," she informed Prince.

"To shop?"

"What else would you do in the Sunrise Shopping Center?"

To delay going indoors she circled slowly in the lot as if

searching for exactly the right parking space. Only when she saw the station wagon come to a halt did she slip the Porsche into an opening some twenty yards away, and begin to apply a new coat of lipstick.

"Just another housewife repairing her makeup," Prince said.

"You got it. They're going inside with those black overnight bags. You watch the car like a good bored husband, and I'll shop around with them."

She wasn't going to let him get near them alone, and Hovde and Agajanian could both observe him here in the Porsche. Once inside, they appeared to know exactly where they were. The dry-runs that Arthur Messinger had required were almost visible, for they walked straight to the men's toilet at the rear. Hance and Wyatt smiled at each other just before they entered the separate booths . . . it was all moving exactly as it had in the three rehearsals.

When they emerged four minutes later, she was stunned. They were both wearing white coveralls and matching plastic "hard" hats—the sort seen on construction workers. She followed them out to the parking lot, slipped in beside Ben Prince. They did not return to their station wagon. Instead, Wyatt and Hance walked a hundred yards and stopped.

"They're looking for somebody," she said.

"What's with the jumpsuits and funny hats?"

"I'll ask them later," she answered sarcastically. The two men paced up and down for several minutes, plainly impatient.

"Somebody's late," Prince said.

"And here comes somebody now. Attention Blue Moon Two and Three. We've got company. '78 BMW, dark blue, Utah plates."

She raised the binoculars, read off the license-plate numbers and saw Stanley Kuziw lean out of the BMW to hand the two waiting men a fairly large tote bag of brown canvas.

"You're almost four minutes late, you stupid—"
"Lots of time. Don't blow your cool," the wheelman told Wyatt. He gave Hance a set of car keys, pointed out the stolen Toyota truck he'd parked an hour earlier. Then he winked, gestured grandly and drove out of the parking lot.

"Coming your way. Pick him up, Blue Moon Three."
"Got him," Hovde said forty seconds later.
The men in the coveralls made their way to the Toyota, unlocked it and rolled down the windows before they put the tote bag inside on the floor. They handled it carefully, as if it contained something breakable, or explosive . . . ?
"The guy in the BMW was wearing the same jumpsuit and hard hat," she thought aloud.
"Uniform of the day."
Fifty-three minutes before the bombs were set to detonate, the men in white drove away from the Sunrise Shopping Center. More jitterbugging, but the general direction seemed to be toward Jaycee Park. Then the man at the wheel—the younger one—drove the Toyota on in the direction of the McCarran air terminal.
"Forty-four minutes," Prince told her.
"Whatever it is, I say it's going down now. What do you say?"
"You're the expert."
What was he hiding?
"Maybe you ought to call Barrett, Ben. He likes you, and he'll believe you."
Prince shifted uncomfortably, and she saw that he was armed. Did he usually carry a .38 Police Special?
"If we stop to phone, we might lose the Toyota," Prince said. The bombers drove around McCarran, but continued onward at a legal speed. Now they were moving away from the concentration of casinos and hotels that comprised The Strip, still zigzagging. She glanced in the mirror at Prince, saw his brow furrowed.

"Twenty-seven minutes. Maybe we *should* call Barrett," he said.

"Too late now. Turning again. Hope they're heading for a better neighborhood—hey, they're stopping."

"Maybe one of them has to take a leak," Prince said irritably—and he was right. Hance spoke to the gas station attendant, was given a key and made his way to the rear of the low building. He returned the key two minutes later, and the Toyota resumed its journey.

"That wasn't Dr. Siegenthaler at the shopping center," Alison Gordon said abruptly. "No, not if Siegenthaler's the brain behind this deal. That guy in the BMW didn't look like any mastermind to me . . . so where the hell is the doctor?"

"Where the hell is the clown in the BMW?"

She was out of range for direct contact with Hovde by walkie-talkie, but she reached Kate Wu at the radio van in the mobile-home park. Blue Moon Three had checked in just moments earlier with word that he was parked near a Pizza Inn at 2850 East Tropicana Avenue, where the BMW driver was "stuffing his face . . . coming out now."

There was no visible pattern, no solid clue as to what the men in the white coveralls planned to do or where. When was easier—nineteen minutes. Something was very wrong. The announced deadline was still days away. It wasn't supposed to happen like this—Kate Wu's voice broke in again, this time in an urgent tone. "Hacienda Hotel, the far end of Las Vegas Boulevard South. *Bingo.*"

"Bingo," she repeated, and saw Prince flinch.

"Maybe that's the last bomb," he said.

"Maybe."

They drove on in silence for another ninety seconds before she realized that the Toyota wasn't jitterbugging any more. It had been on a straight course for almost a mile now, heading directly toward the main cluster of luxury hotels. This course would lead right to the Sahara Hotel. Prince saw it too, asked about it as she dropped back to let Agajanian take the number-one surveillance position.

"What do you think it means?"

She shrugged, found that the Porsche was now within radio range for direct contact with Hovde. The BMW had just turned right in the general direction of the Convention Center. At 12:29, Hovde radioed that the car was in the Center's huge parking lot.

"There could be a bomb there too. I should have told Littlefield," she said.

"I told you that you were terrific last night. Well, you've done a terrific job and already saved who knows how many lives," Prince told her.

"We've got nine minutes."

The Toyota did not slow down at the Sahara Hotel. Hance turned right into the evening traffic on The Strip. There were many more vehicles on this busy multi-lane road, many more chances to lose the bombers in the flow of cars. She reported their location to the communications van, listened.

"Your ears should be burning," she told Prince. "The BMW is now sitting in *another* parking area—behind your hotel."

Prince considered this, loosening his .38 in his holster in an almost abstracted way. "The bomb has already been removed from the Kublai Khan, so this is probably just another pit stop."

"Five minutes to blast off. I'm glad you're not scared."

"I'm scared," he confided, "and I don't enjoy it."

"Welcome to the club, Mr. Prince."

The Toyota suddenly slowed, pulled off the road at the entrance to the Castaways Hotel & Casino. She was too close to the truck to duplicate the maneuver without being noticed so she drove on and radioed Agajanian behind her to take up an observation post a hundred yards before the Castaways. The men in the white coveralls were waiting for someone or something, and in a bit more than three minutes any undiscovered bombs would kill dozens—perhaps hundreds—of people.

"Coming your way," Agajanian radioed, and she scanned the traffic. A Winnebago recreational vehicle, a Coors beer truck, an armored car marked Purolator Inc. and the glittery limousine of a "rhinestone cowboy" performing nightly at the Frontier swept past before the Toyota came into sight. There was little more than one minute left. She let a yellow taxi move in behind the Toyota to mask her vehicle, joined the procession.

Perhaps they had located all the bombs after all.

Maybe nothing was going to happen. If there were no explosions, the man who called himself Dr. Moses Siegenthaler might change or cancel his plan. That would give time to bring in the police, to make peace with Lieutenant Barrett and let him save all the lives and take all the headlines. There didn't have to be violence this sunny afternoon. The Toyota turned right again abruptly, this time down a very familiar strip of concrete.

"Oh, God," Prince groaned.

"This is Blue Moon One. On the driveway to the rear parking area behind the Kublai Khan. It is now 12:30, and we've just run out of time."

As the Porsche turned the corner of the hotel, they saw Hovde in the maroon Mercury, plus the BMW, the Toyota and some thirty other cars. They also saw the armored car at the rear door of the casino, and parked twenty yards away a green van. There was no one in the van, whose rear faced the hotel.

It happened very quickly. Two uniformed casino security men brought canvas sacks out, and a pair of husky Purolator guards in the gray-green attire of their company signed receipts. The casino employees reentered the building, and the guards carried the money sacks to the steel-sheathed truck. When they banged on the rear door, a third guard opened it from inside.

That was when Hance and Wyatt jumped from the Toyota. "Freeze!" they ordered.

They were wearing Frankenstein monster masks, pointing M-16 automatic weapons at the guards. One of the Purolator guards began to raise his hands slowly. The other seemed undecided. The guard inside had no such problem. He jerked the heavy door toward him, dropped to the floor and jerked out his weapon. Alison Gordon zipped open her shoulder bag, jumped from the Porsche as the two M-16's opened fire.

The armored car door clanged shut, and four M-16 rounds hurled the guard with the upraised hands crashing back into the money truck. The other man in the monster disguise was covering the rear door of the hotel. He stopped doing that when A. B. Gordon took the rapid-fire Ingraham machine pistol from her bag and shot three holes in his face, blood seeping through the openings in the Frankenstein mask.

Then Arthur Messinger fired. Wearing the coveralls, mask and hard hat, he crouched in the back of the green van and launched his missile at the armored car. The 60-millimeter rocket flew from the tube just as it had up near the mountain cabin. It blew the rear door of the armored car half open, gutting one chunk of metal and leaving a hot jagged remnant hanging askew from a maimed hinge.

There was a lot of shooting and shouting going on, but she could make out Agajanian's voice. The ex-master sergeant and Lester Wyatt ignored Hance's corpse, charged the Purolator truck—hosing bullets as they came. Now Messinger threw two smoke bombs toward the Porsche, spun to shoot half a dozen slugs from his own M-16 into the eviscerated armored car. Somebody screamed in pain from inside—once. She recognized that noise. Terminal.

Messinger was inside the truck, hurling out bags to the ground. Wyatt was laying down a covering fire, bellowing something over the crescendo of gunfire. Through the smoke she saw that Hovde was crouched behind a car—

shooting. The accountant had taken his firing position behind the protection of a big Cadillac, using its heavy engine as a shield.

"Stanley, Stanley . . ." one of the heist men was shouting.

She heard the sound of an auto engine roaring nearby, was too busy to look. She didn't see Hovde half-rise behind her to take better aim, but Lester Wyatt's spout of M-16 bullets at him caught her attention. She dropped to the concrete, swung the Ingraham. Too late.

A Certified Public Accountant named Andrew Agajanian killed him. Actually, someone else shot him at the same time so perhaps the responsibility—or credit—for the demise of Lester Wyatt at thirty-nine had to be shared. She started to get up and for one moment wondered what Prince was doing, but then Messinger charged from the back of the truck—firing his automatic weapon with one hand and scooping up one, two, three sacks with the other.

"Look out, Al," Agajanian warned.

She turned, saw Ben Prince with the .38 in his hand.

He was pointing it at her head.

CHAPTER 23

He fired.

The blast deafened her, but she did not feel the impact of the bullet. Stanley Kuziw did. The slug sliced his left ear off, and the next round from the .38 shattered the wheelman's left forearm and made him drop the automatic he'd been aiming at her. He slumped back inside the BMW, screaming. She could not make out the words. Perhaps there weren't any.

She thought that this would be an excellent time for nine policemen or the Air National Guard to appear, but they did not so the exchange continued. Messinger tossed two of the sacks into the BMW as it neared, dropped the third. He squeezed off two short bursts in approved U.S. Army style, reached down for the last bag.

"Stanley," he shouted.

The wheelman did not answer. He was hurt and frightened, and it was all going wrong. Who were these strangers, and what the hell was that bitch doing with the weird little machine gun? She looked so damned cool, and the pain of his wounds was awful. Stanley Kuziw had never been shot before. Two bags of money would be enough for him, he decided as he stepped down on the accelerator.

The creep was bugging out alone, no great surprise to

Arthur Messinger. He had never counted on the wheelman to handle the pressure of a firefight, never expected one to develop anyway. The bombs that would distract the police and create the diversion to cover their escape had already exploded. He had not heard the one in the Kublai Khan go off, but a single malfunction didn't matter in the plan. Hance and Wyatt were probably dead, and there wasn't going to be any escape for Arthur Messinger. Not for Stanley Kuziw either. Messinger lifted his M-16 and shot the wounded wheelman three times in the chest.

Stanley Kuziw stopped screaming, but the BMW he'd stolen the night before did not stop moving. It hurtled on between Alison Gordon and Messinger, barely missing her as she leaped back out of its path. She collided with Prince, and they both fell painfully against a parked Peugeot. The BMW crashed into a little red car, which burst into flames.

It had been a good plan, Messinger thought angrily. It would have made them all rich . . . the armored car had already stopped at nine other casinos and was carrying between two and three million dollars. It would have worked if these people had not intervened. Furious at the thought that he must have made some error that betrayed his scheme, Messinger saw only one hope. If he could blow away the woman and the good-looking man beside her, he might get away on the powerhouse Harley-Davidson motorcycle parked behind them.

He aimed at her, pulled the trigger. A single round burst from his M-16 before the clip was exhausted. He wasn't rational any more. He simply wanted to smash these stupid people who had wrecked his perfect operation. He raised the M-16 as if it were a mace or club, ran forward to break open her skull.

"Don't shoot him," she yelled. She didn't seem to be aware of the thin line of blood along her left temple. Hovde, Agajanian and Prince heard her. None of them shot Arthur Messinger. She did. She put a bullet into each of his legs, and he fell in his tracks. He was almost at her feet, glaring up at her with a peculiar mixture of hate and respect.

He still wanted to hit her. He made a desperate swipe at her legs with the M-16, then another. He missed by several inches, tried again until Prince bent down to jerk the weapon from his hands. The security man searched him roughly, found in coverall pockets two more clips for the M-16, another smoke bomb and a grenade.

"Lucky he didn't throw *this,*" Prince said.

She recognized the U.S. Army's Mk-398 "defensive" hand grenade, a nasty blast-effect device that also sprayed fragments up to two hundred meters. She thought of Hovde, who knew much more, swiveled to find him bent over and clutching his stomach in visible pain.

"It's all right," Agajanian assured her.

"A belly wound is never all right. Get an ambulance, damn it."

"Not . . . for . . . me," Hovde said between gasps.

"He's trying to tell you that he was wearing one of those bulletproof fabric vests—right down to his nuts," the accountant explained. "Knocked the wind out of him. Bad bruises for a couple of weeks but he'll be as good as he ever was."

"That's damn good," she replied, and Hovde smiled wanly. She sat on the fender of a white Jaguar, noticed that it was splattered with blood. Now she looked at the Ingraham, saw that it needed a new clip and mechanically reloaded with a fresh one from her bag.

"The war is over, lady," Prince said quietly, and sat down beside her. Agajanian was using his walkie-talkie now, telling Kate Wu to summon ambulances and police and to inform Fanelli and the dog unit about the shootout.

"What are you going to tell the cops?" Prince asked her. She shrugged, pointed at the burning Fiat. Agajanian understood, radioed a request for the fire department too. The rear door to the hotel opened. The security men who emerged recognized Prince, eyed the devastation in awe.

"What happened here, Mr. Prince?" one asked.

"I'm not sure," he answered and looked at Alison Gordon. She put the Ingraham in her shoulder bag, stared down at Messinger. He was the only one alive who knew.

"If you're not cops, who are you?" the ex-sergeant demanded.

"We should have finished him," the accountant argued.

She shook her head. "He might be Siegenthaler." A siren was sounding not too far away. The police cars would be there very soon. More people were pouring from the Kublai Khan. Journalists and TV news crews would be on their way within minutes. All these corpses and burning vehicles and the money sacks would add up to a major story in any city, an even bigger sensation in one as violence-free as this resort.

More sirens, nearer.

"I think I'll tell them the truth," she announced as the first black-and-white screeched into the parking lot. Two police bounded out of the car. Tan pants, dark brown shirts and large pistols in their hands.

"Unbelievable," said the junior officer. The other policeman looked at Alison Gordon and the ravaged armored car and the bodies. "I'm Officer Peabody," he said. "Suppose you tell me what this is all about."

She hesitated, nodded. "There was a misunderstanding, a *serious* misunderstanding," she said carefully. Another police car arrived as Hovde shuddered from the pain in his abdomen.

"A *misunderstanding?*"

"They were trying to rob the armored truck," Prince said. He identified himself and pointed to Messinger as one of the thieves. He was about to continue when he noticed the trickle of blood from her temple.

"You're *hit!*"

She looked into the windshield of the car she was sitting on, saw the blood and reached up to wipe it away.

"You all right, miss?" Peabody asked.

"It's just a scratch," Alison Gordon answered.

Then she fainted.

CHAPTER 24

RED ROSES—the big ones that cost three dollars apiece, massive yellow peonies, splendid chrysanthemums and other dazzling blossoms Prince couldn't name half filled the hospital room.

"I'm glad I didn't bring flowers," he told Alison Gordon and looked for a place to put down the box of bittersweet Godiva chocolates. There was hardly a surface not covered by vases of magnificent blooms. He was about to tell her how well she looked in the mid-morning sun when a nurse's aide carried in another large bouquet.

"I took the liberty of opening the card," the woman in white announced primly. "From a man named Jerry Brown. I think he's the governor of California."

"He thinks so too," Prince replied.

The nurse's aide pointed out other flowers sent by Barbra Streisand, Stevie Wonder, Sir Lew Grade, David Rockefeller, Walter Cronkite, Burt Reynolds and a certain Omar Baroodi.

"Bet he's an Arab prince," she guessed shrewdly and left.

"He's a sheik. Thanks for the candy," Alison Gordon told Prince.

"Hear you're coming along nicely. Good. It all worked out fine, you know."

"I have a very small headache from a minor graze, Mr. Prince. *What* worked out fine?"

The front page of the newspaper that he handed her featured a three-column report on the shootout with a large photo of the battered Purolator truck. The caption identified the three men standing (l. to r.) as Kublai Khan security executive Ben Prince, Officer F. Peabody and Chief of Detectives Lincoln Diamant. The two "subjects" on the ground were "slain perpetrators." She read the first three paragraphs, erupted. "This says hotel security men stopped the robbery, you bastard. Makes heroes of you and your troops. It's a complete lie—"

"No, it's an *in*complete sort of half truth," he corrected affably. "Very popular these days. You see them everywhere. Washington, London, the Riviera—even Beverly Hills. Come in a complete range of colors and sizes for every budget. What are you sore about anyway? I did it for you, you know."

"For *me?*"

"You want to discuss the *real* story with Charlie Barrett? You'd all be indicted on nineteen different charges. This way it's cool. Security men are allowed to shoot it out with dastardly brigands. We may get medals."

She read on, turned to the continuation on page nine.

"Check the picture on the facing page. Your dogs missed one," Prince told her.

The Desert Dream Paint Company's warehouse had burned to the ground after an explosion at twenty minutes to one. Three fire trucks had been unable to stop the blaze from destroying $400,000' worth of paint. Cause of the blast was being investigated.

"At least no one got killed." She sighed and leaned back.

"I think five stiffs behind the hotel were enough. One of the armored car guards will survive, and so will the nasty guy you shot in the legs. That was very humane of you, Miss Gordon."

"Who is he?"

"His prints were telephotoed to Washington, and the F.B.I. reports he's a retired army sergeant with a clean-as-a-whistle military record. Outstanding combat soldier with years of unblemished service. Name of Arthur Messinger."

"A. K. A.?"

The security man shook his head. "Just Arthur Messinger, of Pittsfield, Massachusetts, pearl of the Berkshires—was never Also Known As anything. This was his first crime. The three clowns with him were confirmed perpetrators—now ex."

"You think that's funny?"

"I'm trying to pretend it is. I never killed anybody before." He looked embarrassed.

She remembered the first person she had killed years ago, a paid assassin who had been stalking her for some Iron Curtain espionage apparatus. She couldn't recall which, couldn't even dredge up what the man had looked like. Prince seemed almost boyish now, open and guileless. She knew that neither was true, but she still wanted to console him. She didn't. Why take the chance?

There was another reason. He was talking as if the threat was over. He was pretending that the gun battle which stopped the four armed thieves had settled everything. But no sensible person could accept the illogic of the two totally independent groups menacing Las Vegas with bombs for utterly different reasons at the same time. Even now, the coincidence numbed her—and the case wasn't nearly over.

Had he been told to do this, or was he trying to cheer her up until she was fully recovered? The idea that this young man might be humoring her was appalling. There might be a third organization out there with more explosives and another plan. Why not? All of a sudden she was overcome by fatigue, and a powerful desire to leave Las Vegas and go home.

"I'm tired," she said truthfully.

"And I'm leaving. When are you coming out?"

"Sometime tomorrow, the doctors think."

"You've got a heavy date, so rest a lot and prepare for a very large evening."

He was either sincere or a damned good actor.

"Will it be terrific?" she asked drowsily.

"You've got my word as an officer and a gent."

The nurse's aide returned with ninety dollars' worth of roses from Sanford Mintzer, and messages that Mr. Sammy Davis, Jr., Mr. Kissinger and a woman who said she worked for Mr. Sinatra had called to transmit good wishes. Someone else had telephoned to ask about the patient's health, left no name.

"That's my cue to tango, I've got a couple of calls to make myself," Prince announced, "and a tuxedo to get cleaned for tomorrow night."

He left the building without stopping at any of the pay telephones. He passed half a dozen booths in the two miles that he drove from the hospital to the Helen of Troy Massage Salon, "total satisfaction guaranteed—in your hotel room or our luxurious private treatment chambers."

"You looked real good on TV, Ben," complimented the five-foot-ten-inch-tall blonde receptionist who had a black belt in karate and an affectionate interest in the handsome security executive. She understood why other women would too, and why he had to "lose" annoying detectives employed by jealous husbands this way.

"*You'd* look better," he said without breaking stride. She beamed as she pressed the buzzer that admitted him to the "consulting room," where two of the women who were overflowing their mini-smocks flashed automatic smiles.

"Treatment?" invited a full-blown brunette.

"Helen. I'm her cousin," Prince replied, and pointed his index finger knowingly at the door to the rear corridor.

"Right on, cuz."

He didn't make any telephone calls from the massage

parlor either, nor did he speak to the ex-computer programmer who called herself Helen. He walked through the building, avoided eye contact with a totally satisfied detergent wholesaler emerging from one of the private chambers and let himself out the back door.

He hiked across fifteen yards of concrete, used a key to open the back door of a two-story-high structure topped by a small tower that resembled a church. It even had a bell in it. The sound of organ music greeted and oppressed him. He stopped, peered through a gap in the drip-dry drapes into the large room beyond. There was neither organist nor instrument, the music was taped, but there was a white-haired man in clerical attire facing a couple in their late twenties. The ministerial type was reading from a $175 leather-bound large-type edition of the King James version of the Holy Bible, and the bride clutched the genuine eight-dollar orchid that came with this "moving $55 complete ceremony—including a glass of California champagne."

"In sickness and in health . . . for richer and for poorer . . ."

Prince elected not to stay for the rest of the ceremony. After all, he knew the ending and he had more urgent business upstairs. He walked to the second floor, rapped three times on a door marked "No Admission" and then twice again. The portal sounded as if it were sheathed in metal. It was. The cold-eyed man who opened it looked as if he might be too.

"You're not supposed to come here."

"Nice to see you too. Sit down, Ben. Thanks," Prince singsonged in reply, and lowered himself onto a sagging armchair. There was very little furniture in the room. A studio couch, a small refrigerator beside a table that supported an electric hot plate, a waste basket, two chairs and a battered desk. On its surface rested two telephones, a radio receiver with many dials and a sawed-off shotgun.

"That's new, isn't it?" Prince asked and pointed to the shotgun.

"Birthday present. Listen, our friends are very unhappy about that publicity you got. Now a lot of people know your face, and you'll have to be extremely careful."

"I always am. That's why I'm still in business. That's why we're going to put our hands on all that money," he said.

"The Gordon woman could make waves."

"She's smart enough to make more than waves, but I can handle her. Tell Uncle not to worry. You're getting edgy cooped up here, Carl. You ought to drop downstairs and get married or stop in at the Helen of Troy for their eighty-dollar around-the-world. Loosen you up, kid."

It was a deliberate provocation. He was well aware that the other man was intensely puritanical, lusting only with a desire to seize the millions and leave this permissive and hedonistic city. Radio Moscow's most righteous critic of capitalist corruption could not despise this resort half as much, but then he had not endured the same religious upbringing. Concealing their headquarters in the Eternal Bliss Wedding Chapel still offended Carl Leibnitz, even though it was recognized as one of the Top Ten among the dozens of swift-service chapels in town. He was a stranger here, and Prince's assurance that the Eternal Bliss was right up there with the Always and Forever, Silver Bell, Little Church of the West, Hitching Post and delightful Wee Kirk o' the Heather had not helped.

"When is the Gordon woman leaving, Ben?"

"What do you care? Never mind. I know. Sexy women make your palms sweat, Carl—right?"

The other man stood up angrily.

"If we didn't need you—"

"You need me, Carl, and you're afraid that she'll screw up this operation somehow or other. You're half right. She could. She's a dynamite broad, blew away those hoods at the armored truck as if they were dust. Okay, I'll answer your question. I don't know when she's splitting. She's a foxy lady."

The other man remembered that he'd left a mug of instant coffee cooling, took a sip and found it too cold. He put it down sadly. "How foxy?"

"Mintzer is trying to talk himself into believing that those pistoleros might have been the people who sent the big bomb and blew up the cars. Be nice if that was true, and he's hoping that the pressure to raise five million is over."

"Nice for who? Not us."

"Whom," Prince corrected. "Moving right along, A. B. Gordon is much too foxy to buy that nonsense. She's a very realistic and logical lady, a credit to the C.I.A."

That was another intentional jab—Prince knew that he loathed the cloak-and-dagger organization.

"Foxy, Ben?"

"To the tenth power. Medically, she could leave town in two or three days, but she'll probably hang around to track down the people who *really* sent the note."

Carl Leibnitz shook his head several times.

"We can't risk that, Ben. That would be bad."

"Gonna get worse when Mintzer gets the instructions on when and where to deliver the money. Should be coming in any day now, I imagine."

"So do I. We've been planning this operation for a long time," Leibnitz reminded, "and this woman can only make trouble. Get rid of her."

"Kill her?"

"You've got a filthy mind. Where did we find you—in a toilet?"

Prince clapped his hands together several times in a parody of applause, then took a thick square envelope from his pocket and dropped it beside the shotgun.

"I came here to deliver *that.* Figured the tape might be urgent," he said, and turned on his heel.

"Thanks for bringing it."

Prince unbolted the heavy door, strode into the corridor that now echoed to another wedding.

"Wait a minute, Ben!"

He slammed the metal portal behind him, started down the stairs. That idiot Leibnitz probably thought that he was emotionally involved with Alison Gordon, a woman he hardly knew.

". . . Do you, Jane, take Raymond for your lawful—"

He locked the rear door behind him with the key, looked around cautiously. The bright sunlight jarred him, made him blink. His eyes adjusted, and he looked at the city. He liked Las Vegas as much as Leibnitz despised it, and soon he would have to leave. There would be no choice after the money was in their hands. The men who actually owned the Kublai Khan didn't have nearly as much polish as Sandy Mintzer. They had strong measures for those who cost them millions, colorful methods such as dismemberment or tossing people into furnaces. Alive.

He glanced at his watch, saw that he was almost late for his dental appointment. He returned to the Cutlass, drove off at the highest speed that the law allowed. His eyes swept the rear-view mirror again and again. It was a fine clear day, but there was no point in being stupid, and hip-handsome Benjamin D. Prince was a lot too young and charming to die. If he were smart and maintained a positive attitude, he could live and love to ninety-three. After all, there were a lot of clean women and dirty comics to enjoy and who could tell what fine new Chinese chefs, tennis partners or playwrights tomorrow would offer? Ben Prince had intelligence, good skin, a strong sense of self-worth and a genuine gift for lying, a combination that should certainly assure success in the 1980's.

Buoyed by this awareness, he drove skillfully and got to his appointment on time. The dentist kept him waiting for thirty-five minutes, of course. After he finished studying a *Playboy* photo spread featuring voluptuous electroshock technicians employed at major southern hospitals, he closed his eyes and thought about Alison Gordon. She hadn't said a word when he told her how he felt about killing the wheelman. He had shot him to save her life. Not even a "thank you." How many had *she* killed? So many that it didn't matter any more, or was she so numbed that she had nothing to say? It wasn't something that you could ask anybody. That strange little machine gun she had probably said it all—

"Mr. Prince?"

He opened his eyes, looked up at the receptionist-secretary in the bulging uniform and false eyelashes.

"Dr. Temkin will see you now, Mr. Prince."

Half an hour later, Prince was richer with the knowledge that his splendid teeth had no cavities, and poorer by sixty dollars. They would *have* to come up with the millions, he thought as he left the office. Even the Mob could not risk the lives of all those thousands of people. And then his time in Vegas would be over. New dentist, new everything. He looked at the Save the Whales calendar on the wall behind the receptionist's desk, saw that November 6th was just seven days from tomorrow.

One week.

Five million of the Mob's skim money.

"Terrific," he said to the receptionist, who took it as a compliment to her new uplift bra, and departed for the Kublai Khan hotel to continue the greatest con operation in this unusual city's colorful history.

CHAPTER 25

HOLDING THE pink message form in her right hand, Ms. Doris Kraft paused outside the office of The Man With the Shades and made her decision. There were times when males had to be handled—*manipulated* was such an ugly term, and in this case and relationship it was fortunate that she had the knack. It was a talent. Why minimize it? He had been tense and sort of *grouchy* for two days, so she would use the *cheery* approach.

"I have good news and bad news," she said brightly as she walked toward his desk on the thick carpet that confirmed his status as deputy C.I.A. director. He looked up at her and sighed.

"You're supposed to ask what's the good news."

"Doris—" he began in the voice he used when his eyes hurt.

"I'll give you the good news first. I phoned the hospital in Las Vegas, and she's going to be all right. Isn't that wonderful?"

"Who's going to be all right?"

"Alison. Don't you read the papers?"

"I must have missed it," he said, and reached for the message form.

"Don't you care? She was one of the best field agents you ever had, wasn't she? Tell the truth."

"She was better than that," he said and wondered how he had put up with Doris Kraft for eighteen years. She had the voice of an electric pencil sharpener and the charm of an industrial paint remover, but she worked sixteen hours a day without bitching and she was, in her abrasive way, utterly loyal.

"Somebody shot her, and she shot a couple of them. Five people were killed."

He nodded noncommitally, accepted the fact that she wasn't ready to give him the message form and put his hand on the desk.

"What does that nothing nod mean?"

"Par for the course. She gets into these situations, Doris. Fine woman, great agent, talented sculptor—but not too lucky. People seem to die in groups wherever she goes. Not all the time, but too often. Maybe I should say she's extremely lucky. She always does the impossible and survives, and the others get buried."

"She's just a widow trying to support herself."

He resisted the impulse to throw something.

"No, Doris, she's a highly attractive, successful and well-paid businesswoman who has an active social life and a net worth of more than half a million dollars. Her house alone would bring four hundred thousand, so drop the hearts and flowers."

"You envy her, don't you?"

He kept his control. "Doris, I've had enough of the good news. Now please give me the bad."

She knew what would happen, but she tried.

"Please don't swear," she admonished, and handed him the message form.

"Son of a bitch! Son of a bitch!"

She understood that his eyes were bothering him again and the Singapore situation was disturbing, but there were limits. "That's no way to speak to an executive secretary. Actually, I really should be an administrative assistant by now. Everyone says so."

She saw that he was thinking, and she guessed that he was giving serious consideration to the promotion as he had promised. She was wrong.

"Please ask Lou Jefferson to come see me?" he said.

"Sure. Don't swear at him though. He's black and sensitive."

When Jefferson arrived a few minutes later, the deputy director told him about the F.B.I. report. "One hundred and twelve female passengers on a DC-10 from London, and four cleared customs at Kennedy before anybody stopped them. We lost her, Lou."

Jefferson lit a cigarette, shook his head. "No, F.B.I. lost her, and it's up to them to find her. They know it too. Domestic security and counter-espionage is their baby, so they can handle the dirty diapers on this one."

The deputy director was proud of his assistant. Jefferson had learned the bureaucratic game well. It was shrewd not to denounce the F.B.I. for this screwup. Their own guilt and need to redeem their pride in the endless, and idiotic, rivalry would goad them more effectively than any C.I.A. blast.

"They're sweating it now, Lou."

"Probably flooded the airport with fifty agents. That's their style. They move in herds, just like the Sovs."

The deputy director tapped the message form on his desk.

"They're playing computers too," he reported. "Tracked down three of the women. All seem to be clean. Still looking for the last one. Kirsten Evensen."

"Norwegian?"

"Traveling on a Norwegian passport anyway. Don't have much of a lead. Found a United Air Lines clerk who thinks that she might be the woman he sold a ticket to Las Vegas."

"If she's one of Attila's gang, she won't be using the same

name any more," Jefferson said.

"You got it. There was no Kirsten Evensen on the passenger list. Of course they've alerted the F.B.I. bureau in Vegas to meet that flight to spot a woman who matches the description of this Evensen woman."

"Maybe she's not the one we're looking for. Whole thing could be a bum steer. Hell, Attila's never operated in the U.S. before."

Maria Desdemona Velez was considering a different question. On her rounds as a cleaning woman on the day shift at the United Air Lines terminal at Kennedy, she had mopped the floor of the *damas*—as they called the ladies toilet in her native Colombia—and begun to empty the used towel container. Under the heap of crushed paper she had found a blonde wig. She had discovered all sorts of things in this lavatory before, but never a hairpiece of this quality. *Madre de Dios,* it must have cost more than one hundred dollars. Women had left underpants, purses, shoes, raincoats and even a leather case containing whips and manacles—none of them of any use. This wig, on the other hand, Maria Velez could give to her cousin who was alone since her husband had left her. It was an elegant thing that might attract the eye of a man, and a new man was what Josefina needed.

For one long moment, the honest cleaning woman thought that no one would deliberately abandon something so fresh and valuable and she pondered her duty to turn it in to the lost and found department. Then she told herself that some spoiled daughter of a rich man had tossed it away, and that it would look lovely on her cousin. She put it under the extra cloth in her sack of cleaning supplies, and went back to work.

It was in her plastic shopping bag as she left the terminal at 4:15 to go home. No, it was not right. She reentered the building and brought the hairpiece to her amiable bald supervisor. He listened, grunted at the thought he would have to walk almost a quarter of a mile to turn it in at the office.

"Keep it, Maria. People don't drop wigs into the trash by accident. On the floor, maybe—but not under the towels. It's yours, Maria," he told her, and turned away before she could argue. She took the wig home to 135th Street and Second Avenue, and that very evening gave it to her cousin. Josefina was very pleased, and she thanked her profusely. It made her look younger, more sophisticated, more New York. She would wear it to the dance on Friday night, and perhaps some good would come of it. It was, after all, something special.

CHAPTER 26

THERE WERE six F.B.I. agents watching the United Air Lines passengers enter the terminal, but Heidi Friedheim only spotted two. That was enough. Grateful that they still dressed compulsively—and conspicuously—in suits, white shirts and ties, she avoided eye contact and moved closer to a quartet of women who seemed to be together. Following right behind these teachers of the deaf, she tried to appear to be part of their group.

She was not aware of either the assassination or the wire-tap in London, or that these federal police were looking for the blonde woman who had entered the U.S.A. as Kirsten Evensen. Well trained and experienced in covert operations, she assumed that she was the target and automatically applied evasive tactics. They worked, or, they *seemed* to. She had to be sure, and she could not compromise the others or the base. Carlos had taught her the priorities well. The Brigade and the struggle came first.

When she came out of the terminal twenty minutes later with her suitcase, she saw Eric Adler at the wheel of the tan van. Anyone watching her would not observe a look of connection or recognition on either face. She told a taxi driver to take her to the Hilton.

"Which Hilton?"

She hesitated, annoyed at this problem. They should have told her that there was more than one. Such details were important. Carlos would not like this sloppiness.

"The *big* one . . ." The ability to improvise, to handle the unfamiliar or unexpected was essential. The instructors in the training camp in South Yemen—K.G.B. men by their speech—had emphasized that, and Carlos had himself drilled it into all of them again and again. Carlos would be pleased by the way she reacted.

The van followed the taxi to the Hilton at a discreet distance, hanging back to observe whether anyone else had her under surveillance. That was another of Carlos' standard precautions. She paid off the cabbie, watched a dozen new arrivals seek the assistance of bellboys. She was not surprised that these others received attention first, for not only was she passive and quiet but aware that service employees operated on the premise that men tipped more generously. Another bellboy joined the bustle. He liked plump females such as Heidi Friedheim.

"Checking in or out, miss?"

"Out. Here's my friend now."

He loaded her bag into the van, expressed the hope that she would patronize another Hilton soon and accepted her dollar bill—all in thirty-five seconds. It was a short drive to the house by the cemetery; the traffic flowed swiftly. Adler told her about the radio news of the shooting at the London hotel, and of the telephone call confirming that Carlos would arrive tomorrow.

"That's good, Eric. Have there been any problems here?"

"Why do you ask that?"

Why did he sound almost defensive?

"There were police waiting when I got off the plane here. F.B.I., I think. Perhaps they were looking for someone else, but I don't like it." She checked the rear-view mirror again.

"There's no one. I would have spotted them on the way in from the airport. You're right to be careful, Heidi. After what happened to Peter in London . . . who do you think did it?"

She waited until he put down her suitcase in the living room of the rented house before she asked the question.

"Drink?" he offered briskly.

"Not now. How are things going here?"

"Under control." He reached for a bottle of Scotch. She hung her jacket over the back of a chair, sat down on a blue loveseat that had seen better days and spoke to him firmly.

"What's wrong? Please—I can tell."

He poured two inches of the White Horse into a glass, replied with his back to her.

"It's all right now."

"Turn around and tell me what happened—every detail."

He faced her, swallowed a gulp.

"So it was that bad?"

"I bought the Smirnoff quarts, just as he said. I followed his instructions to the letter. Not more than two in any liquor store. I got fifty-six quarts—half a dozen extra for spares, just as he wanted."

He paused, sipped more Scotch and shuddered. "I've been all alone here for weeks. No one to talk to. Just that TV set with those imbecilic movies and game shows. No companionship, just a phone call at a pay booth every six days. The house got messy. I didn't want you all to find a filthy place when you arrived. He hates that, you know."

"So you hired a cleaning woman?"

"Not exactly. I went to a folk music concert at the university. There's a good university here. It's not just a famous basketball team. This was to raise money for a Third World Arts Festival."

"And you met a girl."

He looked at her as if she were a witch, nodded.

"Rosa. Her mother named her after Rosa Luxemburg."

"Very pretty with long blonde hair, and she talked about

changing the system? That's the kind of girl you meet at such concerts, isn't it?"

Now he seemed frightened.

"She appeared sympathetic, and kind—"

"And you wanted someone to talk to—in bed."

"It wasn't just that, she said that she earned extra money by cleaning houses at $3.50 an hour, so I thought it might be a good idea—"

"It was a terrible idea. You knew that no one else was to enter this house. Let's get to the point. You're making *me* nervous now. What happened?"

He finished the whiskey before he replied.

"After we were . . . finished she said that she'd start on the house right away. Naked, so she wouldn't get her clothes dirty. It was sort of a joke. She did the dining room and the living room."

Not too well. Heidi Friedheim rubbed one finger over the frame of the loveseat, felt dust but said nothing.

"It happened when I went to the bathroom. She must have gone into the kitchen to get a soft drink or something. There was no soft drink in the fridge, so—"

He stopped in mid-sentence, unable to say the rest. He gestured, and Heidi Friedheim followed him into the kitchen. He pointed at the large freezer that stood beside the refrigerator, tried to speak again and failed. He stepped forward, jerked open the freezer door.

The college girl didn't look quite so pretty any more. Her long blonde hair was still attractive, but her face was twisted in pain. The butcher knife protruding from her chest was presumably the source of that terminal agony. The corpse filled the front of the freezer, but Heidi Friedheim could see the neatly stacked Smirnoff bottles behind the doubled-up body.

"She looked in the freezer," Adler managed to continue. "I can't imagine why. You don't keep soft drinks in a freezer. Maybe she thought it was another refrigerator."

"Doesn't matter."

"Doesn't matter," he agreed. "She saw all the bottles. First she giggled and said something about how crazy I must be for vodka . . . how her friends would be impressed that a fellow had forty or fifty bottles. Then she noticed the color of the contents wasn't the same as ordinary vodka, asked if it was something special. There was only one thing to do. I tried to think of what Carlos would do, and this was it."

"You did the right thing, Eric. Close the door."

The girl whose progressive mother had admired Red Rosa Luxemburg would be missed, and—worse—someone might have seen her with Adler. This entire mess was not necessary, but there was no point in lecturing him now. Carlos would do much more than that tomorrow, she thought as she led the red-haired man back into the dining room.

"I'll have that drink now," she said.

"Brandy? Gin? Scotch? There's no vodka. I poured it all down the sink."

"Brandy will be fine," she told him. First they spoke of various ways in which the body might be disposed of and when. Then they discussed the next step in the plan of the May 5th Brigade to destroy the casinos of Las Vegas.

CHAPTER 27

"NAME, RANK and serial number, huh?" Alison Gordon asked.

"That's what the cops say," Prince told her. "He wouldn't admit that he was Siegenthaler, even though the auto rental people positively identified him. All the ol' sarge would tell anyone was his name, rank and serial number." The doorman of the Kublai Khan bowed in greeting.

"He's crazy."

"Could be his mind snapped," Prince agreed, "because he's playing it by the military code—just as if he's a prisoner of war."

"What war?" she said as they entered the hotel.

"His private war on the armored truck—the one you screwed up. In case you're interested, his name is Arthur Messinger and he's a registered Republican."

"Who cares?" she said bitterly, then felt a twinge of embarrassment. It was her anger at having stumbled into this irrelevant assault upon the money truck speaking, her rage at the senseless carnage that barred compassion for this sick, doomed man. He wasn't even important enough to be tragic.

"Shouldn't have said that," she admitted. "I'm just bitter about all the time we lost tracking the wrong people. Somebody probably cares, or should. Family or a doctor or some priest. I wish I could, but I can't."

The throng of gamblers and tourists and the hubbub were overwhelming. It was eight P.M.; Hovde and the accountant should be searching Prince's apartment now. Breaking and entering were among the skills they had not lost since leaving the C.I.A. payroll.

"Don't worry about it," Prince counseled and pressed forward through the massed legions of energetic optimists. "He's not that special. Lots of guys out to lunch like the Ol' Sarge, guys who never served in any army or saw the horrors in 'Nam. It's not your table, not mine either."

Their table was, of course, the best in the top-floor restaurant named The Ming Dynasty. The view of the sprawling city was excellent, the glittering display of huge flashing signs on the hotels and casinos below quite dramatic. The walls were covered with red silk, and Asian waiters were attired as warriors from the Ming era. The bus-"boys" who assisted them were all Caucasian females whose smiles showed fine teeth and whose plunging necklines exposed eye-catching breasts.

Prince saw her negative reaction to this use of women, gestured to the headwaiter. "Just the Vegas touch. Little flash of skin never hurt anyone, and it adds some spice to the dining experience. Makes the high rollers feel like Chinese emperors, or something like that . . . All right, it's a *tiny* bit vulgar but people love it."

"Follow the crowd and you can't go wrong," she said sardonically. They would be going through all the drawers, checking desk pads and closets. Agajanian and Hovde were thorough, patient.

"Let's *forget* the crowd," he urged, "and take a night off from judging people. You're just out of the hospital. That kind of heavy-duty social commentary could be too much for you."

She finally allowed a small smile.

"Come on," he pressed as the headwaiter neared, "you're much too nice to spend all your time throwing the first stone. You can do that tomorrow. We'll set aside from ten A.M. to noon for putting down Vegas. Okay?"

"Okay," she replied, and wondered whether it was her fatigue that made his appeal seem genuine.

"As the Chairperson of the Sociology Department at UCLA and noted authority on the grape, your input on the choice of wine would be a valuable contribution to the committee," Prince announced grandly.

"He lies a lot," she told the headwaiter.

"But only to beautiful women. I'll send over the sommelier when you're ready, Miss Gordon," the headwaiter said as he put down menus.

"See, you're a famous person, Miss Gordon. I hope you're a hungry one too."

"Ravenous. Hospital food is . . . well, it's hospital food."

"What a way with words you have. Champagne?"

There was something more than mischief behind his grin.

"You're planning to get me drunk?"

"And steal your first edition of Veblen's masterpiece on conspicuous consumption. I've always had the hots for masterpieces."

"That doesn't surprise me. What are we celebrating?"

"Your good health, the fact that Mintzer is paying for all this and my wonderful fortune in sharing this evening with you. It's going to be very educational."

About to light a Sobranie, she paused. "Educational for whom?"

"For me." He deftly torched the end of her cigarette with his own lighter. "A night with the chairperson is bound to teach me plenty about the . . . the cultural and moral malaise facing contemporary American society. You like that?"

"The chairperson will hit you with a chair if you don't knock it off. Actually, I do know a fair amount about wine, Mr. Prince."

"I hope you're not one of these snobby Californians who go around putting down French and German wines. Those Europeans have made a lot of progress in the past ten years, and this stuff's not half bad now."

"Order the goddamn champagne." How could he have known that she was an enthusiastic consumer of California wines, that half of the 300-odd bottles in her cellar contained vintage California creations?

Prince signaled his own knowledge by instructing the leather-aproned and chained sommelier to bring Chandon Brut, the superior champagne that the Moet people are producing so successfully and discreetly in California. After two glasses of the sparkling drink that couldn't legally be called champagne at Moet's French headquarters because it was not made in the Champagne district of the Motherland, Alison Gordon found that the style of Las Vegas was not nearly as interesting as the sixteen-page menu—Szechuan, Hunan, and Cantonese cuisines were all represented at length.

"Let's eat everything and drink too much," Prince proposed as he refilled her glass. It was half-past eight. They would be photographing his telephone bills, checking for hidden safes or double-bottomed suitcases by now.

"This is your top restaurant?" she tested.

"Kublai Khan's finest. You'll find it amusing, or should I say impertinent?"

"You're impertinent. How good is this cooking?"

He placed his right hand over his heart. "Scout's Honor. Almost as good as the Chinese food in L.A. . . . in other words—"

"Mediocre," she supplied with a cheer she didn't quite understand. After they agreed on appetizer, soup, a shrimp dish and others featuring beef and chicken, she selected a '77 Pinot Chardonnay and a big '75 Zinfandel from California vintners whose wines were among her favorites. Then they ate too much and drank to excess, and he told her some funny stories about tourists and gamblers and the University of Nevada in Las Vegas' hotel administration school. Even as she laughed, she wondered whether she would remember any of these tales the next day.

"I'm not drunk, Mr. Prince," she announced over her fourth cup of tea. He looked around warily, then leaned forward confidentially.

"I'm not surprised. *They water the tea,"* he whispered.

The Grand Marnier was not diluted, however. It was warm and strong, and the glow in her stomach was as pleasant as the taste of the orange brandy-liqueur itself.

"I'm not even *half* drunk," she told him.

"Sorry, but I did keep half my word. The cooking was mediocre. Give me credit for that."

Watching him sign the bill with a flourish, she wondered where Thomas Arroyo and Kate Wu were this evening on their first date. No, it wouldn't be a date but a time alone together. Thomas was beyond the "dating" ritual. Fanelli would be celebrating with the younger Wu sister, and Alison Gordon didn't care what O. K. Littlefield was doing and to or with whom. She saw Prince put a $20 bill on the table, hand a ten to the headwaiter as they left. He played by the rules, and one of the twenty-three commandments in the Las Vegas testament was that one does not stiff the service staff, even on house tabs.

"Right this way, please, and no dawdling. The show must go on," Prince said.

"What show?"

"Thought you'd never ask. The super-extravaganza ten o'clock show in the glorious Marco Polo Room of the Kublai Khan—a must for any visit to glamorous Las Vegas. It's a million-dollar production, and Mr. Mintzer would be heartbroken if you missed it. Naked girls! Elephants! Flaming egg rolls! Fountains! Chinese acrobats! Trained swans swimming in unison!"

"The breast stroke, I presume?"

"Australian crawl. Come on, live a little."

The Marco Polo Room was just a bit smaller than Victoria Station, and had fewer Swedish students with backpacks hunkered down waiting for trains to Dover. The setup was the usual one for Vegas show rooms, with many long tables —each seating a dozen or more ticket holders. Alison Gordon and Ben Prince were escorted to a front-row-center table, the special one for Mr. Mintzer's personal VIP guests. There were more than 1,200 people in the vast room, with four captains in charge of traffic control.

"They're making a bundle," Prince confided. "Each captain is picking up a hundred or a hundred and fifty bucks a night in tokes. Tips, under-the-table loot to give certain customers good tables. It's a ripoff, but we can't stop it. If Caesars couldn't, we can't. They tried to automate the whole seating process with computers, but the waiters and captains wouldn't stand for that—am I telling you more about show business than you want to learn?"

"Yes."

A waiter appeared with stemmed glasses and a bottle of chilled Piper, and then the extravaganza began. It was everything that Prince had promised. Also very loud. Lots of trumpets and saxophones and drums. A dozen and a half tall showgirls parading topless, and half bottomless. About 90 percent of each young woman's rump was exposed. Somehow, the effect of all this flesh was less than erotic as the leggy ladies with the appliquéd smiles moved briskly through their numbers. They were quite pretty, graceful and businesslike, to be fair.

The elephants were delightful, the "boy" and "girl" singers fine and the line of smaller female dancers impressive in their choreographed precision. It was all very dazzling, with flashy lighting, costumes and other effects, including the waterfall and the shadow ballet portraying the construction of The Great Wall of China. When the production was over at 11:45, the patrons applauded again and stood up to adjust their clothes.

They entered the lobby of Caesars Palace at ten minutes after midnight, immediately heard her name over the wall of sound produced by the gamblers. It was a metallic voice from the powerful loudspeakers overhead.

"Miss A. B. Gordon . . . Miss A. B. Gordon."

She found a house phone, recognized Hovde's unique whisper seconds later.

"Clean," he reported succinctly.

"Develop the film and get some dinner. Any problems?'

"No."

"Good night—and thanks."

"Welcome."

Turning from the house phone a moment later, she sensed that the photos of bank statements, telephone bills, letters, notes and check stubs would probably produce nothing. As a trained security specialist himself, Prince would be much too prudent to leave any obvious to covert associations around his apartment. He was clever, and charming in his fashion.

"Nightcap?" he proposed when she rejoined him.

"Think I'll turn in. Thanks, it was fun."

"Tomorrow night will be even better. Sinatra's opening here, and I'm very tight with the citizen who runs security at Caesars. It will be a tough ticket, but I can swing it."

She nodded, and they started across the lobby toward the steps leading to Cleopatra's Barge and the bank of elevators that served the North Tower when a handsome gray-haired man with the face of an over-aged baby stopped them, pointed his cigar.

"You all right?" he asked in a voice of concern.

"Fine, Marty. Lost some weight, I see. Looks good."

He stepped back, tapped off the ash and eyed her critically.

"You ought to be more careful, Al. *He* was worried. We all were."

"It was only a crease. We're just on our way to try to book seats for the early show tomorrow night. Oh, this is Ben Prince. Ben, I'd like you to meet a friend from Beverly Hills."

"Don't you ever check your mailbox?" the man with the cigar asked impatiently. "You've *got* a pair—at *his* table. Nice to meet you, Mr. Prince."

And then he was gone, leaving behind the scent of a $1.30 Monte Cruz and a startled Ben Prince.

"Sorry he had to run, Ben. Busy man. Lovely wife too. He's—"

"One of the top lawyers in the country. Why didn't you tell me you were tight with him and Old Blue Eyes? Why did you let me make an idiot of myself with that big talk about the security man here?"

"You're not an idiot, Ben," she told him, and wondered how long she had been calling him by his first name. On the way up to the ninth floor she explained her reluctance to impose on either clients or friends to use their influence for favors.

"That's the show business game, and I'm not playing it. I'm no good at it anyway," she said. For no reason that she could identify, she suddenly found herself speculating about the missing forty-seven sticks of dynamite. It was preposterous to be so compulsive, to let such considerations intrude into a pleasant social evening. She blinked, pushed the thought from her mind.

"What is it?" the observant security man asked.

"Fatigue," she lied. She was actually feeling rather light and airy, a state that probably reflected all the champagne, wine and liqueur that she had consumed. Ben Prince had been rather entertaining and civilized himself. Ben? It might be wiser to keep things on a Mr. Prince basis. Now she was feeling a bit tired, in a nice way. The glow continued on the way to the ninth floor, and as they reached the door of her room. She unlocked it, swallowed to submerge an incipient yawn. They exchanged "good nights," and she began to turn toward her room.

Then she remembered. "One thing I want to ask you—"

"Certainly," he said and stepped forward. His arms were around her, and she realized that she was not resisting. Now his lips were against hers, and she was kissing as boldly as she was being kissed. It all seemed to make sense. No, there was no question of sense—and it was more than lust. She couldn't tell what it was. She didn't care. Somehow or other they were inside her room, and one of his hands cupped the back of her head very tenderly—then fiercely. His other hand moved down her spine to the small of her back.

How did he know? How could he know that the small of her back was a special place for her, something indefinable and irresistible? She began to move, to squirm, to press against him. Startled by the speed of what was happening, she fought for control. She broke the embrace, looked up into his eyes.

"Wait a minute. This is crazy—"

"Crazy," he agreed and swept her back into his arms.

It was wild again, and then it was gentle—and then a torrent. Nothing could stop or save her. Her whole body felt on fire. Hands caressed her flanks, she moaned as she pressed and twisted under his touch.

The kissing never stopped, the room was dark and her mouth was open, and she shuddered as he stroked her neck and shoulders. Gentle kisses moving across her face and eyes were almost more than she could bear. She began to shake, to dig her fingers into his back. He cupped her breasts so gently, and as he stroked her hard nipples she heard him say her name . . .

They were on her bed, and there was nothing between them now. She did not recall undressing, but they were naked, skin against skin in a tangle of limbs, and the gasps that sounded in the blackness said there was no turning back. She was heaving and groaning, hips moving in rhythm as his delicate fingers moved down across her middle to the wetness. Her head twisted back and forth on the pillow. Those animal sounds were her own—deep and urgent.

He entered so very slowly, so very gently. Small concentric coils of electric heat began to spin inside her. The hairy man was heavy and deliberate. He made love with a wondrous grace, and his weight upon her was right. The roaring in her ears grew louder, but over that she heard herself crying out again and again.

It was happening. It was blotting out and lighting up everything the way it should. How could it be this way with a man she barely knew—*"Now,"* he said hoarsely into her ear. "Yes, *yes!"* she celebrated and hurled herself against him in desperate union. They crashed against each other a dozen times before the spasm deep inside her made her scream. It didn't stop. Neither did he. The throbbing, flowing went on inside, and then he thrust again and made the unmistakable sound of completion. She felt the gush, wrapped her legs around him even tighter, and sighed.

She felt his weight. The invisible stubble on his face was rough against her smooth cheek. She didn't mind the scratchy surface, she breathed deeply as he kissed her eyes, ears and lips. She lay there listening to her heart pound in the room lit only by the moon rays streaming in the window. She ran her hands down his broad back, enjoying the man and the quiet and the hot peace that was now inside her. He had big shoulders and a thick, muscular neck. She hadn't noticed that before. How had it happened? She remembered. At the door.

"I want to ask you something," she said.

"What?"

"I was going to ask you . . . before."

"Sure," and he laughed and he began to make love to her again. It was like a dream—a good dream. The whole thing happened once more, more slowly but just as inexorably, and splendidly. The kissing, the touching, the excitement, the crying out and the deep whirlpools that spun them faster and faster until the moment of fierce completion.

There was more tenderness and gentle talk when it was over. He got her a glass of cold water, and he kissed her shoulder as she drank. Then they got under the covers, and she fell asleep in his arms.

CHAPTER 28

ONLY A handful of people were awake in Phoenix. A few lights shone in all-night diners, in radio and TV stations and in the printing plant turning out the morning edition of the *Arizona Republic* on East Van Buren Street. A skeleton force manned the police stations and radio cars, but there was almost no one aside from cleaning crews in the office buildings of this prosperous, industrial city of 710,000.

Howard McGhee, the night supervisor at the offices of the Federal Bureau of Investigation in the fourteenth largest municipality in the United States, was awake at 2:40 A.M. It was quiet here on the sixth floor of the Americo Towers building, but the few Special Agents on duty were all busy with a variety of cases, chores and reports. The teleprinter stuttered only now and then, and there were hardly any telephone calls. McGhee heard a phone ring across the hall, speculated that it was probably either a crank sounding a UFO alarm or an informer.

"Informer," announced Special Agent O'Donnell when he entered the supervisor's office ninety seconds later. "Pretty reliable fellow—up on the Navaho Reservation. Helped us with straight stuff five or six times. We carry him on the books as Peter Green."

"What's Peter got this time?"

"Tip on that explosion up there, sir. There's a young Indian with a big mouth and a thirst to match who's making noises that a cousin did that job."

"Possible?" McGhee asked.

"Definitely, sir. He's a demolition expert, Peter Green says, with army training. The cousin and his pickup truck disappeared within a day after the blast. Word is that the cousin was one of the strong defenders of that valley as a sacred place."

The supervisor meshed his fingers.

"It's going to be lousy," he predicted. "Lousy for the Bureau. However this turns out—whether we catch him or not, we come out as the bad guys. Persecuting Indians—and God knows those Navahos have been screwed fifty-nine ways from Sunday in the past century—or failing to protect property and a strategic mineral the country needs. Either way, we're the heavies."

"I guess so, sir."

McGhee reached for the sugar-free mints he was using to kick the nicotine addiction, popped one into his mouth.

"We used to be heroes," he reminisced. "Whole TV series about the Bureau, and lots of films. Big-budget features, and plenty of books. Now we're the turkeys. It's the media. Wasn't very hard for them to snipe and smear. Things were done in the past—*certain* things by some well-meaning *top* people—that made it easy to do a hatchet job on us."

Special Agent F. X. O'Donnell did not expect the night supervisor to go into specifics, and McGhee didn't.

"Turkeys," the older man grumbled, "and just about every day's Thanksgiving. So much for self-pity. What have you got on the cousin and the truck?"

"I thought we'd get his military record and prints from Washington, and the license-plate numbers from the state computer. Then we could put a 'wanted for questioning in a federal felony' on the wire. How far would he go?"

"Five hundred or a thousand miles. No more," McGhee

judged. "Right, that's a sound approach. Set it down with the informer's report in a memo, and I'll initial my approval. I want to see it before we go off duty at eight."

"Yes, sir."

"And I want those license-plate numbers on the wire to every Bureau office west of the Mississippi by ten. You don't mind putting in some overtime, do you O'Donnell?"

"No, sir."

With efficiency rating time a bare week away, the younger agent made certain to have the memo on the night supervisor's desk by four o'clock—not eight. The license-plate numbers of Thomas Arroyo's 1972 pickup were on the F.B.I. teletype by half-past six. Bureau offices moved quickly to pass on the "want," and by the time that Alison Gordon first began to stir at nine A.M. a special agent attached to the F.B.I. unit in Las Vegas was preparing to relay the information to the local police. Then the word would go out to all eighty-eight detective cars, ninety-nine uniform cars and seven hundred and fifty officers. If the truck was in Las Vegas, they would find it within two or three days. If the Navaho was with it, they would find him too.

They handled this sort of chore a few times a week; it was strictly routine and usually peaceful. Only infrequently did someone merely wanted for questioning resist. People did get shot, but the Las Vegas P.D. abhorred excess force. There had not been a fatality on a federal "want" here for more than seven months. That hadn't been an *Indian.* No, sir, that was a *Mexican* who had assaulted an immigration inspector in San Antonio with a fish-scaling knife. He'd been crazy.

CHAPTER 29

BEN PRINCE looked at the sleeping woman beside him, and enjoyed her serene smile. Sprawled out in a position that was utterly relaxed and somehow fundamental, she was all ripe curves like one of those Rodin bronzes of lush earth mothers. She was much smaller, of course, but more splendid. Even covered by the sheet she appeared naked.

He wondered what she would be like when she awakened. He had slept with so many women that he could usually predict what they would do and say in the morning. Alison Gordon was not a type, however. She fit in no category or mold. He did not know her very well, but he knew enough about women to be confident of that. This was a special person—beyond the "new" woman so glibly touted and dissected in the media. If anything, Alison Gordon was the new "new woman," and only a fool would say that she thought like a man. She was genuinely feminine, and she thought more quickly, realistically and profoundly than any of the men Prince knew.

She stirred, and Prince could not help himself. He reached out to touch her hair. Even in her sleep she felt the caress, and turned over, seeking warmth, to press against him. She shaped herself to his body and burrowed her head closer . . . closer. He stroked her hair again, then caressed her neck. She opened one eye and blinked. Then she opened both, and she remembered. She hesitated for only a moment before her whole face—still flushed and pink-plump from the deep sleep—lit up with some inner fire.

Prince reached out to embrace her, but her arms encircled him first. They kissed several times before she rubbed her cheek against his, and now he smelled that perfume again. His fingers moved down her spine. When they reached the small of her back, she moved and sucked in her breath—and pulled away.

"There was something I wanted to ask you," she said.

"Later." He kissed her ear.

"When?"

"How about next Tuesday?"

He didn't wait for a reply, and after a few moments she didn't care. It was as good as it had been the night before. Thank God that he was not one of those Beverly Hills sex technicians who pressed all the right buttons like engineers, she thought, as she rested her head on his shoulder.

"Good morning, Miss Gordon," he said.

"I think you can call me Alison."

"You sure?"

"Not really. I don't really know that much about you."

"You know I've got great taste," he pointed out as he stroked her hip. "I think you're terrific, remember?"

"Great taste and good skin," she said, "and you don't talk about pre-Columbian art or real estate like most of the men I meet."

"That's because I don't have any pre-Columbian art or real estate," he confided, stroking her belly. "If I did, I'd no doubt be as big a nerd as those other guys."

She shook her head. "I don't think so. I'm reserving judgment on you till I know more, though. You're brighter than most and a better lover than almost anybody—but what else?"

"I'm a native-born American, free of contagious diseases and twenty-eight years old."

"I'm thirty-five."

"Cradle snatcher."

"I've slept with men younger than you."

"But no better. I've never been on a television game show, arrested, or married."

"I was married. I'm a widow."

"I'm a Democrat, which is almost as good but only every four years. You forgot to mention that you're a fine sculptor, outstanding with machine guns and a very loving lady. You are a lady, you know."

"What do you care?"

Prince sat up, held her head in his hands and kissed her.

"I happen to care about that, and I don't mess with dumb women either."

"Don't mess with me. Be decent, be candid and be here. Don't look so uneasy, Ben. I don't expect the absolute truth all the time. Just keep the lies to a minimum."

Now her hands wandered down his shoulders and chest.

"I may not even be a widow. My husband disappeared on a government mission in Asia eight years ago, and he's legally dead. He might show up at any minute to defend my honor, so be careful."

"He'd better be careful. I'm a good shot, and quick on the draw. Probably runs in the family. Had an uncle who was very large in the organized crime business, as you know."

For a moment she speculated on whether he really knew that she had investigated his background or was guessing, and why he mentioned it so casually now. Before she could reach any conclusions the telephone rang.

The sheet fell away as she sat up to take the instrument. "Gordon," she identified, then listened, aware that Prince was studying the upper half of her body.

"Don't say any more. I'll be there in thirty, forty minutes

. . . Yes, I'm all right . . . sure . . . thank you for the flowers . . . good-by."

As soon as she hung up the phone she leaped out of bed and faced Prince, hands on her hips.

"Take a good look. Study the whole body, Mr. Prince."

"Beautiful. Is that a merkin?" he asked, and pointed at the bountiful pubic growth.

"That's me, it's *all* me."

"All magnificent, and you're so smart too . . . *mens sana in corpore sano,* as Mick Jagger used to say."

"Get dressed," she answered, and outran him to the shower where he joined her under the spray.

"What the hell are you doing here?" she demanded.

"Looking for my watch."

"It isn't here—or *there* either," she replied as he stroked her.

"How would you know? You've got a face full of suds. Pass the soap, will you?"

Minutes later as he was knotting his tie he saw her reflected in the mirror—reaching for the .357 magnum.

"That's quite a cannon."

She did not answer.

"Be easier if you mounted it on a half-track."

"Be nicer if you shaved," she replied, and jammed the heavy revolver into her holster. Prince stroked his face, nodded in agreement.

"Can I borrow your straight razor, or a machete?"

"Very funny." She put on a raw silk jacket, buttoned it to cover the gun and pointed at the door.

"My mother told me there'd be women like you," Prince said, and stroked his stubble again. He picked up his blazer, and followed her to the elevator.

After they had ordered orange juice and coffee in the Noshorium, she left him to make the call that she could not make from the tapped phone in her room.

"Who's this?"

"Andy," said the accountant who had the morning shift at the command post. "Just had a call from the Dog Man, maybe fifty-eight seconds ago. Wants to know when he can—"

"Pick up his money. He can't. Not yet."

"You mean it *still* isn't over? After all that, there's *more?*"

"It's only just begun."

"Hey, Paul Williams wrote that lyric. Talented little guy," Agajanian said.

"He's adorable," she said, and returned to the coffee shop.

"What do you want to fight about?" Prince inquired.

"What?"

"All over your face. Something's steaming you, beloved," he told her as the waitress neared with the juice and black coffee.

"Why did you call me that?" Alison Gordon asked.

Prince glanced at the waitress, shrugged.

"Why, Ben?"

"It seemed like a good idea at the time." They drank the juice in silence, and were halfway through the first cups of coffee before she spoke.

"It's the phone call."

"Why? You were expecting it, weren't you?"

"Sure. Weren't you?"

"Of course, if it's the expensive one I think it is."

"That's the one." She smiled.

"Did I do something right?"

"You didn't play games with me. You told the truth."

He finished his coffee, and winked.

"I can tell the truth two or three times a day, Miss Gordon."

She drained the cup, and stood up suddenly.

"Alison. You can call me Alison, if you want."

"I want."

She looked fine and she knew it. The reflection she saw in the coffee shop window confirmed it. People looked at her as Prince steered a path through the casino to the front door, and recognized that rosy flush. This woman had not slept alone. The up-to-date high-school and liberated college kids would say that she'd "had sex," and her older sister would describe it as "making love." Alison Gordon thought that the latter was closer to the truth, but it might be too soon to know. The irony of the situation was that in a little while it might be too late.

"I'll say it again," Prince told her as he unlocked the Cutlass.

"Yes?"

"You're terrific. You look, and you are. People were staring at you in the hotel."

She squeezed his hand. Hovde would be checking on those long-distance phone calls and letters right now and forty-seven sticks of dynamite were missing and some bastards were tapping her phone, but that didn't affect her sense of glorious well-being. She was still glowing ten minutes later when they reached the third floor office of the man whom she despised.

CHAPTER 30

"RUN IT back. I want to hear that last part again," she said. Mintzer pressed the button that put the cassette machine on rewind. The man who ran the Kublai Khan looked at the hotel's assistant security director and all but sniffed. It was obvious that Prince's unshaven and rumpled appearance did not meet the standards of this luxury resort.

"This is about halfway. Sure you don't want it from the top?" Mintzer asked.

"That won't be necessary. I'm taking the cassette with me," she announced. Mintzer halted the rewinding, pushed down the forward button.

"Two aluminum-sided overnight cases . . . —not canvas, *aluminum* .. the kind your couriers use. You got that, Four Eyes?" It was a nasty voice.

"I hear you," Mintzer's voice replied stiffly, "but I don't know how to find that kind of money. Even a fifth of that would be an immense strain—"

"Not you, idiot. The vampires and money lords you work for . . . the parasite millionaires . . . they've got fortunes. We just want a little piece of that."

"You've been reading comic books."

"It will be the end of Las Vegas. Thousands dead, famous

hotels devastated and a massacre that will make Jonestown look like a Girl Scout picnic. This whole city . . . the money machine itself . . . will be ruined forever. No one will hear the name Las Vegas without feeling queasy. It'll be like My Lai—"

She gestured and Mintzer stopped the machine. Prince sensed that she had heard *something* on the tape that Mintzer had not noticed.

"My Lai? You think he's serious?" Mintzer wondered.

Prince waited for her to identify the something. She merely nodded. Mintzer thought that she was answering his question.

"I believe that we must proceed on the assumption that this man and his associates are quite serious," she said carefully.

"You think it's a group?" Prince asked.

"Why don't you have a couple of those aluminum cases ready, Sandy, and don't panic."

"No reason to," Mintzer said. "Your people found those other bombs, and I'm confident that you'll cope with these just as well. Nobody could really blow up twenty-five or thirty hotels and casinos at the same time, could they? You'd surely find the bombs with those dogs Ben told me about."

"Do our best," she promised. She took the cassette, and Prince followed her to the door. "You'll bear in mind that they may be watching you, Sandy."

"Me?" He seemed startled, and not nearly as cool and executive.

"These are bad people. Don't you think so, Ben?"

"The worst, they might even be tied up with some creep who used to work here—"

"Or who still does. Not too likely though. You checked them all out, didn't you, Ben?"

"Twice."

"Do it again, and get a shave," Mintzer ordered nervously.

When Prince and the woman left seconds later, Mintzer went to the window and thought about what she had said. Were these violent men watching him? First there was the threat of surveillance by the I.R.S. and other federal agents, and now the menace of the nameless others. Mintzer looked up over the city and smiled as he saw the familiar silhouette of a 747 jetliner. It was those huge air transports that made the entire Vegas boom and Sanford Mintzer's six-figure salary possible, bringing in the throngs of gamblers, tourists and conventioneers.

For a few moments he thought back to his own flying days, and remembered those B-29 sorties over North Korea. Hell, that big Boeing up there in the sky over McCarran dwarfed the bomber that had carried Lieutenant Mintzer to battle in that dimly remembered "police action"; the B-29 would look like a model beside it. How long ago? Almost thirty years . . . No, he didn't regret leaving the Air Force. He had enjoyed his service as a young man, but all this he had now was more appropriate for this stage of life. It wasn't that one was better, but there was a time for each. Mintzer and Las Vegas had both worked long and hard for this prosperity. They had earned it, and nothing was going to interfere now. It was so well organized, and flowing so smoothly. Everybody worked together for a bigger and better, more popular and more profitable Las Vegas. The state and county governments, the hotels and casinos, banks and unions all cooperated nicely. Yes, they did a fine job together once the airlines brought in the customers.

Thank God for the 747's, he thought, and—in a mixture of mischief, respect and sentimentality—tossed a salute at the plane on the horizon. If he'd stayed in the Air Force he might be a light colonel, maybe even a bird colonel by now. He glanced around his office, and approved. This was better.

Somehow or other they would stop the extortionists.

They would find and destroy them; make an example.

Then everything would go back to normal, and it would be another boon year for everyone—the greatest in the history of Las Vegas.

Well, wouldn't it . . . ?

CHAPTER 31

THERE ARE advantages in renting a house by the cemetery. One does not have a wall of tall buildings blotting out the view. There is also the not insignificant benefit of quiet evenings, and the useful camouflage provided by the daytime flow of cars in and out of the adjacent burial place. Taking advantage of the open vista, Adler looked up from his watch and pointed at the 747 descending to touch down at McCarran.

"I think he's on that plane," Adler said.

"Maybe."

"He's supposed to be on that flight, Heidi."

She smiled benignly, as if he were a foolish child.

"That's exactly my point, Eric. Him?—he's never where he's supposed to be. He changes schedules all the time. That's the only constant in his way of doing things: He realizes that any one of us could be captured and then tortured or drugged. If even we don't know where he is or when he's coming or how, we can't betray him."

"He's good on security," Adler agreed.

"The best. Who else would arrange for breakins to destroy his military service and school records, to burn almost every photo of himself ever taken? Years ago he began to avoid cameras at demonstrations when others were fighting for attention. They're all dead or in prison, but Carlos survives. So he might be on that plane, but he probably isn't."

The doorbell rang. Adler reached under the cushions of a brown-and-white-striped couch and took out a small blue machine pistol—the VZ-61 used by Czech security police. This was the Skorpion, the .32-caliber weapon that Red Brigade gunmen had used to kill Italy's Aldo Moro.

"It's a delivery truck. You expecting anything from People's Hardware?" Heidi Friedheim asked.

"It could be the models."

"Delivery man in gray coveralls is standing with a clipboard by the door."

"You talk to him and I'll cover you," Adler said. The heavyset man in reflecting aviator glasses was riffling through the sheaf of invoices on the clipboard. He looked at the number over the door again, then shifted his weight as if his feet hurt. Looking bored, he rang the bell a second time.

"Ready, Eric?"

"Open the door."

She picked up her purse and flicked the catch to give instant access to her pistol. Then she unlocked the door. The delivery man was peering down at his clipboard. She couldn't see his face.

"Archer?" he asked.

"No one here by that name."

"This 431?"

"Yes."

"You got no Eric Archer? This says 431."

"Eric *Adler?*"

"I got twenty-six boxes for this . . . my invoice says Archer."

Heidi felt that there was something wrong. She signaled to Adler and stepped aside to give him a clear field of fire. Her fingers inched into her purse.

"Dead."

They both spun and found themselves facing another man in coveralls. He had a machine pistol aimed at Adler's midriff.

"You'd both be dead." He was a dark-complexioned man in his thirties, nearly six feet tall. He had glossy black hair, thin lips and deep-set eyes that resembled two pieces of ebony.

"I told you a hundred times, cover both doors. I could have cut you two down with one burst."

"Sorry, Carlos," she apologized as the grinning "delivery man" strode past her, closed the door behind him.

"Like the new mustache, Heidi?" he said.

"I heard you were in Libya, Willi."

"I got tired of training hysterical Arabs, and Carlos thought my three years of college in this country gave me just the right Yankee speech for this operation. Where do you want the boxes?"

"Eric will help you bring them in," Carlos said. "How could you be so careless, Eric?"

The red-headed American opened his mouth, closed it and gestured vaguely with the Skorpion before he finally spoke.

"No excuse, Carlos. It was stupid . . . I've been sort of . . . there's been a lot of pressure . . . no one to help. I'm . . . I'm glad you're here," and he hurried out to help unload the truck.

Carlos looked at Heidi and lowered the muzzle of his weapon. "What's the matter with him?"

"Eric wasn't trained for this sort of operation. He was an American who wanted to join our cause, and he had the inside information about this situation here. He was only on one mission with us in Europe, the time we blew up that British military warehouse near Hamburg. He's doing his best, Carlos."

"Let's have the rest of it."

There was only a slight trace of Hispanic accent in his

speech. Carlos Fabrega Salinas, brilliant, creatively homicidal son of one of Mexico's richest lawyers, was gifted in languages; he spoke four besides Spanish, all very well. That skill had also helped keep him alive as he changed passports and identities routinely while police in a dozen countries searched for him.

"There was a problem with a young woman, a student."

"What young woman?" he asked.

She led him into the kitchen, opened the freezer door.

"I'm listening," Carlos said. Halfway through her account, he closed the freezer door and stood silently until Heidi completed her report. Then he sat down on a kitchen chair and sighed.

"He shouldn't have brought her here," said the man whom the C.I.A. had code-named Attila. "I understand why he did, but I don't approve of it. It was weak. A lot of people are. We have to liberate them—"

"We will," she said loyally, and took a cold bottle of his favorite beer from the refrigerator. She had remembered his fondness for dark Lowenbrau. Heidi Friedheim was a bit pillowy and overweight, but she was a faithful comrade, as well as an adequate mistress.

"He created the problem, but I guess he solved it," Carlos said, sipping the beer. "Once she saw those bottles, there was probably nothing else he could do. That's promising. Maybe when all this is over, we can send him on a training course. He might develop into a good revolutionary fighter."

"He'd like that . . . you look weary, *liebschen.*"

"We flew into Houston instead of New York, and bought the truck there. Even taking turns driving, it's a long trip from Houston to Las Vegas."

They could hear Adler and Willi Gehrke manhandling the boxes in the front of the house. Carlos unzipped his coverall and rubbed his eyes.

"Coffee or bed? I've made our bed for you."

It was touching the way she said "our bed." The sex and the sleep would do him good. Three hours. No more. He got up, patted her rear and made his way to where they were attacking the boxes.

"You did the right thing, Eric."

Adler looked at him uncertainly.

"It was wrong to bring her here, but then you did the right thing. We'll talk about the body later. Two o'clock."

He yawned and pointed at Gehrke. "You get some rest too."

He followed her upstairs, thinking how dark people found light-skinned ones so attractive and vice versa. Heidi was much more intelligent than his previous mistress, whom the French police had gunned down at the Lyons roadblock, and brighter than the other men in the group too. Too bad her cooking was mediocre, he reflected, as he took off his shoes beside the large bed. He draped his clothes over the chair and stared out the second-floor window for a moment before she flicked the blinds shut. He thought about the strange city outside. He had driven through part of it, but it had hardly seemed like a city—no European or Latin American metropolis anyway. How could there be more than four hundred thousand people out there? Where were they—hiding?

It did not matter. It was the surprise they had planned so meticulously that counted. He lay down on the bed beside her. She rolled over to press against him immediately. The kisses and caresses followed in the usual sequence. She was loyal and shrewd but not so inventive in bed—they carried out the sexual ritual as correctly as if it were some ancient rite. Afterward they talked briefly about what had happened in London and decided when the transmitter would be tested.

The transmitter was important. It was the key to the big surprise.

"Wake me at two," he told her—and then he was asleep.

CHAPTER 32

"SCREW HIM!" Alison Gordon yelled into the telephone.

"He says—"

"Not a chance. That bastard will be paid with everyone else. Tell him to go play with his dogs and leave me alone—"

"Al—" Fanelli protested.

"Don't argue. Tell him." She crashed down the receiver, stormed out of the hotel room.

The man wearing the headset in Room 921 winced, took off the earphones and cursed. The woman in 907 was crazy. Goddamn female tantrums. She'd probably smashed the eavesdropping device in her outburst. She'd been so cool until this morning but now she was flying off the handle over nothing—like his brother's second wife. She ought to be in good spirits after that night in the sack. He'd have to get the damn thing checked, and they wouldn't like that. . . .

Some fifty minutes later the short woman in the maid's uniform cautiously unlocked the door to 907 with her passkey. She called out twice. When there was no reply she chained the door shut behind her. She looked around, made certain that there was no one in the toilet or shower and hurried to the phone. The mini-transmitter was broken. She deftly removed it, clicked in the replacement device and reattached the cover.

She did not see the man who was watching her through the tiny hole drilled in the closet door. As soon as she left, Hovde spoke into his walkie-talkie.

"Leaving now. Female, Caucasian, about five-one. Standard Caesars maid uniform . . . Fair skin, lousy legs, brown hair—"

"Got her," Agajanian said from the end of the corridor, then watched her rap on the door of 921, twice . . . then once . . . then three times.

"921," the accountant said softly into his transmitter. "You come take the room, Don, and I'll stick with her when she comes out," he told Hovde.

At a quarter of one Andrew Agajanian met Alison Gordon on the steps of the museum of the University of Nevada in Las Vegas.

"It worked," he said.

"You ought to check out this museum—not the Prado, but some interesting stuff."

"Don't you want to know where she went? Would you like to try a guess?"

"Of course. Let's see, Andy. It's a large town, spread out to hell and gone."

"You'll never guess—but try."

She lit a Sobranie. "Three hundred Las Vegas Boulevard South?"

Agajanian stared.

"I guessed, it figured."

"You knew. Come on, let's have the rest, Al."

She admired the modern buildings of the university rising behind him.

"I hate it when you do the cat-that-ate-the-canary bit, Al. All right, you're a super fox with feminine intuition."

They walked to the Porsche parked across the street.

Agajanian asked the question as she swung open the car door. "Why would they wire your phone?"

"Don't know. I'm not holding out on you. All I've got is a hunch. You can help me check it out tomorrow after the meeting," she said as she slid in behind the wheel and Agajanian sat down beside her. "It's at four in the afternoon Pick up a silencer from Hovde. He's got the arsenal."

She started the engine, abandoned the Sobranie in the dashboard ashtray and checked the rear-view mirror.

"You serious about the silencer, Al?"

"And find a range. I want everybody to sharpen up."

"It's that bad?"

"It will be."

Her account of the extortionists' latest threat had ruined Agajanian's appetite. When they reached the fried chicken restaurant he barely nibbled at one breaded leg as he thought about what she had reported . . . "There's something funny about that Prince, Al. You think you can trust him?"

"Only for certain things . . ." She ate four big pieces of chicken and hummed through every bite, and still there was that special little smile when she finished her second cup of coffee and signaled for the check. . . .

Some thirty-one miles away, Thomas Arroyo was receiving his bill at a roadside Tex-Mex chiliburger "ranch." It had been a pleasant drive out to the historic mining town in the desert, a genuine relic and not one of those modern imitations. He had told Kate Wu about the rocks and stunted flowers and cacti, and she contributed a lot of interesting information from the Nevada history book she had been reading. It was comfortable and comforting to travel with Kate Wu.

He paid the check and started back to the mobile-home park where the older Wu sister was to take over the radio duties in an hour. He could see by her face that this warm and intelligent woman liked him, and he did not mind that she talked a bit more than he did. He had actually spoken more than usual today, and he had enjoyed it. Even now he felt that there was a great deal more to discuss with Kate Wu. . . .

Even though he was relaxed, he was careful to drive prudently and observe all the speed limits and other traffic regulations. He first noticed the police car behind him when his truck was seventeen miles out of Las Vegas, and was puzzled that the black-and-white car was still in sight half a dozen miles later. It was probably a coincidence, or maybe they were waiting for the driver of an out-of-state vehicle to violate some law. Then the radio on his dashboard sounded, and he didn't look back again until his conversation with Fanelli was completed. He scanned the mirror again.

The police car was still there. Perhaps a bit closer. . . .

CHAPTER 33

"THAT STUFF is tricky, isn't it?" Gehrke said as they put the large box on the kitchen table.

"What *stuff?*"

"The stuff in the vodka bottles stacked up behind the woman in the freezer. Remember her, Eric?"

"Don't tease him. He did the right thing," Heidi Friedheim said. She cut the nylon cord that bound the box, put down the poultry shears and ripped away the brown wrapping paper.

"Of course it was the right thing," Gehrke agreed. "Carlos said so, but that stuff is still dangerous, *nicht wahr?*"

"Not if you have certain heart diseases," she pointed out. "That stuff, as you call it, kept my Aunt Clara alive for years."

"And it's killed a lot of people too," Gehrke said. They opened the box, and took great care as they removed fistfuls of fluffy packing material, then took out the three big pieces. Gehrke held up the largest for inspection. It was an excellent small replica of a fuselage, complete with Pan American Airways markings. "Boeing's finest."

It was a model of a 747 jetliner, with one significant modification—the two wings supported a realistic-looking jet engines, but the actual propulsion unit was a one-half horsepower piston motor protruding from the nose of the fuselage. Gehrke gave the stubbly propeller a quarter spin and made a guttural sound to resemble the roar of an engine.

"Don't play with it. It's not a toy," she said in a schoolteacher's voice.

"It's a weapon," Adler said.

"Sure, sure. Where the hell are the wheels?"

They found the wheels in neatly stapled plastic pouches buried in the fluffy batting. There was another small transparent sack with a tube of special glue and a small screwdriver. Adler leaned the empty carton against the wall, clearing the table for Gehrke and Heidi to begin attaching the wings and landing gear. The light wooden wings were each three feet long, the fuselage even longer.

"I'm still uneasy about that stuff in the freezer. I've never used it. What the hell do we know about it?" Gehrke asked.

"It makes a big bang, shock waves and enough heat to cause fires," Adler recited. "When it goes off it raises the temperature at ground zero to 9,000 degrees Fahrenheit; that's 5,000 Celsius."

"I'm impressed, keep talking."

"When it bangs it generates gases that would fill more than 1,200 times its original volume. That adds up to a flash pressure of 20,000 atmospheres, and the shock wave moves at 17,000 miles an hour. That's what's in those vodka bottles, Herr Gehrke—one of the most powerful explosives known. Glyceryl trinitrate, or—if you prefer—nitroglycerin."

"Willi," Heidi added, "this weapon has been carefully designed. Nitro because it offers a lot of blast for a little weight. The same goes for the bottles. The shape of the Smirnoff quarts fits both the interior space and the cargo lift capacity of the model planes. These things have been planned *scientifically.*"

"I'd prefer that it weren't so damn sensitive," Gehrke grumbled, "but I suppose keeping it cool helps."

"Makes it even more sensitive—in the pure state. I've mixed it with another polynitrate, so now it won't freeze unless the temperature gets down to minus twenty Fahrenheit. Rest easy. It's only zero in there. I check it four or five times a day."

Heidi Friedheim looked at her watch and stood up.

"I have to wake him now."

By the time Carlos dressed and came downstairs the wings and wheels were attached. He stood in the doorway of the kitchen for several seconds, silently eyeing the model 747.

"Nice little miniature, right?" Gehrke said.

"The radio-controlled model crowd wouldn't call this a miniature," he said. "A true RC miniature would be much smaller. This is the biggest, a jumbo—top of the line. A miniature would be too small in both size and engine power to fly with our heavy bottles."

"Fuel?" she asked. They all looked at Adler.

"Ordered and ready for pickup anytime today. I didn't want them to know our address . . . we're buying a lot more than any one team in the competition would need."

Carlos picked up the coffee pot and found himself a mug. He poured the dark liquid and swallowed half a mouthful . . . "Let's talk about that body," he said as he leaned back against the sink. This was no time to tell Adler that his coffee was awful, an insult to any Latin American. No, he would quietly ask Heidi to take over the coffee making.

"Eric, why don't you collect that kerosene now?" Heidi suggested.

"We'll still be working this out when you get back," Carlos said.

Whether Adler believed this or not, he took the van keys from his pocket and started for the rear door. "They know she's gone," he said.

"The school or the police?" Carlos asked.

"Both. They're looking. It was on the radio, the one o'clock news."

"Any further details?"

"None that they broadcast. I'll keep listening."

"Do that." When the red-headed American had left, Carlos emptied the coffee down the sink. "Eric's not a bad sort, he's not stupid either, in spite of his mistake," and then they began to discuss whether the corpse should be chopped up into pieces with an axe, disfigured with acid that would burn away the face and fingerprints, doused with gasoline in some isolated desert area and incinerated, immersed in a tub of lye that would consume all the flesh—or just left in the freezer?

Heidi was busy cooking up ham and eggs for her lover's late breakfast . . . "We could bury her in a trunk up in the hills, I suppose. Honey or butter on your toast?"

"I'll try the honey. Willi, what do you think of the burial-way-out-there idea?"

"It'll buy us time, but the problem is we can't be sure how much. You'll like the honey. I had some for lunch."

As Carlos had predicted, they were still discussing how to get rid of the corpse when Adler returned. They had definitely eliminated leaving the body intact in the freezer—it would be discovered within a week of their departure, when the landlord came. The dead woman must not be connected with this house, must be found—if at all—miles away and as long after November 6th as possible. It would be best if she could not be identified—a missing person matter received less attention than a specific homicide.

"So we've finally reached a consensus. Good, that's the reasonable way. We're all agreed that we'll keep her in the box till the night of the fifth, drive her out into some remote spot near the transmitter, do the teeth, pour the acid on face, feet and fingers then and bury her."

"Scars?"

"You're right, Heidi. Does she have any scars or other identifying marks, Eric? You would have noticed them."

Adler's eyes clouded. It was difficult to determine whether he was frozen in painful recollection or was concentrating in an effort to recall the body of the woman he had taken to bed and stabbed.

"Some kind of birthmark on her . . . her rear. Don't remember which side."

"We'll find it," Carlos said, sounding almost benign. "Now for the schedule. We'll go over the escape routes today and start assembling the rest of the RC models tonight. Don't make a sour face, Willi. You can see the . . . decadent night life tomorrow. For political study." He said it with a straight face which told nothing of what he was feeling or thinking.

"When do we see our little friends, Carlos?" Gehrke asked.

"Tomorrow afternoon. We do the test, and then we collect their ingenious gadgets for Eric to distribute. Anything else?"

"The acid, Eric?" she reminded.

"I'll get it at West Chemical on South Maryland Parkway."

"Is there a health food store near there?"

"Not too far away. Why?"

"Could you buy some jam for tomorrow's breakfast?" He promised not to forget, and then they unrolled the map to go over the escape timetable and routes again. Whatever chaos they could leave behind would mask their flight, and killing all those thousands of people would buy a good deal of chaos.

There was even a special anti-materialist irony in the plan. The gangsters would pay the five million dollars, and the bourgeois gamblers would be burned up and blown up anyway. The significance of this would have to be spelled out clearly in the note they must leave for the sensation-hungry journalists who should be made to serve the public-relations interests of the revolution. When all the details of the escape were covered for the sixth or seventh time, Carlos Fabrega Salinas began to draft the manifesto that would go to the press. He had written a score of these in the past nine years, all excellent, but everyone in the kitchen had to admit that this was his best yet—fierce, clear, ideologically impeccable And short enough to be published or quoted in its entirety on broadcasts. The media would love it.

Carlos loved the media

CHAPTER 34

THE TARGET practice with the pistols at the Las Vegas Gun Club went well; if the manager had any questions about the sniper-rifles with the advanced scopes he had the good taste not to ask them. He was spared the automatic weapons, which A. B. Gordon and her associates took to a gully halfway to Hoover Dam for firing. . . .

The show was excellent at the 1,200-seat Circus Maximus, the Caesars Palace showroom adorned with gold-leafed garlands and illuminated shields representing the legions of the Roman army. The superstar was at his super best, playing the audience and singing with the force and authority of a man twenty years younger. After seven songs he introduced the dozen celebrities seated at the front-row-center table reserved for his guests. Alison Gordon was grateful that her name was not mentioned, that her friend on stage knew how much she prized, needed her privacy.

"He sang that last one for you," Prince told her as they left the huge theater.

"Don't be silly."

"He pointed his finger right at you—like a pistol. 'Night and day, you are the one.' He was pointing at you."

She refused to admit it.

"Come on, you know him well."

"Not in the biblical sense."

Prince took her hand and squeezed it.

"I won't pry about your clients."

"Was never a client. I did some work for a friend of his, and he thanked me at one of those Bel Aire bar mitzvahs. Now tell me what you did on *your* summer vacation."

"Ate green vegetables and prayed for a sexy lady detective who would teach me right from wrong."

"How did you make out?"

"So far the right's terrific. I can hardly wait for the wrong."

She smiled in spite of herself, then nodded politely to a man five yards away.

"That fellow who waved to you looks a lot like the seniorest V.P. of NBC."

"Network-dropping, Ben? You're right though. That's Captain Video. A great lay."

"Come off it, Alison, why are you doing this hard-hearted Hannah, toast of Savannah act? For a supposedly tough broad, you're not so tough."

"Aside from a tendency to machine-gun people, I guess I'm a pussycat. Anyway, you think we could take a walk?"

"What for?"

"Balmy fresh air. Moonlight. An escape from the crowds, the noise and the smoke that go with every casino in this town. I'm tired of recirculated, air-conditioned, extra-terrestrial air."

She was steering him toward the front door.

"But nobody walks in Vegas—"

"Nobody walks in Beverly Hills either. The cops pick people up for questioning if they do. But I'm walking here."

"But there's no place to walk, just more hotels and casinos."

She would not be dissuaded. In a conciliatory gesture she led him to the people-mover—the hotel's moving belt that carried them out to the late-night action of The Strip. They turned left into the artificial brightness of electric signs that flashed and glittered as far as the eye could see. They strolled past The Castaways, Frontier and Silver Slipper to the Stardust, noting the lesser casinos along the way and the heavy flow of cars and taxis. They crossed The Strip at a traffic light to the mini-mall of shops, then started back past the Riviera, Desert Inn, Sands, Flamingo and MGM Grand to the Alladin, where they went in to rest their feet and slake their thirst.

"Very interesting," she told him as they walked through the lobby to find a bar.

"What's special about this hotel?"

"Nothing. That's the point. Same slots, same gambling tables, same gang of people, same noise as almost all the other hotels in town. It's interesting that ninety percent of the hotels are offering just about the same scene, with the main difference that the older ones charge less. New is nice, I guess."

"Let's get back to your place, where I can tell you all about my etchings and collection of rare T-shirts."

They found a bar and had two drinks. It was then that she suggested they adjourn to his apartment instead of the nearby hotel.

"I have a two-part plan, Ben. It should avoid the problem of going to work without a shave. The first part is that we go to your place, and lock the door, and pull down the blinds. The second part—"

But he was already waving a twenty-dollar bill at the bartender.

It was 1:40 A.M. when he locked the door of his apartment behind them. The pair of table lamps he'd left on cast a warm light over most of the large area that served as living and dining rooms. The furniture was good quality, not pseudo-chic, and the plants on the windowsill and floor all looked healthy. He went to the blinds, lowered the slats and turned. She was seated on the couch, her open purse on her lap.

"You are the one," she sang. Her voice sounded nothing like the superstar's, and there was another difference. She was not pointing her finger, but a .32-caliber Beretta.

"I want to ask you something, Ben."

"Show and tell time, huh?" He sighed.

She gestured toward the armchair, he sat down.

"This isn't fair, you know. You lure me up here *à deux* with steamy promises, and now—"

He felt the cold metal oval at the back of his neck.

"À trois and more, Ben. I believe that you fellows met at our get-together with the armored car gang."

Prince shifted his glance to the right, recognized Agajanian reflected in the wall mirror.

"How are you doing, Andy? Say, that's a fine-looking silencer. And here's Donny Boy. Any more nifty surprises?"

Standing in the doorway to the kitchen, Hovde moved his right arm and suddenly the throwing knife dropped into his hand.

"Knives, I hate. Just take the credit cards and the etchings; I won't call the cops or anybody—"

"Cut the shit." Agajanian pushed the silencer into his neck.

"You've got terrible friends, Alison, and you're making a big mistake. I don't have any diamond cuff links, there's practically no cash—"

"$1,108 in a checking account at the Pioneer Citizens Bank, and $805 in a savings account you never closed at the First National Branch out at Nellis," Agajanian reported.

"Last month you called your sister in Atlanta, Dr. Naomi Velkoff, twice, and phoned your mama in Miami three times," she said. "You hardly made any calls at all from this phone. Why?"

"Is that the big question you've been panting to ask?"

She shook her head.

"My theory, Ben, is that you call from pay phones because you're up to your appendicitis scar in some very covert risky operation. You're afraid of a tap. There's a lot of that going on, I hear."

"You've got the wrong man—"

"Would you believe that some son of a bitch is tapping *my* phone, lover?"

"That's illegal. Call the fuzz. Use my phone, if you want—"

"I don't care for people who play those games, Ben. We've got a complicated situation here. The question on the table is whether you're one of the very bad people, or a lesser variety."

He was sweating. He could feel it trickle down his spine. "Who are the very bad people?"

"I didn't know myself until yesterday . . . the ones who mean to blow up all those tourists in the casinos."

Prince sat up abruptly. "You know who they are?"

"Not really. People use certain expressions. Words can be like fingerprints—trademarks. If you read anything more than *Variety* you might have recognized those phrases on the cassette yesterday. 'Money lords.' 'Millionaire parasites.' Only one bunch uses that rhetoric: the May Fifth Brigade."

"Those West German crazies?"

"They aren't all Germans. They're the most homicidal of the far-left splinter groups, pious maniacs who claim to be the purest Marxists. May fifth, 1818 was the day Karl Marx was born."

Prince squirmed. "Politics was never my bag. Would anybody mind if I took a leak?"

"Yes. Andy would mind so much he'd shoot you."

"I'll wait. Let's get something straight. Whether you're right or wrong about these terrorists, I have nothing to do with them. Why would you possibly think I was hooked up with those maniacs?"

She put down the Beretta and took out the box of Sobranies. It was empty.

"Because they must have an inside man, Ben."

"Or woman. Maybe a precocious teenager. Kids are very political these days. It could be any one of one hundred or maybe eight hundred people. The hotel has a big staff."

"My friends think it's you. You're in the right spot. My idea, on the other hand, is that you're with the *other* crowd —the lesser variety . . ."

He grew very still, he hesitated before continuing in the same indignant tone . . . "Whoever they are, *I* don't know them. I'm just a $27,000-a-year guy trying to keep one hotel clean of chiselers and thieves. This is a straight town. Gaming Control Board makes sure of that—"

Hovde stepped forward, but she held up her hand and he stopped.

"Kill him!" Hovde said.

Three things happened quickly. Prince started to stand, Agajanian jerked him back by his hair, and the Beretta was aimed at his chest again.

"Your friend is kind of crazy," Prince said. "They're *both* crazy."

"Not as crazy as you," she said. "You're going to tell us—tonight."

"Tell you *what?*"

"About those people at 300 Las Vegas Boulevard South—and the woman who isn't a maid and that fellow in Room 921 who is such a good listener. I should have guessed it was you as soon as we found the bug. You were the one who sent the candy before I even checked in. You knew about my room before I did, so it had to be you who tipped them."

"Who's *them?* What the hell are you talking about? For Chrissakes, I've never even been in that building!"

"That's what I told my friends. I said Ben would stay away from that building as if his life depended on it—which it does." She looked at Agajanian questioningly. "What do you say, Andy?"

"If he won't play, he's dead weight, and we don't need that."

"Last chance, Ben. Old friend."

Prince leaned back, shook his head. "I don't have your answers, Alison, and you aren't the sort who just kills people."

She stood up and straightened her dress. "Well, I know someone who does. I'll tell him about your friends at 300, and you'll be dead before cocktail time."

She picked up the phone and dialed the number.

"Kublai Khan? Mr. Mintzer, please."

Prince moved about four inches before Agajanian put the silencer into his right ear.

"Mr. Mintzer? Tell him it's A. B. Gordon . . . They're paging him now . . . Hello, Mr. Mintzer . . . Yes, I have some information that may surprise you."

"You win," Prince said quickly.

She covered the mouthpiece with her hand. "No tricks?"

He shook his head, and she removed her hand.

"I'll call you back," she said. She hung up the phone and waited for Prince to speak.

CHAPTER 35

"I'M GOING to be in a ton of trouble," he began ruefully.

"Better than the bottom of Lake Meade," the man with the silenced pistol said.

"You're going to be in trouble too. They spent a lot of time and money setting this up. It was supposed to be a max-security deal, top secret. I told you the truth. I've never been inside 300 Las Vegas Boulevard South."

"They contacted you at Nellis, before you left the Air Force, right?" she asked.

"How did you know?"

Agajanian moved the gun away from Prince's head, and perched on a chair two feet away.

"Thanks. They must have checked me out pretty well. They knew about my uncle, my whole family and me. They knew a lot about me. They did quite a sales job."

"Internal Revenue?" Agajanian said.

Prince shook his head again.

"The I.R.S. has an office at 300," the accountant pressed.

"This was the F.B.I.," she said flatly. "That's ten you owe me, Andy."

"F.B.I.," Prince nodded. "Must have done a lot of digging. Found out about my cousin who teaches ethics at Harvard, and my grandma who was so ashamed of the Shtarker uncle she wouldn't see him on her deathbed."

Prince was silent for a few seconds as he remembered. "Well, these F.B.I. guys talked about how rotten the Mob was and how awful it must be for my family to carry that disgrace. They pointed out that I was an outstanding Air Force officer—yeah, they said *outstanding*—so I had to care about the country. The old Jack Kennedy bit—what can you do for your country, Ben?"

"And they said you're the only guy who could do it?"

"Sounds like *you* tapped *their* phones. But you're right, that was it . . . been trying for years to nail these racketeers, I'd be a rat and a traitor if I didn't do my share . . . they laid some guilt trip on me. You know anything about Jewish guilt?"

"I live in Beverly Hills, Ben. That's a guilt-free zone."

"Well, anyway, that bit you did with Mintzer scared the hell out of me. Gucci loafers are my style, not cement boots. God . . . I'm in some mess now." He ran his hand through his hair twice and took a cigar from the humidor on the sideboard. He puffed several times before going on.

The F.B.I. had learned that the Kublai Khan was secretly owned by the Mob, and that the hotel's assistant security chief was moving on to a more lucrative job in Atlantic City. Prince's uncle was near death from cancer at the time. Perhaps his old cronies would hire the nephew out of sentimentality, as well as esteem for young Prince's Air Force security expertise. It worked. A special autonomous F.B.I. unit was established with its own communication center manned around the clock.

"I was supposed to find the skim money—all the cash that they never report to the I.R.S. or anybody else. It's millions from the Khan alone each year. How do they cook the books, where do they stash the money and how do they launder it —all for noble Ben to dig out by himself. I broke my hump for a year and a half without much to show for it. Then that note came in with the bomb, and everybody said, 'Whoopee.' "

Hovde slipped the knife back into its sheath.

"What a break. If I stayed close, I might come up with something big when Mintzer had to produce the cash. Even if we didn't locate the main conduit, just catching these characters with the five million would leave them with big tax troubles . . . where did you get that bread, Sandy? . . . You want to do five years in the slammer, Sandy? No? Then talk to your Uncle Sam? . . . Hurray for the goddamn extortionists."

"Suppose they won't pay the five?" she asked.

"They have to. People who can burn up cars can do hotels too. That talk about ruining the town's name? That's real money talk. Despite what you may think, this really is a great town for fun and entertainment, a sort of three-dimensional movie. Thousands of people, and not just Mob types, have built this into a money machine. It's like a cow that gives milk twenty-four hours a day. Nobody can risk the city's reputation as a *safe,* fun place—not even them."

"You're wrong," she said.

"You're nuts. Who would risk ten thousand lives?"

"The man who hired us . . . one of the people who give Mintzer his orders. They don't want to pay. It's a matter of principle. Nobody shakes them down."

Prince held a finger up, and she half smiled.

"Yes, Benjamin, you may go to the lavatory—but hurry back."

Agajanian followed him to the toilet, and trailed him back a minute later.

"He watched me. Is he some kind of pervert?"

"He doesn't trust you, Ben. You're a pretty tricky guy."

Prince relit his corona. "Don't want to hurt your feelings, but we were *not* glad to hear you were coming. The F.B.I. knows about you and your . . . well, they called it a three-ring circus. They didn't want you screwing up this opportunity."

Agajanian laughed. "The government didn't want us to catch the extortionists because that would make it tougher to wreck the skimming . . . What about the *bombs?*"

"They said nobody drifty enough to take on the Mob could slip that many in without getting nailed, that it could never happen. There was no idea about these May 5th maniacs who specialize in stunts and massacres."

"Unbelievable. I may vote Socialist next time," the accountant said.

"Lot to do, and just three days to do it," she said, and pointed at Agajanian. "Get the dogs out with Thomas again first thing in the morning. We sweep every damn hotel and casino, again."

The accountant shrugged.

"I know, Andy. We aren't likely to find these bombs because this May 5th mob is a lot slicker, more dangerous, than those armored-car people, but we'll try. You try too, Ben."

"I'm no bomb expert—"

"The F.B.I. is, and they're loaded with manpower and detection equipment. You tell them it's Carlos 'Attila' Salinas and the May 5th Brigade. That ought to bring them running. You tell your principals, and I'll tell mine. My client ought to be kept informed."

"Let him sweat too," Hovde said.

"He probably forgot how. All right, it's been a long but rewarding evening. Big day tomorrow. Good night, gentlemen."

She made no move to rise. Instead, she kicked off her shoes. She waved as they left, then turned to Prince.

"You're quite a ballsy guy, Benjamin. That guilt rap did not convince, you know."

"I didn't know."

"You are a good citizen who is to be admired. I, for one, admire you."

"And I, you . . . would you like to see my etchings?"

She stood up, unhooked her skirt, which rustled to the floor.

"I thought you'd never ask."

They kissed, then walked to the bedroom. There really were several framed etchings on the wall—a Braque and a Chagall and an El Greco.

She had only brief glimpses before he took her in his arms. She didn't really get to appreciate them until after breakfast the next morning.

CHAPTER 36

"THEY'RE LYING," she said matter of factly.

"They've already called Washington for extra manpower."

"You're being *had,* Ben," Alison Gordon told him as she tugged together the lapels of the short gown that exposed more than it covered.

"Why don't you turn that set off?"

"Watching TV from bed is one of my vices—like these damn chocolates." She finished the last dark truffle in the candy box and tried to figure out whether the candidate being interviewed on the news program was the Democrat or the Republican.

"They'll be getting a go-ahead from D.C. *any minute,"* Prince insisted.

"Don't hold your breath. You are the honored recipient-elect of the official U.S. Government Mark-12 shaft, the red, white and blue screw. And I am not sloshed. Two bottles of Carlsberg just loosens my vixen tongue."

"They will call back . . . tonight . . ." he trailed off.

"Not tonight, and not this week. Your Washington bosses don't believe you. You've never seen this May 5th gang here or anywhere else. I'm not sure I'd believe you either. They figure you're getting close to the skimmers, so you ought to stick to that and leave anti-terrorist stuff to the experts."

"The skim money finances dope deals, buying politicians, porno rings—the works!"

"I'm with you, and so are you as long as you stick to their orders. It could be that your F.B.I. friends don't think even these mothers could pull it off. *They've* never tangled with the May 5th Brigade either. Maybe some bureaucrat wants to show up the I.R.S. by doing what the Treasury agents never could do here, or perhaps it's just budget-hearing time in six weeks, and wrecking the Mob's skim setup would pull some great press."

"Balls."

"Don't take it personally, Ben. I haven't done that well either. It's six P.M. Our dogs haven't found a thing and my piano-playing client isn't answering *my* calls. Could be he'll phone later tonight when the rates go down."

"You scared?"

"Can't you tell?"

Now some sports announcer was at somebody's training ring, carrying on about the "major heavyweight battle," set for the arena Caesars Palace operated near its tennis courts. The security man was not listening. He walked to the toilet, from which he dimly heard the voices in the background as he washed his hands, pleased that the running water drowned them out. He reminded himself that she was probably still cynical about the F.B.I. because of that organization's chronic conflicts with the C.I.A., where she had worked for years. Now that he saw the situation in its proper context, he felt better. He dried his hands and returned to the bedroom.

"Son of a *bitch,*" she said, and jumped out of bed.

"What's wrong?"

"Not wrong—*right.*" She was looking intently at the television set. Prince turned to the screen and saw a crowd of people looking up at two little planes. His U.S.A.F. recognition-training helped him identify one as an R.A.F. Spitfire interceptor and the others as an American Mustang fighter-bomber—vintage World War II machines now collectors' items. The camera panned the people on the ground.

"That's it." She tossed off her robe, grabbed up the telephone. "Clean living, that's what does it," she said as she dialed. "Jackpot. We have lucked out, Don . . .. He's here . . . I'm dead certain . . . right . . . everybody out of the pool. I want the whole team to meet us in half an hour at Channel 3 . . . the TV station . . . Where is it, Ben?"

"Boulder Highway, at about the four-thousand block."

"You know anybody there?"

"Janette Hamilton, assistant news director. What's this all about?"

"Don, it's out on Boulder Highway. Around four thousand . . . Right . . . Fanelli . . . Thomas . . . the radio sisters . . . Hell, no, he isn't here alone . . . not that prick . . . thirty minutes."

She hung up and began dressing swiftly. "*Now* we've got a shot, lover."

"At what?"

"At *whom,* you mean. Call the Hamilton woman. Ask her to hold a tape of that news spot. We need her help at the station right away. Life and death, except in this case it happens to be the truth. Where's my bra?"

Prince pointed, then called Janette Hamilton to say he was on the way. As he hung up, Alison straightened her dress, stepped into her shoes and fluffed out her hair as she reached for her purse.

"Come on, Ben. I'll give you answers on our way. I'm almost positive I recognized someone on that video tape."

Channel 3—the NBC affiliate in Las Vegas—was at 4100 Boulder Highway. When Janette Hamilton saw Ben Prince enter the reception area, she realized that the emergency was genuine. She had known him for nearly three years—most always bright and easy. He certainly had never looked this grim before.

Janette Hamilton was pretty, smart and ambitious. She was also puzzled. Prince had introduced this strange assortment of people so quickly that she hadn't really caught their names. The woman with him seemed to be in charge . . . God, it was that Beverly Hills detective who'd been shot during the robbery . . ."You want to explain this, Ben?"

"It's a great story. You'll get an exclusive," Alison Gordon answered for him. The control room was crowded, the atmosphere urgent.

"Roll tape," Janette Hamilton told the young engineer.

The overhead monitor filled with the final moments of the boxing sequence, and now they saw the throng of people—men and women of various nationalities, according to the off-camera narrator—and flags of several countries.

"It's coming now," Alison Gordon said. The TV reporter was speaking to an Italian couple who had come "all the way from Milan to compete for the $15,000 first prize in this world championship sponsored by Circus Circus." The husband pointed out that the U.S.A. had many more radio-control model activists, with some seventy thousand members in the Academy of Model Aeronautics and twice that many in local clubs. Britain's Society of Model Aircraft Engineers was also bigger than the Italian organization, but Marcello Bonomi had won third prize there last year and hoped to do better with his new plane . . .

"Don, Andy . . . this is it."

The next shot was up at a radio-controlled Stuka being guided by a young Hamburg history teacher, and then they saw the Spitfire and the Mustang. The camera swung to the teams operating the multiple-channel transmitters that controlled the flights. A long pan of the other entrants and their families followed, showing their reactions.

"There, freeze it," Alison Gordon said.

"Freeze frame, Arnold. Roll it back ten seconds and hit the button when she yells."

The engineer complied.

"There. In the back with those two Asian men—see him?"

"Sort of," Hovde answered in his gravelly voice.

"Could you blow it up some?" Agajanian suggested.

"No problem."

Maxine Wu was the first to speak.

"They're Japanese."

"It's him, isn't it?" Alison Gordon said.

"Looks like him," Hovde said guardedly.

"It's him," said Agajanian, "and I don't believe it. You were right, Al. You said he'd show if the brigade was in for a big score."

"Is that it?" Janette Hamilton asked. Prince looked at Alison and they both nodded. The engineer departed for his bowling date.

"Who is this 'he' and what's my big exclusive story?"

"Number-three junk dealer in the *world,"* Prince improvised. "Handles almost a ton of heroin a year."

"What's his name?"

"Come on—this cat's got eight names and ten lives. Both Interpol and the drug-enforcement people here have been after him for years. Right, Al?"

She nodded in assent, and appreciation. The way he'd implied that she was working with the federal agents was a neat and helpful piece of work.

"I'm not authorized to speak for the D.E.A.," she told the news executive truthfully. "I'm not a government employee any more. I'm just helping out on this one. I can say that Washington has been trying to put this s.o.b. out of business for years. This is all confidential, of course."

"I can keep my mouth shut."

"She's all right, Al. Jan's good people. You've just got to let her know—exclusive—when the bust is going down."

"She's got it," A. B. Gordon vowed solemnly, and the two women shook hands. Ms. Hamilton gave Prince a farewell kiss that hinted they had been more than bridge partners, and Alison Gordon told herself that his past escapades were hardly her concern. In the parking lot outside, she spoke out on what lay ahead.

"I said before that we've got a shot now. That's right, but we'll need shooters. The F.B.I. doesn't believe that there's a serious bomb threat from real terrorists and my former employers are highly unlikely to risk either a jurisdictional war with the F.B.I. or a lot more rotten press by intervening. We may need our own shooters to take these terrorists, Don."

"How many?"

"Five or six. Top marksmen with experience in night firing. We can supply infra-red or low-light scopes, can't we?"

"I have a few."

"We'll pay five hundred a day for two days. They've got to be here by noon tomorrow, so you'd better start phoning. You might try Country and Jo-Jo Williams. We want the best."

"You'll get 'em—"

Prince erupted.

"You can't do this. You can't just roll in like gangbusters with a private posse and start shooting. Even if it is the guy you call Attila, you can't pull this vigilante stuff . . ."

She put a cigarette in her holder and Agajanian lit it. "What we really need is our own army and our own air force."

"It's illegal, damn it," Prince protested, "and we'll all go to jail—"

"I don't think so."

"Why the hell not?"

"Because you're going to help us make it all nice and legal," she said. She explained her plan over dinner. The Italian food was only so-so, but he had to admit that the plan was extraordinary.

"Of course, they'll never buy it," he predicted.

"They've got to." She stood up and reached for her handbag.

At 6:50 P.M. in the Langley, Virginia HQ of the Central Intelligence Agency, a bone-weary deputy director with hurting eyes was locking his torch-proof wall safe for the night when the phone rang.

"Yes?" he asked wearily.

"It's Alison."

"Put her on, Doris," he told his secretary.

The exchange of amenities was guarded. It was like two former lovers speaking for the first time after many years. He wanted to tell her that he missed her and she wanted to ask about his eyes. Instead, she told him about the situation and the plan.

"This your idea?" he stalled.

"Of course. Who else would come up with a scheme like this? Isn't that what you're thinking?"

She was still too damned smart, still too right too often ... "Yes. An operation like that would be ... interesting. You know, I wouldn't believe this story from almost anyone else ... there's very little *hard* proof ... it's a big risk."

"There's no choice, and you know it."

Right again.

"It's not the money, that's no problem. It's the planes. If you're wrong, it will be a disaster."

"You've got to get the planes. I know you will."

He took off the dark glasses, rubbed his sore eyes.

"What makes you so sure?"

"Because of all those lives ... *and* you never could pass up an opportunity like this to lord it over the F.B.I. or the Pentagon. What about the courier?"

"All right, we'll send the package out by fighter ... should be in your hands by eight in the morning. I'll call you back about planes in a couple of hours."

She gave him the telephone number of Caesars Palace. "I

knew that I could count on your . . . intelligence." She laughed. "And . . . well, it's been so long . . . I mean I'm sorry about the way I spoke, I didn't mean to hurt your feelings."

They both laughed ruefully and ended the conversation. He sat there with his ruined eyes shut for a full minute, suffering and computing. Then he picked up the phone again and asked Doris Kraft to get him Lieutenant General Feist at the Pentagon.

CHAPTER 37

NOVEMBER 5TH, 1:50 P.M., clear and warm.

Lieutenant Charles Barrett, head of the police bomb squad, was returning to his office after a wholesome but not quite satisfying lunch of cottage cheese and bean sprouts when he saw Ben Prince and the Gordon woman leading a group of people out of the building. The strangers, five men and a black woman in her late twenties, had a very business-like air. Something told him they were not tourists, gamblers, salesmen or curiosity seekers visiting police headquarters.

"Lieutenant Barrett," Alison Gordon greeted in a reasonable imitation of pleasure. "Just the man I—we—wanted to see."

"Who's we?"

"Mr. Prince and I. Oh, these other people are new employees of the Khan who've just been deputized."

They did have the look of security professionals. Barrett remembered seeing the black woman before. "Jo-Jo Williams . . . you shot here five or six years ago in the rifle championships. Took the women's title, didn't you?"

"Bull's-eye."

"But half a dozen new security people at once?"

"We've got a problem, Lieutenant Barrett. Would you step over here for a second? It's sort of delicate."

Barrett walked with her and Prince until they were out of earshot of the others.

"Yes?"

"There's been a bomb threat, lieutenant. Man phoned that he'd blow up the Kublai Khan unless he got a *lot* of money. Then he called again and said he'd blast a dozen hotels—those were his words—if the $500,000 wasn't paid tomorrow."

"That's a lot of money. When did the second call come in?"

"An hour ago. It was actually the third," she said. "Mintzer tells me that this fellow phoned to claim he'd blown those airport cars. My firm was hired to check it out."

"I didn't think you were here to shoot craps," Barrett said. "Wouldn't have hurt if you'd come clean with me at the beginning."

"I owe you an apology. Ben said I should tell you, but he was overruled."

He shrugged. "Hotel going to pay?"

"I doubt it," Prince told him. "We don't believe in paying extortionists, and it's a ton of money. We're not even sure how real this threat is. We haven't heard anything about where or when the payoff is supposed to be made, so maybe it's a scam."

"Maybe it isn't," she said.

"Lady's right, Ben. We'll roll our dog teams and search units on the double, and you let me know if there's any further word from anybody about anything. My God, you know what a bomb could do in any one of those hotels?"

Without waiting for an answer, Barrett rushed into the building to get his bomb squad into action.

"But I thought we figured the bombs are coming in on those model planes," Prince said.

"Extra insurance can't hurt. Maybe Attila's got a few more

tricks up his cape. He must have at least two. How can he put up thirty or forty RC aircraft—big ones that can carry a significant warhead—without being spotted?"

"Not from the park where the competition is."

"My thought exactly. So they're launching from somewhere else. Where? How far away can these birds be controlled? How big a circle do we have to sweep? How much time have we got to find them?"

"Five tomorrow afternoon is the deadline for payment."

They rejoined the shooters. The former C.I.A. marksman known as "Country" Binks was in earnest conversation with Jo-Jo Williams, who was a foot shorter but knew just as much about ammo loads for target-shooting accuracy.

"These will be moving targets, miss," he reminded as the new deputies reboarded the pair of Hertz station wagons. A Southern gentleman, Binks stepped aside to let Josephine Johnson Williams enter first.

"Thank you, Mr. Binks," she said, and turned to make sure that the case containing her rifle was safely stowed in the rear.

"See you at the command post in an hour," Alison Gordon told them. "That's Room 711—lucky number. Don't talk to strangers, and remember the phones could be tapped. Go."

The shooters departed and she drove Prince back to The Strip to confront Mintzer. By now the V.P. of the Kublai Khan *must* have some fresh orders and final word about paying the money. As they passed the Sahara Hotel a tan van freshly painted with the name "Western Safety Services, Inc." swung into traffic behind them.

The van followed the Porsche as far as the Frontier, where Eric Adler turned off and parked behind the seven-story hotel.

"Western," he said to the salad chef finishing some sort of cigarette at the rear entrance. The cook and the nearby guard noted the snappy shoulder patch on Adler's green coveralls and nodded indifferently. The security man studied his clipboard and asked a sensible question.

"Aren't you early with that thing? You're not due today, Jack."

"Man, I just tote these goddamn extinguishers where they tell me. Your safety chief must have called special, or maybe my dispatcher screwed up again. You've never seen a dumbass like him."

"I've seen worse," the guard said, and nodded permission for Adler to enter with the heavy fire extinguisher. He took the service elevator to the fourth floor, removed an identical-looking extinguisher from a wall bracket and replaced it with the one he had carried from the van.

They were twins in external appearance, and the cylinder Adler hung up would function as a fire extinguisher if, God forbid, somebody tried to use it during the next twenty-four hours. But it had a powerful dormant radio beacon concealed in its top. The Japanese Red Army technicians had done a wonderful job down to the last detail on the outside, and the inside was a first-class weapon. The timer—silent and electro-magnetically undetectable, would kick on the homing device at five the next afternoon, and the transmitter would guide the flying bomb to this target. After the explosion of two quarts of nitroglycerin had done its work, the resulting fires would burn flesh, drapes, furniture, clothes, most anything else.

Hundreds of casualties at each hotel, he thought, as he smiled pleasantly at the security man on the way out of the building. There was little time to savor the thought of the fires and carnage that would be coming, however . . . Adler still had fourteen more homing beacons to put in place before 2:30 the next afternoon.

Actually, November 6th, five P.M., would be the moment of truth, but Carlos wanted him at the launch site no later than half past three. Everything had to be double-checked. The May 5th Brigade never took chances. Every detail had been prepared. The deadly armada of 747's was ready. Nothing, foreseeably, could stop them now.

CHAPTER 38

"OUR ATTORNEY reports that the board of directors is . . . deeply concerned about the possible loss of life if we don't pay," Mintzer announced stiffly.

Alison Gordon crossed her legs and looked sincere.

"Though your dogs found nothing this morning," he continued, "our directors are not convinced that a bombing will not be attempted. What do you think, Miss Gordon?"

"I believe it *will* be attempted."

He coughed and squinted uncomfortably. "Yes, they have . . . ah . . . reevaluated their initial decision, on humanitarian grounds."

"They're going to pay," she translated.

Mintzer cleared his throat, phrased his next statement. "Despite their high regard for principle, they are preparing to borrow the money. The hotel doesn't have that kind of cash, of course."

"Of course."

"After all, the welfare of our guests comes first."

The other senior racketeers had either persuaded or outvoted Spinoza, she guessed, and they were probably worried that the insurance company might not pay off if they didn't give the money to the bombers. The human and property damage awards could be much more than five million dollars.

"The arrangements for securing the money are being made. These matters are complex."

Not half as complex as the creative accounting that would have to conceal where the cash came from. Movieland's alleged "Chinese" bookkeeping would be child's play compared to the numbers game that the Mob's inventive mathematicians would play.

"What about delivery?" Prince asked.

"They'll call tomorrow—no earlier," she predicted. "Idea is to give us as little time as possible to set any traps or alert the police."

Mintzer's pained expression returned. "We have a fine force in Las Vegas, and all of us in the hotel and hospitality community respect our capable department—"

"But they might get ambitious and screw up the payoff," she finished for him.

"Bringing in the police might possibly risk the lives of our guests, Miss Gordon. We are compelled—by safety considerations—to handle this entire matter with our own personnel. With all due regard for your organization, we feel that it might be more prudent for Ben to take care of the transfer."

So you won't have to explain where you got that ransom money, she thought. It was working out. The V.P. was playing into the hands of the F.B.I., and there would be no reasonable way for Spinoza to blame Alison Gordon when it happened. *He* had chosen Prince to handle the money . . .

"All this must be kept completely confidential," Mintzer said, "including the sum involved."

"Of course. You don't mind if I continue trying to find out who the extortionists are, do you?"

"Not at all, Miss Gordon. Go right ahead with your detecting. Just so long as you don't interfere with the payment.

Who knows? You might come up with something that'll be useful later."

"Who knows? . . ." The extortionists, she knew, would be hunted down, and the underworld's code of business practice would be respected—there would be no embarrassing violence in Nevada. If she could identify the people who had dared to shake down the Mob, then so much sooner would the machinery of retribution be set in motion. Weeks later, in some other state, the extortionists would die in some appropriately grisly fashion that would carry a message for anyone else who might be contemplating such untoward behavior. . . .

When she stood up to leave, Mintzer asked Ben Prince to stay behind to discuss "arrangements," so she returned to the command post alone. If Mintzer's bosses had now agreed to pay, that did not bother her a bit. She had signed on to save lives, not skim money—and Spinoza knew it.

Back in Room 711, she took a Morocco-leather-covered notebook from her shoulder bag and went over her checklist.

"Andy?"

"On schedule. The shooters have their scopes, body armor and plenty of ammo. They'll be assembled in two teams at the airport at nine tomorrow morning. Country's leading one unit, Jo-Jo the other."

"You know the drill?"

"Don told us who they are," the black woman said. "You find them, we'll do the rest."

"Good. The choppers will be ready to lift off before nine."

She looked at her watch, and decided that it was time to make the telephone call.

"Thomas?"

"Don and I have the suitcase fixed up. The receiver is tiny, for obvious reasons. You'll have to get the transmitter within a mile or less to activate it."

She turned to the communications expert.

"Everything's cool, Al. We're moving the radio van downstairs here tonight."

Agajanian pointed at the large wall map of Clark County. "Be a lot easier if we knew from which direction those little birds are coming."

"I'm working on that. You have those cars ready to roll, leave the rest to me and our friend with the sun glasses.

Agajanian shook his head.

"Spit it out, Andy."

"Prince told you that he's with the feds, and they're the ones with all forty-eight sticks of that dynamite—right?"

"Yes."

"Took the first one to test it for taggants that could trace where the stuff was bought, and scooped up the rest so nobody'd get hurt."

"That's it."

"Did they trace the stuff, Al?"

"Stolen over near Reno a month ago. Why?"

"How do we know he's telling us the truth?" Agajanian pressed. "He *says* the feds got it, he *says* he's with the feds . . . Al, I realize that you two are tight but . . . don't get sore, I'm just the nervous type—"

"I'm not sore. You've raised an absolutely valid question. Yes, we'll have to provide for that possibility. And I have."

"Al, I didn't mean to—"

"You didn't. Anything else we should discuss? Any old business? New business? Problems?"

"I don't know if it's a problem," Thomas Arroyo said, "but the police have been following me. Every time I've been on the road in the past three days a car has been right behind me. Different car each time."

"You're certain?"

He nodded.

"It's a problem," she told him. "Any idea why?"

He decided to say nothing about the explosions back on

his reservation. "No. They pick me up in the morning. Another car takes over later. They just hang back and follow."

"Are they good?"

"So-so. I think I could lose them," Arroyo volunteered.

"You will—tomorrow at nine A.M. . . . anything else?"

Agajanian and Fanelli exchanged uneasy glances, but said nothing.

"Don't worry. It's going to be all right," she said and left to make her long-distance call from outside the hotel. It wasn't all right.

As she returned to the command post twenty-five minutes later Fanelli looked up grimly at her and threw a switch on the radio. Hovde's distinctive voice sounded from a speaker.

"I lost them, damn it. Don't know how they did it, but . . ."

He had been at the park where the radio-controlled-aircraft championships were progressing, watching the Japanese whom they had seen speaking with Attila on the video tape. Hovde was to follow them to the terrorists. She reached for the microphone.

"Maybe we can find them again," she said. "You know who they are? Where they're staying? Rented car? You must have something."

"Names are H. Takashimi and O. Mitsuya. Supposed to be the Japanese champs from a model-aircraft club in Osaka. Paid their hotel bill in cash this morning. Nobody remembers whether they left in a cab or a car, so you can forget about plates. I blew it."

"Get over to that hotel. You'll find *something,* Don."

"Our best lead, and I blew it. Okay, I'm on my way."

She stared at the Clark County map on the wall. Hovde had reported earlier that it was possible for radio-controlled models to be flown as far as a hundred miles with precise navigation. The newer planes and more powerful transmitters had even greater ranges.

"What do you think?" Fanelli asked.

"There goes Plan A—get them on the ground."

"How about Plan B?"

She considered for several moments.

"Plan B is flashier, Gerry. It's riskier, of course, but it may be all we've got."

"Anything else I can do?"

"Pray."

CHAPTER 39

SHE SLEPT poorly and she slept alone, but she was not weary on the morning of November 6th. The knowledge that it was coming to a boil—that it would be settled before the sun set—filled her with enormous energy. The fact that such vitality was rooted in tension and danger did not bother her. She had lived with them daily for a long time. Maybe so long that she depended on them.

Everyone was in position. The Wu sisters were at the long-range transmitter in the radio van behind Caesars Palace, the shooters were standing by with two curious helicopter pilots at Sky Harbor, Ben Prince sat waiting for the extortionists' call in Mintzer's office and Hovde and Agajanian were tracking the missing Japanese. A. B. Gordon paced the command post and lit another cigarette.

"It's only a quarter after eleven," Fanelli pointed out, "and you've wiped out almost a pack already. What the hell are you doing?"

"Going over Plan B and trying to figure out why the money had to be packaged in those aluminum cases. I have a hunch that it's water."

"Water?"

"Metal's waterproof, more so than canvas. The delivery probably involves water. I'm not sure, I don't know, and those cars following Thomas bother me."

"Maybe they're Internal Revenue," Fanelli suggested, and walked to the electric urn to pour himself the fifth cup of coffee since dawn.

"That stuff is addictive," she said.

"Impossible. Been drinking it for years."

"I'll take a cup," Agajanian announced as he followed Hovde into the large room. The expressions they wore said it all. They had struck out.

"No luck?" she asked.

"We've got bad news and bad news. Which do you want first?" Hovde asked.

"You did your best."

"All right, we'll start with the bad news. We phoned Osaka and found out that Mr. Takashimi and Mr. Mitsuya are in a hospital there. Somebody poisoned them a week ago, just two days after they each got very convincing cables announcing the competition here had been canceled."

"Tricky. Whoever the two Oriental gentlemen who showed here are, they know about RC aircraft. They made the quarter-finals."

"Using an extremely long-range transmitter," Agajanian reported as he dropped two lumps of sugar into his bitter brew. "According to the sharp guy I met who edits *Model Aviation,* the rig that the Japanese had was an ultra-sophisticated system, digital proportional for continuously variable positioning of the controls. It's a seven-channel job that can easily work out to seventy or eighty miles. One channel for ailerons, one for throttle and so forth."

Agajanian paused to sip at the coffee, added another sugar.

"And now for the real bad news," Hovde said. "There is not a clue as to where these guys have gone. Somebody thinks that they might have loaded their transmitter into a small truck—no color specified—carrying plates from another state—also unspecified. I told you, Al. I blew it."

"Homing beacons," Fanelli said suddenly.

She nodded and ground out the Sobranie. "The way that the May 5th people and their Japanese allies are going to hit targets from twenty or fifty miles out. They'll guide the little birds in to the edge of town, and then the planes will home on beacons planted in each hotel."

"We can sweep the frequencies and find 'em."

"Maybe. I called Barrett three hours ago. His people are searching and sweeping and they haven't found a damn thing," she told them. "The beacons probably haven't gone active yet."

"How long have we got to wait?" Hovde asked.

"Turn it up, Gerry," she ordered. He twisted a dial, and they heard the voice of Mintzer's secretary telling a Mr. Baird that the executive V.P. of the Kublai Khan would have to call him back.

"Tap's working. Who's Baird?"

"Prince's boss. He was out of town for a while. Mintzer's keeping him out of this. Fewer people who know, the better, I suppose."

In the next two hours, the group in the command post overheard twenty-two phone calls, consumed six sandwiches and three candy bars, drank seven cups of coffee and got on each other's nerves. At ten minutes to two, Mintzer's telephone jangled again.

"Tell him it's Mr. November," the caller instructed.

Everyone in the command post recognized the voice. They had heard the cassette of the previous call several times.

"Mr. November on line two," the secretary announced.

"I'll take it."

This conversation was much shorter than the earlier ones. The extortionist asked whether Mintzer had "the two packages," and when he said he did he was told that a letter with delivery instructions had been left for a Mr. Gewirtz at the concierge's desk.

"Tell Thomas," Alison Gordon ordered.

It took no more than fifteen seconds to make radio contact.

"It's going down right now," Fanelli told him. "He'll be on his way to the concierge's front desk any second."

Prince was still looking out the window when Mintzer emerged from the closet with two of the common aluminum suitcases the casino used for its transfers.

"Follow their instructions to the letter. We're all counting on you, Ben."

They shook hands, and Prince left with the twin containers. Mintzer watched him cross the casino on the closed-circuit TV, then lost sight of him as he walked from the gambling area to the front desk.

Prince put down the aluminum cases, asked for the Gewirtz letter. Arroyo moved swiftly. He stumbled, set down a pair of identical-looking pieces of metal luggage. The switch took only a moment. No one but Prince and Arroyo saw it happen.

Prince reread the instructions, put the folded sheet of paper in his jacket pocket and picked up the cases that Arroyo had left for him.

Eric Adler, watching from a nearby phone booth, saw Prince come out of the hotel and climb into his car for the first leg of his journey. As soon as his vehicle disappeared into the traffic, Adler dialed the number of the other booth outside the city where Willi Gehrke waited.

"Just left. Brown Cutlass, '78 model, I think. About six feet tall, seems to be alone. It's the guy I told you about, Prince . . . He was hired about seven weeks before I quit . . . Big man with the women . . . No, I couldn't tell whether he's armed . . . I've still got two more of those to install, and I'll be seeing you by 3:30 as planned . . . Bye."

When Adler ended the call, Gehrke walked from the booth to a four-wheel-drive Scout and drove three miles to the hilltop where the others were busy inserting the last bottles of nitroglycerin in model 747's. They were working inside a large plastic bubble, an instant shelter kept inflated by air pressure. Gehrke heard the noise of the pumps and had to shout his question to one of the Japanese over the clatter.

"Where's Carlos?"

The Japanese gestured out toward the right. Gehrke followed his direction, circled a boulder and almost collided with the terrorist leader. Another of the Japanese was digging a grave, and before he could stop himself Gehrke saw the acid-ruin of the dead woman's face.

"That's deep enough. Thanks," Carlos said to the man with the spade, then turned to Gehrke. "Give us a hand."

Reluctant to touch it, Gehrke forced himself to pick up the corpse's still frozen feet and they succeeded in dumping the body into the excavation. Carlos took the shovel—a calculated display—and began to heave earth into the hole as Gehrke reported.

"Sounds all right, but you'd better get over to cover Heidi in case she needs help. Take the hunting rifle with the scope —and be careful, Willi."

Gehrke took the long gun and departed in the Scout. Carlos and the Japanese reentered the bubble a few minutes after they had tamped down the soil and covered the grave with rocks. There were the planes, row on row. Some of the 747's carried the markings of Lufthansa, others British Airways, others Japan Air Lines or Pan American. A balanced international capitalist armada, Carlos thought with some satisfaction, as he began to count—26 . . . 27 . . . 28, that would have to do. There should be no problems if everyone obeyed his instructions . . .

Ben Prince was following them to the letter. Driving at forty miles an hour as ordered, he took the Henderson turnoff and proceeded six miles to the Coors beer sign. The envelope with directions for the next leg was taped to the back as promised. Prince started his car, and repeated the contents of the new message aloud. He hoped that the transmitter Fanelli had hidden under the dashboard was working, and that the May 5th Brigade did not travel with unscrambling equipment.

The various notes sent the Cutlass zigzagging back and forth, so it wasn't until half past three that he guessed where he was being guided. It was Lake Meade, the largest man-made reservoir in the United States, one hundred and fifteen miles long with five hundred miles of shore, created almost half a century before when President Roosevelt had dedicated a huge dam honoring his Republican predecessor—the 727-foot-high Hoover Dam that sealed off Black Canyon and domesticated the Colorado River. Thirty miles from Vegas and publicized as "the eighth engineering wonder of the world," the immense dam was a success in both flood control and hydroelectric power production, and popular with swimmers, boatsmen, fishing enthusiasts and thousands of tourists who just came to look and tell friends that they had driven across Route 66—on top of the dam.

Now he saw the dam and the lake, both overwhelming. He drove another twelve minutes to the hollow tree, where he found the promised rolls of waterproof tape and sealed the aluminum cases tightly. There was the rowboat he'd been told to use. He climbed in, saw the orange buoy 150 yards offshore and began to row slowly toward it.

He assumed that he was being watched by someone with a gun, and he was right. Concealed in the shrubbery, Willi Gehrke had him in his sights every second.

Prince unobtrusively pressed the arming buttons that looked like rivets on the side of each case, took a deep breath and tied the metal containers to the nylon cords floating from the buoy. The whole thing reminded him of setting out fishing tackle. He let his eyes wander in a wide arc, not surprised when he saw no one. In accord with the instructions he rowed back to the shore and pulled the small craft up on the beach. No doubt they would come out from hiding to collect the cases as soon as he was out of sight. Perspiring from the afternoon warmth and the rowing, he took off his jacket and laid it on the front seat of the Cutlass. It was only as he started the motor that the temptation overcame him. He half turned for a final glance at the buoy.

The brightly colored marker bobbed at the same spot.

The cases that had floated beside it were gone.

"It went off like clockwork!" Heidi Friedheim said proudly as they put the cases at their leader's feet.

"Thanks to our female fish here," Gehrke added.

"Excellent. What did you do with the wet suit and scuba gear?"

"Just what you told us, Carlos. We buried it in a gully half a mile from the lake. It's a beautiful lake."

"I saw the pictures Eric sent with the maps. It seemed splendid." He reached for one of the cases.

"I think it's all there. We took a quick look when we checked inside," Gehrke told him.

Carlos opened the lid and stared admiringly at the stacks and stacks of $50 and $100 bills. "Eric, come take a look. Bring our Red Army comrades with you."

The three men emerged from the plastic igloo, studied the mounds of money.

"We *did* it, Eric. Look at that. That's a great bonus for the revolution—thanks to you and our allies from Japan."

Adler was so moved by this praise from his hero that he could only nod and grin, but the Japanese terrorists bowed slightly and spoke of their satisfaction in working with such a noted anti-imperialist fighter in the struggle against the enemies of the people. They bowed again when Carlos told them that they could collect their one million as soon as the planes were launched.

"It's time to launch," he said. "Twenty to five. Our beacons will be sending in ten minutes."

Moving carefully to avoid injuring the delicate wings of the models, they started to bring the 747's out to the sandy, scrubby plateau on top of the rise—their airfield for the bombing of Las Vegas. It was not large enough to accommodate all the mini-aircraft at once, so the plan was to launch in waves. There would be a three-minute interval between each wave, with four nitro-laden 747's in each strike force.

When the planes were properly positioned, the Japanese withdrew to their transmitter and began manipulating the dials. The one-half-horsepower engines kicked on, stuttered and then growled, sounding like a chorus of chain saws. Compared to the roar of the old piston-powered aircraft of the past or the ear-splitting shriek of modern jets, these first sounds were insignificant—almost ludicrous. Still, this mini-thunder was the prelude to the first air attack upon an American city. A real attack, whatever the size of the attackers.

The planes began to move. In moments they were lifting off, slowly rising on the air currents from the valley below. The Japanese experts handled them deftly. First they swung them in a gentle circle as the models climbed to 400 . . . 500 . . . 600 feet, and then they turned the machines on a course that would take them directly to the center of the city twenty-eight miles away. The 747's were still climbing as they shrank to dots on the horizon. Now they were out of sight. The attack had begun.

CHAPTER 40

"COMRADE LEADER to radar control. Come in, radar control," the pilot chanted. On the left shoulder of his flight suit was the red star of a Soviet Air Force pilot, and the needle-nosed 1,300-mph interceptor was painted in the camouflage pattern of Warsaw Pact military aircraft.

"Radar control to Comrade Leader. No target yet. Continue sweep in Delta Sector."

Ten seconds of silence, and then the flier heard the voice of his wingman.

"Comrade Two to Comrade Leader, we're well out of our exercise area. What the hell is going on? We're carrying live ammo, full combat loads, missile warheads armed—and over Clark County? What kind of 'exercise' is this?"

"This is no exercise, Lenny. This is the real goddamn thing. Tighten up the formation, Comrade Three."

The third jet moved up a bit closer, and the radio crackled again.

"—This is McCarran Tower to unidentified jets. You are intruding into approach pattern. Urgent you return to military air space over Nellis range immediately."

"Nellis to McCarran. Nellis to McCarran. Classified military operation in progress. Repeat, classified high-priority flight in progress. Request you clear air space for national-security mission."

"McCarran to Nellis. This is the approach control supervisor. Is this a joke?"

"Negative. We cannot discuss classified mission further on clear radio channel. Suggest you telephone Nellis commander immediately and reroute inbound commercial traffic."

"You bet your ass I will," the head air traffic controller at McCarran said indignantly.

The Northrop F-5E's flew on. Painted to resemble Sov-block interceptors, these were planes from the special "Aggressor" unit—the crack 64th Fighter Weapons Squadron that helped train U.S. pilots at Nellis. The F-5E Tigers had been picked for this unusual duty because they looked like MIG-21's, and the men who flew them were skilled in the combat tactics of Warsaw Pact air forces.

"Radar intercept control to Comrade Leader. Our ground vans in Charlie Sector have your targets. Altitude 1,400 feet. Air speed less than 100. Do you read me?"

"Okay, we're on our way."

Eight vans carrying low-level air-search radar gear had ringed the desert resort since noon, two hours after the astounding orders had come from the three-star general who commanded Air Intelligence from the Pentagon. Their antennae had swept the skies for five hours without result—until now. Moving at 900 mph some 16,000 feet above the ground, the Tigers turned sharp left toward Charlie Sector and began to dive sharply. At that speed, it took two and a half minutes to reach their enemy.

"This is Comrade Leader. Reduce air speed to minimum cruise. There they are, about 2,000 feet below us."

"What the hell are they, toys?"

"They're too small to hit with Sidewinders. We'll have to use cannon," the flight leader said. He took the F-5E's down to 1,500 feet and moved up behind the radio-controlled models. Even with the F-5E's dangerously close to stall speed it was going to be impossible to keep from overrunning the little RC craft.

"They're baby 747's," the wingman called out.

"With warheads. Let's swing out and fall back to at least 1,000 yards before we start blasting. Lucky we're still out over open country. I'll take the left bird, the next one's for you, Lenny, and the third's for Chuck . . . Further back . . . You're too close, Chuck . . . Okay . . . Okay . . . Attack!"

The 20-millimeter cannon in the noses of the fighters hosed out bursts of tracers and high-explosive shells. Two of the 747's blew up almost simultaneously, with the shock waves from the nitroglycerin jarring the fighter pilots as if they'd been punched. One F-5E staggered as the flier fought for control. The interceptor veered off, as the pilot added more power to keep from stalling out, then slid back into the V formation.

"What the hell are they carrying?" the startled aviator asked.

"Comrade Leader to Comrade Flight. Okay, prepare to resume attack . . . let's go."

The helicopters were already airborne from Sky Harbor. Alison Gordon peered ahead anxiously from the lead craft, then glanced down at Las Vegas off to the right. The black chopper pilot suddenly raised his right hand from the controls to show a pair of fingers. "They've wiped two. This is fantastic."

She pointed west and he nodded. Sure, the vicious little machines were coming in from that direction so their base must be out there . . .

The second wave of flying bombs took off at 5:08, on schedule.

"Thomas to Blue Moon Leader. Heading west toward Parker Peak. Signal getting stronger," Arroyo radioed from his moving truck.

"We're on our way." Alison Gordon looked around the helicopter and saw the shooters resting in their seats. Waiting to do their job. One had his eyes closed, another was studying an erotic photo monthly named *Beaver,* and Jo-Jo Williams was applying a fresh coat of lipstick. She finished, and returned to reading the Fodor travel guide to Greece.

The whirlybirds chugged on for several minutes before Nellis tower radioed that the first group of models had been shot out of the sky and that radar had just picked up another from the west. The F-5E's were moving west to engage.

Nineteen miles away, Gehrke and Adler were loading the last of their gear into the van and delivery truck.

"Hurry it up," Carlos ordered. "We want to be gone from here in ten minutes. Heidi, start deflating the bubble." . . .

"New targets bearing one-one-zero. Attack," Comrade Leader called out.

"I've got the left one . . . watch it, Lenny . . . get him . . ."

Three miles away this time, Alison Gordon and her assault team heard the blasts. Their pilot was listening to the frantic air-traffic controller at McCarran warning off a puzzled DC-9, and shouting at some Hollywood star's private Gulfstream to "Get the hell up to 8,000 feet and *stay* there."

At 5:11, the third group of 747's was airborne. Clouds were scudding in across the mountains now, and the sounds of explosions rolled in like the beat of a distant kettle drum. Carlos Fabrega Salinas and the other terrorists smiled. Las Vegas was being smashed. The communique was in the mail, and tomorrow the world would know that it was the May 5th Brigade that had devastated this Sodom in the sands.

"Look," Jo-Jo Williams said.

The third wave of RC aircraft was passing by about two hundred yards to the right at 700 feet, still climbing. That meant the field they were launched from was probably less than a mile ahead. Alison Gordon picked up the microphone.

"Stand by, assault team. Look's like we're almost there."

The shooters put on their steel helmets, as did Agajanian and Hovde. Alison Gordon was the last to do so. She was not carrying the small Ingraham this afternoon. The weapon that rested on her lap was an Israeli Uzi, the paratrooper's gun used by the U.S. Secret Service to protect American presidents. Hovde and the accountant carried the same nine-millimeter gun, and each wore an ammunition bag with additional forty-round magazines. They understood that Attila and his people would not be taken alive.

Heidi Friedheim was the first to hear the helicopters. She could not see them at first, but suddenly they broke out of the clouds at 140 miles an hour, less than a mile away. She shouted and reached for her gun. Gehrke and Adler had Scorpions in their hands within moments. The helicopters dropped down to twenty feet, swooped in and divided. One slid in behind a rocky outcropping ninety yards from the camp, while the others clattered above the parked vehicles. Gehrke fired two wild bursts from his Czech machine pistol before Jo-Jo Williams put a bullet through his head.

Hovde threw a concussion grenade that sent Adler sprawling but, though dazed, he rolled behind the van with his nose and ears bleeding, still holding tight to his weapon.

"Okay, I can see you. I can see you up there," Arroyo radioed, and stepped on the gas. No one had the time to answer. A. B. Gordon led the shooters from her helicopter, jumping out before the machine even touched the ground. They knew what to do without any instructions from her. They fanned out and took cover like veteran snipers, which several, indeed, had been. This was no occasion for a massed charge. This was "target of opportunity" time, and the shooters were professionally selecting them. . . .

With Attila laying down a covering fire, the Japanese squatted behind two large rocks to launch the fourth wave. This time it was half a dozen of the mini-bombs. They were airborne before the attackers quite realized what was happening, before they could turn their attention from the fierce firefight raging atop the hill. Country Binks was the first to react, a tribute to his years of Louisiana duck hunting. He raised his piece automatically, sighted in three seconds and almost instinctively allowed for the model's speed and angle of climb.

His first round missed. His second didn't. The blast was deafening. Chunks of rock and sandy earth rained down—but five more of the radio-controlled warheads were still flying. Alison Gordon squeezed off a long burst from the Uzi that shot away the tail controls of one of the 747's. The small machine shook, went into a twisting dive and crashed halfway down the slope. The shock wave from the explosion caught Arroyo as he was climbing out of his truck, threw him reeling for several yards.

Carlos pointed in the opposite direction, and the Red Army specialists from Japan understood. They turned four of the 747's around, sent them up the far side of the hill to gain altitude and then swung them back toward the city. They reached 300 feet before Hovde and Agajanian saw them, interrupted their exchange of bullets with Heidi Friedheim and turned their attention to the rising models.

It was impossible to tell whether Hovde or the accountant fired more accurately. One of them blew up the last plane, and an instant later that blast detonated the nitroglycerin in another. The twin thunderclaps knocked down the shooters working their way up the far ridge. Falling rocks broke the glasses of one of the Red Army men. With one lens starred by cracks and the other in slivers embedded in his face, he bounced two grenades down the slope. As he rose from his crouch to throw, a Carolinian who had shot on the U.S.

Olympic team at Munich put a bullet into his stomach. The grenades skipped down the hill. The shooters on their way up scattered, but one took a clump of fragments in his legs that turned his pant legs bloody . . .

"Comrade Leader, this is radar control. More targets on the way. Altitude 1,100 feet and climbing. Approaching boundary of Charlie Sector."

"Roger, this is Comrade Leader. Preparing to engage."

"Comrade Two to Comrade Leader. I've got a fuel problem. Gauge shows one of the pumps isn't working. I may have to go home."

"Not yet, you don't, Lenny. You'll fly that damn thing till it's bone dry or stone cold."

"Then what—*eject?*"

"Hang tough."

"Up your's, Comrade Lead— . . . *hell,* there they are at nine o'clock . . ."

The general in command at Nellis heard the radio exchange and reacted swiftly. Klaxons sounded. Three more "Aggressor" pilots hurried to their planes. . . .

The firing on the crest grew more intense. When Adler tried to start his van two of Alison Gordon's snipers shot him. He spun like a quarterback making a handoff and fell half dead. Three more 747's left the ground, and Heidi Friedheim threw two more grenades. Carlos was moving toward the People's Hardware truck, expertly getting off short bursts as he zigzagged to the vehicle.

Several more explosions in the distance signaled that the F-5E's were doing their job. Heidi took up Adler's machine pistol and wounded Country Binks with two rounds that tore his rifle from his shoulder. She was reloading when Jo-Jo Williams shot, and killed her.

Two more 747's were now rising as the shooters closed their circle. Alison Gordon left that problem to the others. She wanted Attila. Where was the bastard?

The marksmen were concentrating on the Japanese at the transmitter now. One had been hit in the arm, another in the chest. They tottered, but kept from crumpling. One was reaching for another 747 when three rounds from Hovde's Uzi ripped into it, and the twin Smirnoff bottles detonated. Pieces of him rained down in an eighty-yard arc. . . .

Adler was groaning in pain. Alison Gordon ignored him. Attila would be going for the money. Where *was* he? She heard the sound of an engine, ran to the crest.

And there he was. He had worked his way down to Arroyo's truck and was now driving wildly down the stoney path. "He's getting away," Agajanian shouted. She saw that the aluminum cases glittered beside him. She ripped open her shoulder bag, grabbed the small transmitter.

"Get him, *get* him."

She pressed the switch. The plastic explosive that Hovde and Arroyo had concealed inside the lining of the case blew up. Carlos Salinas was a dead man even before the ruined truck rolled over and its fuel tank erupted in flames. Only a handful of the five million in bills were blown clear of the inferno.

Attila was dead. The dirty, sweaty, dry-mouthed members of the assault force wandered through the chaos and carnage on the crest, finally gathering around the one remaining 747. They shook their heads and breathed in gulps of air as they tasted the coppery flavor of tension and fear they had all shared. They were not ashamed, just tired. These were the things that came with facing death.

"I guess we got them all," Hovde said.

He was wrong. One of the 747's had slipped through the screen of fighters in the clouds. Neither Alison Gordon nor the shooters could see or hear it, it was too far away. Instead, somewhere in the distance was a chorus of sirens. The five police cars arrived minutes later, and it was only as Lieutenant Barrett stepped from the first black-and-white that Alison Gordon realized one of the flying bombs must have gotten through to Las Vegas. The explosion was barely audible, but she knew.

How many had died?

CHAPTER 41

NOVEMBER 7TH, 9:30 A.M.

"We were *lucky,"* she said.

The flying bomb had not hit any of the crowded hotels. It had struck the antenna tower of one of the TV stations, knocking it off the air in the middle of an *I Love Lucy* rerun. A piece of the tower had fallen within yards of a passing school bus.

"Very," Ben Prince agreed.

"Thomas will be out of the hospital tomorrow," Agajanian reported as he started to remove the charts and maps from the wall of the command post.

"Shooters are gone," Hovde said. "All but the one who got hit. He's in the room next to Thomas. It's over."

"Uh . . . not exactly," Prince said. "I'm afraid Thomas has a slight problem. The F.B.I. is going to pick him up tomorrow."

"I don't think so," Alison Gordon said.

"You don't understand, Al. There's been a hold-for-questioning out on him for days. Something to do with blowing up a valley on the reservation. They've had the local law tailing him, and he'd be inside right now if I hadn't persuaded them to wait till this deal was finished."

"You don't understand. I'd better talk to those people. I

know where I can make a toll-free courtesy call—direct."

He shook his head. "They don't want to talk to you, Al. They want you to go away without any more headlines."

"What room was it, Andy?"

"It was 921. Can I watch?"

"No."

She rapped on the door of 921 a minute later, using the same coded sequence of knocks Agajanian had seen the "maid" use. The shirt-sleeved man who opened it a moment later was blue eyed, neatly dressed and surprised.

"My name is A. B. Gordon. Can I use your phone?"

"What?"

"You've been playing with mine for ten days, Sam, so it's my turn."

She pushed past him, jerked the door shut behind her.

"What's the number, Sam?"

"I think you're in the wrong—"

"The number at 300 Las Vegas Boulevard South. I want to talk to the mastermind—"

The woman was hysterical, but Special Agent R. J. Young was too well-trained to let her fluster him.

"Who?"

"The boss, the Special Agent in Charge of this Bureau. Never mind."

She found the number in the phone book, dialed swiftly.

"Special Agent in Charge. Tell him it's A. B. Gordon."

She was speaking with him moments later. He had a deep voice, one intended to radiate calm and competence.

"Yes, Miss Gordon?"

"*No.* You got that? There is no possible way you're going to bust Thomas Arroyo. Go catch some bank robbers or Polish spies."

"This is a matter involving a felony, Miss Gordon—a felony on an Indian reservation. The Bureau has a responsibility to protect reservations, and we intend to discharge it."

"What's your name?"

"Newkirk. If you have any complaints, Miss Gordon—"

"Listen, Newkirk. I've got five million reasons why Thomas Arroyo is going to walk, and why this whole thing's going down the toilet. If it doesn't, Mr. Newkirk, you and your Bureau do."

He carefully considered the implications of what the agitated woman had said . . . "Is that some sort of threat?"

"Of course not. I'm just going to let the press and the politicians and the public find out that you knew about these notorious terrorists for days and simply refused to act on it. You'll be on a sled dog unit in Alaska after that, Newkirk."

More silence.

"Now, Miss Gordon, there's no point—"

"You've got my word, Mr. Newkirk, Alaska. Now you get on the horn to D.C., and put this across. Three-ring circus? I'll give you a real one."

"Perhaps there's been some misunder—"

"I'm in a pretty good mood. You've got two hours, clock's running."

She slammed down the instrument and turned to confront the agent who had manned the wiretap.

"That gadget wired into my phone?"

His silence answered the question, and she started across the room to the equipment.

"That's federal property," he protested.

She threw it to the floor with a crash.

"Put it on my tax bill."

Much of her rage had subsided by the time she reentered the command post. Fanelli and Maxine Wu were there to say good-by, holding hands in a way that moved something inside her.

"Sis sends her best," the pretty Chinese-American said.

"She's over at the hospital seeing Tom. The dog man split as soon as he got his money, Al. You know, it was just like Don promised me."

Gordon thought, and remembered. "Weird and dangerous?"

"That's it. So long."

As they left, she sat down and lit a cigarette. "Ben, I think it will be all right with Thomas. I had a good talk . . . a candid discussion . . . with the Bureau chief here."

"He agreed?"

"I explained how it would serve the national interest. Very intelligent group in the Bureau. As you know." She walked to the telephone. "We've agreed that the tap is no longer necessary. The phone's clean now," she announced as she dialed. After a brief conversation with a pleased Doris Kraft, she heard the voice of The Man With the Shades.

"I called to thank you for the planes and the registered money we used for the switch and to let you know how it came out," she said. "The skim money we recovered is key evidence . . . so the F.B.I. will owe you one."

"I appreciate your good manners. Still the lady. That's hard to do."

"Harder every day."

"Whole world knows how it came out," he told her. "It was on every news broadcast, every front page. The Agency and fifty other intelligence organizations couldn't find them, but you did—and you took them out."

"They would have killed a lot of people if you hadn't gotten us some Air Force. Nobody else believed me."

"You should have called sooner, Alison. I always believed you. You know . . . if you ever get tired of that private-eye stuff . . . No, that's foolish, isn't it?"

"Not foolish. Just impossible. Can't go home again . . . listen, if you should get out to Beverly . . . no, that wouldn't work either . . . Andy and Don are fine . . . we're all in great shape. Great . . . thanks again."

Agajanian and Hovde looked at her and each other, and decided to pack their bags. There was nothing that they could say to her that would help.

"Why don't you go ahead?" she suggested.

"You want to drive back alone?"

"Clear my head. See you at the office tomorrow."

Now she was alone with Prince. They embraced and he felt the .357 in her belly holster.

"That thing's still coming between us."

"I'm afraid so," she said and they separated.

"You're going, I know . . . The F.B.I. has the five million that we saved in the bag switch, but I'm the only witness that it came from Mintzer. You're clean with the Mob and I'll keep it that way. I'm going into protective custody while they put the heat on him. They think he'll sing rather than serve five or six years."

"I wouldn't bet on it. You've taken five million of their skim money anyway—a full week's profits. You're a good citizen, Ben, and a decent man—better than you'll admit."

"Don't exaggerate. It's what I told you—guilt."

She smiled, and patted his cheek.

"I'm glad we met, Ben."

They embraced again, and his hands moved down her spine to that place in the small of her back. She broke away.

"Not now."

"They'll be here any minute, Al."

She didn't have to answer. There was a rap at the door, and three of those healthy young men in medium-priced suits and white shirts with ties appeared. Ben Prince nodded and started to leave.

"Alison, when this is all over and I can—"

"Sure."

She looked around the command post, now empty and bare, and once again just an impersonal room in the city's deluxe hotel.

It was finished for her. The sole survivor of the terrorist group would eventually tell the F.B.I. the whole story, starting from how he had discovered the Kublai Khan's underworld link back when he worked there as an electrician.

With no one to help or encourage him, Adler would crack under efficient and patient interrogation.

She was—like Eric Adler—a survivor, and alone now. She packed her suitcases, paid her bill and got into the Porsche. Everyone knows that Las Vegas gets only four or five inches of rain per year, but it began to drizzle as she drove away from Caesars Palace out onto The Strip.

She didn't care. She did not mind leaving this city. She was less unsympathetic to the desert resort than she had been two weeks ago, but it was time to go. The drizzle turned to rain. It was pouring by the time she crossed the Clark County line.